PAMELA FRANKAU

(1908-1967) was the younger daughter of the prolific novelist Gilbert Frankau and his first wife Dorothea (Drummond-Black) Frankau, who divorced when she was a child. She was educated at Burgess Hill School, Sussex and thereafter lived with her mother and sister in Windsor. Declining a place at Cambridge she decided to devote herself to writing. Her first two fictional attempts were rejected and, forced to find employment because of her mother's illness, she took a job at the *Amalgamated Press*, making use of the journey to write.

This time she found success: *The Marriage of Harlequin* (1927) appeared when Pamela Frankau was nineteen. The next few years were prosperous — she was promoted to sub-editor on the *Woman's Journal*, found a ready market for her articles and stories, published three more novels and became friends with Noel Coward, John van Druten, G.B. Stern and Rebecca West. This halcyon period was shortlived. The story market slumped, Pamela broke off an engagement and, ill and unhappy, retreated to the South of France to finish *She and I* (1930). She later recorded these differing fortunes in an autobiography, *I Find Four People* (1935).

In 1940, Humbert Woolfe, whom she had loved for nine years, died suddenly. Devastated by his death, she travelled to America for some months. On her return she worked for the Ministry of Food — where she became a great friend of Lettice Cooper — and later the ATS. In 1942 she converted to Catholicism. Three years later she married an American professor, Marshall Dill Junior, and moved to California. Their child died in infancy and the marriage collapsed after seven years.

The best-known of Pamela Frankau's thirty novels include *The Willow Cabin* (1949), *The Winged Horse* (1953), *A Wreath for the Enemy* (1954, also dramatised for television) and *The Bridge* (1957). She also published non-fiction, three collections of short stories and was a critic for BBC radio.

For the last decade of her life, until her death from cancer, Pamela Frankau shared a Hampstead house with the theatrical producer Margaret Webster.

VIRAGO
MODERN
CLASSIC

NUMBER
272

PAMELA FRANKAU

A WREATH
FOR THE ENEMY

WITH A NEW INTRODUCTION BY
RAFFAELLA BARKER

Published by VIRAGO PRESS Limited 1988
20-23 Mandela Street, Camden Town, London NW1 0HQ

First published in Great Britain by William Heinemann 1954
Copyright © Pamela Frankau 1954
Introduction Copyright © Raffaella Barker 1988

British Library Cataloguing in Publication Data

Frankau, Pamela., *1908-1967*
A wreath for the enemy.—(A Virago modern classic).
I. Title
823'.912[F]
ISBN 0-86068-633-8

Printed in Great Britain by Cox & Wyman of Reading, Berks

INTRODUCTION

When I was twelve, I wrote a letter to Somerset House requesting that my name should be changed to Jackie. I did not receive a reply, and never quite feeling that the ring of authenticity would be there without the changed birth certificate, I continued to squirm as Raffaella, with a never-ending stream of amusing (to my contemporaries at any rate) alternatives such as Ravioli, Rafia and Rat.

The yearning for conformity which is felt by children can drive them to absurd depths of humiliation and dissimilation. The children who rejoice in their individuality are as rare as the adults who accept their banality. Pamela Frankau described in her autobiography, *I Find Four People*, a school bicycle trip which she insisted on gracing with her presence despite her inability to ride a bicycle. The occasion was punctuated by her frequent clashes with the tarmac, and left her ostracised, pretending not to notice and cultivating "a dreamy, and she hoped, a poetic expression".

A Wreath for the Enemy is about nonconformity and the discomfort it causes. From her autobiography it is not difficult to see that Pamela Frankau suffered as a child through her nonconformity. That she triumphed over the petty attitudes of her contemporaries is a salutory thought for any miserable fourteen-year-old who may happen upon this novel. The heroine, Penelope, given a free rein, does not take advantage of it. Don Bradley, suffocated at home by parents who shift uncomfortably and change the subject if abstracts are brought up, develops into a wholly philosophical and emotional character. The message of the novel is clear; for the purposes of growing up it is essential to shed the chains of family entrenchment.

Born in 1908, Pamela Frankau was brought up in London, where she lived with her mother and sister, her parents having separated. This in itself set her apart from other children, divorce not being at all common at that time. She was sent to boarding school at the age of eleven, where she achieved academic, if not social success. The reader of her autobiography gleans a picture of a precocious child, who longed to disappear into the ranks of average schoolgirls, but was unable to do so, having been deemed by them deplorably conceited. While conceit is too strong a word, plainly Pamela Frankau had a high opinion of her own worth, not perhaps without reason, as she excelled at her schoolwork, in swimming and in her enthusiasm for the Girl Guides. She left, aged seventeen, with first class honours in her School Certificate, a feat she accomplished by one week's exhaustive cramming just before the exams.

Notwithstanding this triumph, Pamela Frankau took a step which she later regretted, and turned down the offer of a place at Girton College Cambridge. Instead she returned to her mother's house in Windsor, determined to write a novel. This ambition was fired not only by her passion for the English language, but also by her heritage. Rebecca West said of the Frankau dynasty, "There never was a family which so indefatigably furnished material for phd theses." While this in itself is arguable, what is undeniable is that they were prolific. Pamela's father, Gilbert Frankau, was himself a novelist of some repute. His influence on his daughter's work took the form of sporadic bursts of encouragement followed by long periods when she didn't see or hear from him at all. Her paternal grandmother wrote sprightly Victorian novels under the pseudonym "Frank Danby"; and her great-aunt was Mrs Aria, a journalist acclaimed for her humour. During her school-days Pamela Frankau had little to do with this side of her family as she and her elder sister Ursula spent all their time with their mother, Dorothea Drummond–Black, a woman lauded for her wit and well-known for her extravagance.

In the year after she left school, Pamela Frankau realised her long-standing ambition and wrote two novels, both of which were rejected by publishers. This did not perturb her, and but for a remark by a family friend, she might well have remained in Windsor for years completing novel after novel without success. However, a visitor to the house told her that she could not make a success of writing at her age and that she should have a job. So at eighteen Pamela Frankau went to work at the Amalgamated Press newspaper offices in Farringdon as a sub sub-editor.

There she met Edgar Wallace's daughter Pat, who became her best friend, and began to write a third novel on the train to and from Windsor every day. This novel, *Marriage of Harlequin*, was published when she was nineteen, to excellent reviews and sales. Others followed thick and fast; by the time Pamela Frankau was twenty-seven, she had published twelve novels. During this period she was introduced to many of London's leading literary figures by her Aunt Eliza (Mrs Aria). To the young author, Aunt Eliza represented "the centre of a world where one longed to be", and it was through her that Pamela Frankau began her association with Rebecca West (who was a mentor throughout her life), Michael Arlen, Sybil Thorndike and countless others who made up the patchwork world of literature and theatre in the twenties and thirties.

Pamela Frankau's literary career was taking off. Her agent thought that she had achieved over and above the success of her forebears. When he read her first novel, he told her, "'You are the third. And you will be the best.'" Heady stuff for an eighteen-year-old. Those readers who are more than eighteen and are still stuck on the first sentence of their first novel might be excused for the sensation of extreme bitterness which is doubtless overcoming them. However, it can be tempered by the knowledge that this period, to which Pamela Frankau refers in her autobiography as her season of "Oysters and Champagne", passed. By the time she was twenty-eight she had had a nervous breakdown — or as she said "something of the sort" — lost all her conceit, embarked upon an unhappy love life and was starting to write much better novels.

It is difficult to enlarge upon the theme of Pamela Frankau's amours. Her opinion in her autobiography was that to write about emotions is to betray them. She did, however, record her passion for a young playwright, which came to nothing, and her subsequent "on the rebound" engagement to a sketchily described young man called Jan. This relationship inevitably broke down and there is no mention of any later romance except for one with a much older man in France. In 1934, however, she met and fell in love with Humbert Wolfe, and never recovered from his death nine years later. Her novel, *The Willow Cabin*, published in 1949, is a testament to their affair and is dedicated to him. Still shattered by this event, Pamela Frankau married an American called Marshall Dill Junior, and went to live with him in California. The marriage was not a success, so Pamela Frankau returned to England and never remarried.

Her own experiences are drawn upon freely in *A Wreath for the Enemy*, in which Penelope, at eighteen, is brimming with fantasies about love, none of which involve the physical aspect. The account of her first sexual experience is moving because of her detachment. Pamela Frankau deftly conveys her feeling of emptiness while giving a sense of Penelope's passion, which is as yet untapped. That Penelope's overriding obsession is for a middle-aged and unimaginative man is no surprise; it is the subsequent twist in the tail of the tale which gives this novel its individuality.

In the course of her own life, Pamela Frankau achieved only two satisfactory relationships. The first was her love affair with the English language. She wrote more than thirty-five novels and countless short stories as well as working sporadically on newspapers and as an advertising copywriter. She wrote at least three thousand words a day, outstripping the rest of her family and many others in quantity if not in quality. An obiturist in *The Times* said of her that "None of her novels, though they are better than most, is as good as she was." This may well be true, although the volume of her work commands respect. Pamela Frankau wrote because it was the thing she loved best. Her sheer enjoyment in the freedom of her pen is reminiscent of an adolescent dog let off its leash in a field peppered with interesting smells. In her novels ideas and arguments, emotions and quotations dance around simple tales of love and

viii

death. Her idiom is often pleasingly arcane, and her characters are given to uttering quaint and idiosyncratic phrases like "a doom" or the "Spoilers-of-the-Fun", which give them an air of likeable pomposity.

Pamela Frankau's witty use of language is her strongest asset and is a manifestation of her own *joie de vivre*; the element she is most remembered for. She had an extreme delight in all things hedonistic, and once confessed that she would never put anyone in her novels who "did not use a footlong cigarette holder, drive a Hispano Suiza and have peaches for breakfast". This remark was made soon after she published her first novel, and while much of her early work may be thus embellished, it is not without relief that I am able to report few sightings of any of the above affectations in her later novels. What is consistently apparent throughout is Pamela Frankau's loathing for the pedestrian and her passions for gambling (several times she bet herself heavily into debt), for the French Riviera, and ultimately for Catholicism. It was with the Catholic church that she had her second fulfilled relationship.

Pamela Frankau had a rich if heterogeneous spiritual life. Born of a Jewish family, but brought up in the Church of England, she converted to Catholicism at the age of thirty-four. Her novels are thick with crises of faith and religious debates, and if occasionally the weight of these themes threatens to bring down the fragile structure of her work, she does, when confining herself strictly to the thoughts and words of her characters (rather than imposing well-rehearsed but two-dimensional arguments upon them) make some salient points, "The racist would do well to remind himself once a day that Our Lord was a Jew," remarks Don Bradley, in *A Wreath for the Enemy*.

Pamela Frankau became a Catholic after Humbert Wolfe died. Having loved him so greatly, she described his death as "a bereavement which had the power to put out the sun". She spent two years adrift from any faith and "drifted into emptiness, self indulgence and despair". Finally, however, she realised that she could not suffocate her faith, try as she might, and returned to the church and into the arms of Catholicism.

It is the strength gleaned from the church, and the basic courageous humour of her own character that give Pamela Frankau's novels their substance. She said once that "Autobiography disguised as fiction is the butt of the sophisticated writer. It has, nevertheless, gone to the making of some good books." Her novels often reflect her own experiences, and it is from them, as much as from her autobiography, that one can draw a picture of a gregarious and vivacious woman, who throughout her life "lost her enemies and kept her friends", but who never quite lived up to her own expectations. Despite publishing so many novels, Pamela Frankau's real desire, which she wrote of in her autobiography, was to write good poetry, an ambition which never came to fruition. She died, aged forty-eight in 1956, and might have considered her own humorous parody of a popular song her epitaph:

> I'll be writing rot, always.
> Rot that's rather hot, always.
> Written for the dense
> It does not make sense.

Pamela Frankau's autobiography was written while she was recovering from a nervous illness in a nursing home. Throughout the book it is evident that she has strong views on many subjects, and not least on writing. Towards its end she records her own fourteen commandments of the pen. She points out that her standards may slide and her tastes change in years to come, but it is nonetheless interesting to note how many of these maxims, though they were coined when Pamela Frankau was only twenty-seven, are alive in *A Wreath for the Enemy*, written nineteen years later. In order to give substance to my subsequent points, it is necessary for me to lay the pertinent maxims before the reader:

Introduction

The presentation of a consecutive scene should be given through the eyes of only one character taking part in the scene.

Topical references, e.g. to hotels, plays, songs and makes of car cheapen the story. If these must appear, their accuracy is essential. Semi-disguises of such names are mistaken.

Qualifications, e.g. "slightly", "faintly", "A kind of" and "rather", should not be permitted.

An author finding it easy to write natural dialogue should be careful to

discipline the flow against the temptation to record colloquial chat for its own sake.

To discuss all fourteen commandments would be more than pedantic. Some are concerned with correct grammar and the use of particular words such as "but", or "quietness" and throw no light on Pamela Frankau's writing except to show that she is a stickler for proper English. Rather more alarming to the present writer is her insistence on the removal of qualifications from the printed page. What is more relevant to Pamela Frankau's own work is her belief that "the presentation of a consecutive scene should be given through the eyes of only one character taking part in the scene". While never deviating from this in *A Wreath for the Enemy*, Pamela Frankau introduces different sections and various voices, some with more success than others, to explain and uphold the themes of the novel. Each character represents a different aspect of youth, and it is perhaps only in Penelope that the reader finds a more complete picture, and the first half of the book, where Penelope narrates, is the most successful. This structural device, which she also used to some extent in *The Willow Cabin*, may serve as a reflection of Pamela Frankau's fragmented vision of herself. This suspicion is confirmed by her autobiography, in which she presents herself in four different guises, each of which represents Pamela Frankau at a different stage in her life.

As to her youthful view that topical references cheapen a story, and if used at all must be accurate: by virtue of the fact that so much of her work is autobiographical, and that she spent a not inconsiderable amount of time in cars and hotels, Pamela Frankau had no option but to include topical references. She does, however, take considerable pains to ensure their accuracy, and her descriptions are often humorous. Where she describes a car it is used as a device to improve the readers impression of the character to whom the car belongs, such as Livesey Raines' smart and solid new black Rolls Royce; a perfect vehicle for this kind but unimaginative man.

Pamela Frankau's statement concerning dialogue is particularly pertinent to *A Wreath for the Enemy*. None of her dialogue ever suffers from banality. Indeed it is one of the triumphs of her writing, and is the device by which her excellent incidental characters come alive. These characters appear, luminous but fleeting, to considerable effect, and with them Pamela Frankau develops humorous scenes dependent on conversation. One of the best of these is a bohemian tea party, which takes place half way through the novel.

"Crusoe, darling — oh, my darling, how are you? I did mean to come to lunch . . . I did try to come to lunch . . . I was deflected."
She was as lovely as a Madonna and she wore trousers. Crusoe said, "Bless you. But it's quite alright. I didn't ask you to lunch."
"You didn't?"
"No, darling."
"Then I have wasted hours of guilt. Hullo, Johnny dear." I had risen to give her my chair. "Oh, but how kind of you," she said, as though I had rescued her from drowning.

This wayward madonna is a typical example of Pamela Frankau's ability to bring her characters instantly and seductively alive. Although the dialogue is often unbelievable, it is always natural, whether uttered by central figures or by those who appear but briefly.

Her opinion that "repetition of the physical characteristics of persons in the story is unnecessary and irritating" and "descriptions of clothes worn by the characters should never be made" are both

confounded in the novel *The Willow Cabin*, where there are repeated references to Caroline Seaward's personal appearance. The
effect is indeed tedious, particularly as neither her clothing nor her
physiognomy vary throughout the book, even though eighteen years
elapse. *A Wreath for the Enemy*, however, remains true to these
maxims. The heroine Penelope's appearance is sketched in the
vaguest terms with comparisons to bush babies, which can only
confound most readers who probably have no idea what a bush baby
looks like. The other characters have similarly shadowy physical
outlines and all are brought to life through their thoughts and
conversation.

That Pamela Frankau was fond of maxims (the apophthegm, not
the machine gun) is quite clear. She was not content with confining
them to her opinions on writing alone. Throughout her books, and
in particular *A Wreath for the Enemy*, her characters deliver maxims
on a plethora of subjects. Some are worthy of noting for their pithy
accuracy, such as Crusoe Raines' remark that "After middle age,
you'll find that you cultivate a pitying affection for your own body
which comes from realising that no one else is going to care for it
again." Others are misguided, in particular a subsequent thought
from Crusoe: "One of the signs of true unhappiness is a regular
placid relief at the sight of one's own bed; to be at peace with the
knowledge that the day is over." (Most would agree that to remove
the prefix "un" from the word "unhappiness" would serve to render
the sentiment true.)

Pamela Frankau remains faithful to the themes of love and death
in all her novels, perhaps in an attempt to exorcise her own experiences. In *A Wreath for the Enemy*, the essential dichotomy lies
between the constraining demands of expectation and the wayward
inclinations of a free soul. It is there in the story of Penelope, a young
girl brought up in a bohemian manner on the French Riviera. Instead
of revelling in her freedom and in the fact that her father and
stepmother treat her as an adult from her earliest youth, Penelope
develops into a careful and naive adult, who "knows everything but

the facts" and is imbued with "a wholly middle aged sense of proportion". Her apparent sophistication owes little to experience but much to the books she has read and to the stream of glamorous guests who pass through her father's hotel. Thus she grows up with a horror of chaos which she conceals guiltily as a child but comes to terms with as she approaches adulthood.

Parallel to Penelope's development runs that of Don Bradley. In him, Pamela Frankau exposes the struggle of a sensitive child born to parents who are the apotheosis of the bourgeois. Don Bradley's teenage suffering, as he befriends an extraordinary man and begins to despise his parents, is delicately portrayed by the author. Pamela Frankau's ability to confront these two opposed rites of passage and to tie them up at the end in a morass of religious compensation shows her sensitivity and her recollection of her own youth.

Death, as in many other of Pamela Frankau's novels, is a major theme of this novel. She explores the remorse, the inability to understand, that is so common amongst those who lose someone dear to them. As in *The Willow Cabin*, a central character dies half way through *A Wreath for the Enemy*. Echoing the earlier book again, his memory is kept alive until the end, and his philosophies are maintained by those who loved him. Pamela Frankau is successful in her portrayal of adolescent attempts to cope with and inability to comprehend the death of a friend. Penelope, left alone in her first experience of mortality, tidies the room and maintains a vigil over the corpse in an attempt to reveal her love and her regret.

To go into greater detail would serve to give away much of the story to those who read introductions before reading the novel. It would serve no purpose whatsoever to those who have read the book and are now reading the introduction because they have nothing better to do. In reading *A Wreath for the Enemy* I was reminded of two other books which are about delightful, precocious adolescents, *I Capture the Castle* by Dodie Smith and *The Constant Nymph* by Margaret Kennedy. Both these books, like *A Wreath for the Enemy* could have been written for children as much as for adults and have struck chords of longing or of recognition into many. Pamela Frankau may not have achieved the renown that Margaret Kennedy has, nor have her books been made into films by Walt Disney like Dodie Smith's, but her sense of humour and her courage have imbued her writing with a charm that has brought about this new edition and the republication of *The Willow Cabin*. This charm will doubtless inspire many initiates to haunt second hand bookshops in pursuit of her other thirty-three novels.

Raffaella Barker, London, 1988

To

JOHN VAN DRUTEN

In loving gratitude for all the years
and all the moods of our friendship.

CONTENTS

I

THE DUCHESS AND THE SMUGS

Told by Penelope Wells

I SAT still at the table, with the blank paper before me. I went back; I remembered; I thought my way in. It was the sensation of pulling on a diver's helmet and going down deep.

Presently, on the sea-floor, I began to find lost things; to raise the moods that were mine when I was fourteen years old, sitting in this garden, writing my Anthology of Hates.

I would begin there.

I

There had been two crises already that day before the cook's husband called to assassinate the cook. The stove caught fire in my presence; the postman had fallen off his bicycle at the gate and been bitten by Charlemagne, our sheep-dog, whose policy it was to attack people only when they were down.

Whenever there were two crises my stepmother Jeanne said, "*Jamais deux sans trois.*" This morning she and Francis (my father) had debated whether the two things happening to the postman could be counted as two separate crises and might therefore be said to have cleared matters up. I thought that they were wasting their time. In our household things went on and on and on happening. It was an hotel, which made the doom worse: it would have been remarkable to have two days without a crisis and even if we did, I doubted whether the rule would apply in reverse, so that we could augur a third. I was very fond of the word augur.

I was not very fond of the cook. But when I was sitting on the terrace in the shade working on my Anthology of Hates, and a man with a bristled chin told me in patois that he had come to kill her, I thought it just as well for her, though obviously disappointing for her husband, that she was off for the afternoon. He carried a knife that did not look particularly sharp; he smelt of liquorice, which meant that he had been drinking Pernod. He stamped up and down, making speeches about his wife and Laurent the waiter, whom he called a *salaud*

3

and many other words new to me and quite difficult to understand.

I said at last, "Look, you can't do it now, because she has gone over to St. Raphael in the bus. But if you wait I will fetch my father." I took the Anthology with me in case he started cutting it up.

I went down the red rock steps that sloped from the garden to the pool. The garden looked the way it always looked, almost as brightly coloured as the postcards of it that you could buy at the desk. There was purple bougainvillæa splashing down the white walls of the hotel; there were hydrangeas of the exact shade of pink blotting-paper; there were huge silver-grey cacti and green umbrella pines against a sky that was darker blue than the sky in England.

I could not love this garden. Always it seemed to me artificial, spiky with colour, not quite true. My idea of a garden was a green lawn and a little apple orchard behind a grey stone house in the Cotswolds. It was my Aunt Anne's house in the village of Whiteford. I saw that garden only once a year, in September. I could conjure it by repeating inside my head—

> 'And autumn leaves of blood and gold
> That strew a Gloucester lane.'

Then the homesickness for the place that was not my home would make a sharp pain under my ribs. I was ashamed to feel so; I could not talk about it; not even to Francis, with whom I could talk about most things.

I came to the top of the steps and saw them lying around the pool, Francis and Jeanne and the two novelists who had come from Antibes for lunch. They were all flat on the yellow mattresses, talking.

I said, "Excuse me for interrupting you, but the cook's husband has come to assassinate the cook."

Francis got up quickly. He looked like Mephistopheles. There were grey streaks in his black hair; all the lines of his face went upward and the pointed moustache followed the lines. His body was dark-brown and hairy, except that the scars on his back and legs, where he was burned when the aeroplane was shot down, did not tan with the sun.

"It's a hot afternoon for an assassination," said the male novelist as they ran up the steps together.

"Perhaps," said Francis, "he can be persuaded to wait until the evening."

"He will have to," I said, "because the cook is in St. Raphael. I told him so."

"Penelope," said my stepmother, sitting up on the yellow mattress, "you had better stay with us."

"But I am working on my book."

"All right, *chérie*; work on it here."

The lady novelist, who had a sparkling, triangular face like a cat, said, "I wish you would read some of it to us. It will take our minds off the current bloodcurdling events."

I begged her to excuse me, adding that I did not anticipate any bloodcurdling events because of the battered look of the knife.

Jeanne said that the cook would have to go in any case, but that her love for Laurent was of a purely spiritual character.

I said, "Laurent is a smoothy, and I do not see how anybody could be in love with him."

"A certain smoothness is not out of place in a head waiter," said the lady novelist.

I did not tell her my real reason for disliking Laurent: he made jokes. I hated jokes more than anything. They came first in the Anthology: they occupied whole pages: I had dozens and dozens: it was a loose-leaf book, so that new variations of hates already listed could be inserted at will.

Retiring from the conversation, I went to sit on the flat rock at the far end of the pool. Francis and the male novelist returned very soon. Francis came over to me. I shut the loose-leaf book.

"The cook's husband," he said, "has decided against it."

"I thought he would. I imagine that if you are really going

to murder somebody you do not impart the intention to others."

"Don't you want to swim?" said Francis.

"No, thank you. I'm working."

"You couldn't be sociable for half an hour?"

"I would rather not."

"I'll write you down for R.C.I.," he threatened.

R.C.I. was Repulsive Children Incorporated, an imaginary foundation which Francis had invented a year before. It came about because a family consisting mainly of unusually spoiled children stayed at the hotel for two days, and were asked by Francis to leave on the third, although the rooms were booked for a month. According to Francis, R.C.I. did a tremendous business and there were qualifying examinations wherein the children were tested for noise, bad manners, whining, and brutal conduct. I tried to pretend that I thought this funny.

"Will you please let me work for a quarter of an hour?" I asked him. "After all, I was disturbed by the assassin."

"All right. Fifteen minutes," he said. "After which you qualify."

In fact, I was not telling him the truth. I had a rendezvous at this hour every day. At four o'clock precisely I was sure of seeing the people from the next villa. I had watched them for ten days and I knew how Dante felt when he waited for Beatrice to pass him on the Ponte Vecchio. Could one, I asked myself, be in love with four people at once? The answer seemed to be Yes. These people had become a secret passion.

The villa was called La Lézardière; a large, stately pink shape with green shutters; there was a gravel terrace, planted with orange trees and descending in tiers to a pool that did not sprawl in a circle of red rocks as ours did, but was of smooth grey concrete. At the tip of this pool there was a real diving-board. A long, gleaming speedboat lay at anchor in the deep water. The stage was set and I waited for the actors.

They had the quality of Vikings; the father and mother were tall, handsome, white-skinned and fair-haired. The boy and girl followed the pattern. They looked as I should have preferred to look. (I was as dark as Francis, and, according to the never-ceasing stream of personal remarks that seemed to be my lot at this time, I was much too thin. And not pretty. If my eyes were not so large I knew that I should be quite ugly. In Francis' opinion, my face had character. "But this, as Miss Edith Cavell said of patriotism," I told him, "is not enough.")

Oh, to look like the Bradleys; to be the Bradleys, I thought, waiting for the Bradleys. They were far, august, and enchanted; they wore the halo of being essentially English. They were Dad and Mum and Don and Eva. I spied on them like a huntress, strained my ears for their words, cherished their time-table. It was regular as the clock. They swam before break-fast and again at ten, staying beside the pool all the morning. At a quarter to one the bell would ring from the villa for their lunch. Oh, the beautiful punctuality of those meals! Some-times we did not eat luncheon until three and although Jeanne told me to go and help myself from the kitchen, this was not the same thing at all.

In the afternoon the Bradleys rested on their terrace in the shade. At four they came back to the pool. They went fishing or water-ski-ing. They were always doing something. They would go for drives in a magnificent grey car with a white hood that folded back. Sometimes they played a catching game beside the pool; or they did exercises in a row, with the father leading them. They had cameras and butterfly-nets and field-glasses. They never seemed to lie around and talk, the loathèd recreation in which I was expected to join.

I took Don and Eva to be twins; and perhaps a year younger than I. I was just fourteen. To be a twin would, I thought, be a most satisfying destiny. I would even have changed places with the youngest member of the Bradley family, a baby in a white perambulator with a white starched nurse in charge of it. If I could be the baby, I should at least be sure of growing up and becoming a Bradley, in a white shirt and grey shorts.

Their magic linked with the magic of my yearly fortnight in England, when, besides having the grey skies and the green garden, I had acquaintance with other English children not in

the least like me: solid, pink-cheeked sorts with ponies; they
came over to tea at my aunt's house and it was always more fun
in anticipation than in fact, because I seemed to make them
shy. And I could never tell them that I yearned for them.

So, in a way, I was content to watch the Bradleys at a
distance. I felt that it was hopeless to want to be friends with
them; to do the things that they did. I was not only different
on the outside, but different on the inside, which was worse.
On the front page of the Anthology I had written: 'I was born
to trouble as the sparks fly upward,' one of the more consoling
quotations because it made the matter seem inevitable.

Now it was four o'clock. My reverie of the golden Bradleys
became the fact of the golden Bradleys, strolling down to the
water. Dad and Don were carrying the water-skis. I should
have only a brief sight of them before they took the speedboat
out into the bay. They would skim and turn far off, tantalising
small shapes on the shiny silky sea. Up on the third tier of the
terrace, between the orange trees, the neat white nurse was
pushing the perambulator. But she was only faintly touched
with the romance that haloed the others. I mourned.

Then a most fortunate thing happened. There was a drift of
strong current around the rocks and as the speedboat moved
out towards the bay, one of the water-skis slipped off astern,
and was carried into the pool under the point where I sat. Don
dived in after it; I ran down the slope of rock on their side, to
shove it off from the edge of the pool.

"Thanks most awfully," he said. He held on to the fringed
seaweed and hooked the water-ski under his free arm. Now
that he was so close to me I could see that he had freckles; it
was a friendly smile and he spoke in the chuffy, English boy's
voice that I liked.

"It's rather fun, water-ski-ing."

"It looks fun. I have never done it."

"Would you like to come out with us?" he jerked his head
towards the boat. "Dad's a frightfully good teacher."

I groaned within me, like the king in the Old Testament.

Here were the gates of Paradise opening and I must let them shut again, or be written down for R.C.I.

"Painful as it is to refuse," I said, "my father has acquired visitors and I have sworn to be sociable. The penalty is ostracism." (Ostracism was another word that appealed to me.)

Don, swinging on the seaweed, gave a gurgle of laughter.

"What's funny?" I asked.

"I'm terribly sorry. Wasn't that meant to be funny?"

"Wasn't what meant to be funny?"

"The way you talked."

"No, it's just the way I talk," I said, drooping with sadness.

"I like it awfully," said Don. This was warming to my heart. By now the speedboat was alongside the rock point. I could see the Viking heads; the delectable faces in detail. Mr. Bradley called, "Coming aboard?"

"She can't," said Don. "Her father has visitors; she'll be ostracised." He was still giggling and his voice shook.

"Oh dear, that's too bad," said Mrs. Bradley. "Why don't you ask your father if you can come tomorrow?"

"I will, most certainly," I said, though I knew that I need never ask permission of Jeanne or Francis for anything that I wanted to do.

I felt as though I had been addressed by a goddess. Don gurgled again. He flashed through the water and they pulled him into the boat.

I had to wait for a few minutes alone, hugging my happiness, preparing a kind of visor to pull down over it when I went back to the group on the yellow mattresses.

"Making friends with the Smugs?" Francis greeted me.

"What an enchanting name," said the lady novelist.

"It isn't their name; it's what they are," said Francis.

I heard my own voice asking thinly, "Why do you call them that?" He shocked me so much that my heart began to beat heavily and I shivered. I tried to conceal this by sitting crouched and hugging my knees. I saw him watching me.

"Well, aren't they?" he said gently. I had given myself away. He had guessed that they meant something to me.

"I don't know. I don't think so. I want to know why you think so."

"Partly from observation," said Francis. "Their gift for organised leisure; their continual instructions to their children; the expressions on their faces. And the one brief conversation that I've conducted with Bradley—he congratulated me on being able to engage in a commercial enterprise on French soil. According to Bradley, you can never trust the French." He imitated the chuffy English voice.

"Isn't 'commercial enterprise' rather an optimistic description of *Chez François*?" asked the lady novelist, and the male novelist laughed. Francis was still looking at me.

"Why do you like them, Penelope?"

I replied with chilled dignity, "I did not say that I liked them. They invited me to go water-ski-ing with them tomorrow."

Jeanne said quickly, "That will be fun. You know, Francis, you are becoming too intolerant of your own countrymen: it is enough in these days for you to meet an Englishman to make you dislike him." This was comforting; I could think this and feel better. Nothing, I thought, could make me feel worse than for Francis to attack the Bradleys. It was another proof that my loves, like my hates, must remain secret, and this was loneliness.

II

I AWOKE next morning full of a wild surmise. I went down early to the pool and watched Francis taking off for Marseille in his small, ramshackle seaplane. He flew in a circle over the garden as he always did, and when the seaplane's long boots pointed for the west, I saw Don and Eva Bradley standing still on the gravel terrace to watch it. They were coming down to the pool alone. Offering myself to them, I went out to the flat rock. They waved and beckoned and shouted.

"Is that your father flying the seaplane?"

"Yes."

"Does he take you up in it?"

"Sometimes."

"Come and swim with us," Don called.

I ran down the rock slope on their side. I was shy now that we stood together. I saw that Eva was a little taller than Don; that she also was freckled; and that they had oiled their skins against sunburn as the grown-ups did. Don wore white trunks and Eva a white swimming suit. They laughed when I shook hands with them, and Don made me an elaborate bow after the handshake. Then they laughed again.

"Are you French or English?"

That saddened me. I said, "I am English, but I live here because my stepmother is a Frenchwoman and my father likes the Riviera."

"We know that," said Don quickly. "He was shot down and taken prisoner by the Germans and escaped and fought with the Resistance, didn't he?"

"Yes. That is how he met Jeanne."

"And he's Francis Wells, the poet?"

"Yes."

"And the hotel is quite mad, isn't it?"

"Indubitably," I said. It was another of my favourite words. Eva doubled up with laughter. "Oh, that's wonderful! I'm *always* going to say indubitably."

"Is it true," Don said, "that guests only get served if your father likes the look of them, and that he charges nothing sometimes, and that all the rooms stay empty for weeks if he wants them to?"

"It is true. It does not seem to me the most intelligent way of running an hotel, but that is none of my business."

"Is he very rich?" asked Eva.

Don said quickly, "Don't, Eva, that's not polite."

"He isn't rich or poor," I said. I could not explain our finances to the Bradleys any more than I could explain them to myself. Sometimes we had money. When we had not, we were never poor in the way that other people were poor. We were 'broke', which, as far as I could see, meant being in debt but living as usual and talking about money.

"Do you go to school in England?"

"No," I said, handing over my chief shame. "I am a day boarder at a convent school near Grasse. It is called Notre Dame des Oliviers."

"Do you like it?"

"I find it unobjectionable," I said. It would have been disloyal to Francis and Jeanne to tell these how little I liked it.

"Do they teach the same things as English schools?"

"Roughly."

"I expect you're awfully clever," said Eva, "and top at everything."

How did she know that? Strenuously, I denied it. Heading the class in literature, composition, and English poetry was just one more way of calling attention to myself. It was part of the doom of being noticeable, of not being like Other People. At Les Oliviers, Other People were French girls, strictly brought up, formally religious, cut to a foreign pattern. I did not want to be they, as I wanted to be the Bradleys: I merely envied their uniformity.

God forbid that I should tell the Bradleys about winning a special prize for a sonnet; about being chosen to recite Racine to hordes of parents; about any of it. I defended myself by asking questions in my turn. Eva went to an English boarding-school in Sussex; Don would go to his first term at public school this autumn. I had guessed their ages correctly. They were just thirteen. 'Home' was Devonshire.

"I would greatly love to live in England," I said.

"I'd far rather live in an hotel on the French Riviera. Lucky Penelope."

"I am not 'lucky Penelope'; I am subject to dooms."

"How heavenly. What sort of dooms?"

"For example, getting an electric shock in science class, and finding a whole nest of mice in my desk," I said. "And being

the only person present when a lunatic arrived believing the
school to be Paradise."

"Go on. Go on," they said. "It's wonderful. Those aren't
dooms, they are adventures."

"Nothing that happens all the time is an adventure," I said.
"The hotel is also doomed."

They turned their heads to look up at it; from here, through
the pines and the cactus, we could see the red crinkled tiles of
its roof, the bougainvillæa, the top of the painted blue sign
that announced '*Chez François*'.

"It can't be doomed," Don said. "Don't famous people
come here?"

"Oh yes. But famous people are more subject to dooms than
ordinary people."

"How?"

"In every way you can imagine. Important telegrams con-
taining money do not arrive. Their wives leave them; they are
recalled on matters of state."

"Does Winston Churchill come?"

"Yes."

"And Lord Beaverbrook and Elsa Maxwell and the Duke of
Windsor and Somerset Maugham?"

"Yes. Frequently. All their signed photographs are kept in
the bar. Would you care to see them?"

Here I encountered the first piece of Bradley dogma. Don
and Eva, who were splashing water on each other's hair
("Dad is most particular about our not getting sunstroke"),
looked doubtful.

"We *would* love to."

"I'm sure it's all right, Eva; because she lives there."

"I don't know. I think we ought to ask first. It is a bar,
after all."

Ashamed, I hid from them the fact that I often served in the
bar when Laurent was off duty.

"Oh, do let's chance it," said Don.

"I don't believe we ought to."

.   .   .   .

Mr. and Mrs. Bradley had gone over to Nice and would not return until the afternoon, so a deadlock threatened. The white starched nurse appeared at eleven o'clock with a Thermos-flask of cold milk and a plate of buns. I gave birth to a brilliant idea; I told her that my stepmother had invited Don and Eva to lunch with us.

It was a little difficult to convince them, after the nurse had gone, that Jeanne would be pleased to have them to lunch without an invitation. When I led them up through our garden, they treated it as an adventure, like tiger shooting.

Jeanne welcomed them, as I had foretold, and the lunch was highly successful, although it contained several things, such as *moules*, which the Bradleys were not allowed to eat. We had the terrace to ourselves. Several cars drove up and their owners were told politely that lunch could not be served to them. This delighted Don and Eva. They were even more delighted when Jeanne told them of Francis' ambition, which was to have a notice: 'Keep Out; This Means You', printed in seventeen languages. One mystery about the Bradleys was that they seemed to like jokes. They thought that I made jokes. When they laughed at my phrases they did not laugh as the grown-ups did, but in the manner of an appreciative audience receiving a comedian. Eva would hold her stomach and cry, "Oh *stop*! It hurts to giggle like this; it really hurts."

I took them on a tour of the hotel. The *salon* was furnished with some good Empire pieces. The bedrooms were not like hotel bedrooms, but more like rooms in clean French farmhouses, with pale walls and dark wood and chintz. All the rooms had balconies where the guests could eat their breakfast. There were no guests.

"And Dad says people *clamour* to stay here in the season," Don said, straddled in the last doorway.

"Yes, they do. Probably some will be allowed in at the end of the week," I explained, "but the Duchess is arriving from Venice at any moment and Francis always waits for her to choose which room she wants, before he lets any. She is changeable."

Eva said, "I can't get over your calling your father Francis. Who is the Duchess?"

"The Duchessa di Terracini. She is half Italian and half American."

"Is she very beautiful?"

"Very far from it. She is seventy and she looks like a figure out of a waxworks. She was celebrated for her lovers, but now she only loves roulette." I did not wish to be uncharitable about the Duchess, whose visit was to be dreaded, and these were the nicest things that I could make myself say. The only thing in her favour was that she had been a friend of my mother, who was American and utterly beautiful and whom I did not remember.

"*Lovers?*" Eva said, looking half pleased and half horrified. Don flushed and looked at his feet. I had learned from talks at school that reactions to a mention of the facts of life could be like this. I knew also that Francis despised the expression, 'the facts of life', because, he said, it sounded as though all the other things that happened in life were figments of the imagination.

"A great many people loved the Duchess desperately," I said. "She was engaged to an Austrian Emperor; he gave her emeralds, but somebody shot him."

"Oh well, then, she's practically history, isn't she?" Eva said, looking relieved.

III

I MIGHT have known that the end of the day would bring doom. It came hard upon the exquisite pleasure of my time in the speedboat with the Bradleys. This was even better than I had planned it in anticipation, a rare gift. I thought that the occasion must be under the patronage of a benign saint or what the Duchess would call a favourable aura; the only worry was Mrs. Bradley's worry about my having no dry clothes to put on after swimming; but with typical Bradley organisation there were an extra white shirt and grey shorts in the boat. Dressed thus I felt like a third twin.

The sea changed colour; the sea began to be white and the rocks a darker red.

"Would you like to come back and have supper with us, Penelope?"

I replied, "I can imagine nothing that I would like more."

"She *does* say wonderful things, doesn't she?" said Eva. I was drunk by now on Bradley admiration and almost reconciled to personal remarks.

"Penelope speaks very nice English," said Mrs. Bradley.

"Will you ask your stepmother then?" she added as we tied up the boat. I was about to say this was unnecessary when Don gave my ribs a portentous nudge; he said quickly, "Eva and I will walk you up there." It was obvious that the hotel exercised as much fascination for them as they for me.

When the three of us set off across the rocks Mr. Bradley called, "Seven o'clock sharp, now!" and Eva made a grimace. She said, "Wouldn't it be nice not to have to be punctual for anything?"

"I never have to be," I said, "except at school, and I think that I prefer it to having no time-table at all."

"Oh, my goodness! Why?"

"I like days to have a shape," I said.

"Can you just stay out to supper when you want to? Always? Without telling them?"

"Oh, yes."

"What would happen if you stayed away a whole night?"

I said that I had never tried. And now we went into the bar because Don said that he wanted to see the photographs again. Laurent was there; straw-coloured and supercilious in his white coat. He began to make his jokes, "*Mesdames, monsieur, bon soir.* What may I serve you? A Pernod? A champagne cocktail?" He flashed along the shelves, reading out the name of each drink, muttering under his breath, "*Mais non; c'est*

terrible; we have nothing that pleases our distinguished
visitors." I saw that the Bradleys were enchanted with him.

We walked all round the gallery of photographs and were
lingering beside Winston Churchill when the worst thing
happened. I heard it coming. One could always hear the
Duchess coming. She made peals of laughter that sounded
like opera; the words came fast and high between the peals.

And here she was, escorted by Francis. She cried, "Ah, my
love, my love!" and I was swept into a complicated, painful
embrace, scratched by her jewellery, crushed against her stays,
and choked with her scent before I got a chance to see her in
perspective. When I did, I saw that there were changes since
last year and that these were for the worse. Her hair, which
had been dyed black, was now dyed bright red. Her powder
was whiter and thicker than ever; her eyelids were dark blue;
she had new false eyelashes of great length that made her look
like a Jersey cow.

She wore a dress of dark-blue chiffon, sewn all over with
sequin stars, and long red gloves with her rings on the outside;
she tilted back on her heels, small and bony, gesticulating with
the gloves.

"Beautiful—beautiful—beautiful!" was one of her slogans.
She said it now; she could not conceivably mean me; she just
meant everything. The Bradleys had become awed and limp
all over. When I introduced them they shook hands jerkily,
snatching their hands away at once. Francis took from
Laurent the bottle of champagne that had been on ice awaiting
the Duchess; he carried it to her favourite table, the corner
table beside the window. She placed upon the table a sequin
bag of size, a long chiffon scarf, and a small jewelled box that
held *bonbons au miel*, my least favourite sweets, reminding me
of scented glue.

Francis uncorked the champagne.

"But glasses for all of us," the Duchess said. "A glass for
each." The Bradleys said, "No, thank you very much," so
quickly that they made it sound like one syllable and I imitated
them.

"But how good for you," cried the Duchess. "The vitalising, the magnificent, the harmless grape. All children should take a little to combat the lassitude and depressions of growth. My mother used to give me a glass every morning after my fencing lesson. *Et toi*, Penelope? More than once last year you have taken your *petit verre* with me."

"Oh, didn't you know? Penelope is on the water wagon," said Francis, and the Duchess again laughed like opera. She cried, "*Santé, santé!*" raising her glass to each of us. Francis helped himself to a Pernod and perched on the bar, swinging his legs. The Bradleys and I stood in a straight, uncomfortable row.

"Of youth," said the Duchess, "I recall three things. The sensation of time seeming endless, as though one were swimming against a current; the insipid insincerity of one's teachers; and bad dreams, chiefly about giants."

Sometimes she expected an answer to statements of this character; at other times she went on talking: I had known her to continue without a break for fifteen minutes.

"I used to dream about giants," said Eva.

"How old are you, Miss?"

"Thirteen."

"At fifteen the dreams become passionate," said the Duchess, sounding lugubrious about it.

"What do you dream about now?" asked Don, who had not removed his eyes from her since she came.

"Packing; missing aeroplanes; losing my clothes," said the Duchess. "Worry—worry—worry; but one is never bored in a dream, which is more than can be said for real life. Give me your hand," she snapped at Eva. She pored over it a moment, and then said briskly, "You are going to marry very young and have three children; an honest life; always be careful in automobiles." Don's hand was already stretched out and waiting. She gave him two wives, a successful business career, and an accident "involving a horse between the ages of seventeen and eighteen".

"That is tolerably old for a horse," Francis interrupted.

"Sh-h," said the Duchess, "perhaps while steeplechasing; it is not serious." She blew me a little kiss: "Penelope I already know. She is as clear to me as a book written by an angel. Let me see if there is any change," she commanded, a medical note in her voice. "Beautiful—beautiful—beautiful! Genius and fame and passion are all here."

"Any dough?" asked Francis.

"I beg your pardon?" said the Duchess, who knew perfectly well what 'dough' meant, but who always refused to recognise American slang.

"I refer to cash," said Francis, looking his most Mephistophelean. "My ambition for Penelope is that she acquire a rich husband, so that she may subsidise Papa in his tottering old age."

"Like so many creative artists, you have the soul of a fishmonger," said the Duchess. She was still holding my hand; she planted a champagne-wet kiss on the palm before she let it go. "I have ordered our dinner, Penelope. It is to be the *écrevisses au gratin* that you like, with small *goûters* of caviar to begin with and *fraises des bois* in kirsch afterward."

I had been anticipating this hurdle; she always insisted that I dine with her on her first evening, before she went to the Casino at nine o'clock.

"I am very sorry, Duchessa; you must excuse me. I am having supper with Don and Eva." I saw Francis raise one eyebrow at me. "I really didn't know you were coming tonight," I pleaded.

"No, that is true," said the Duchess, "but I am very disappointed. I have come to regard it as a regular tryst." She put her head on one side. "Why do you not all three stay and dine with me? We will make it a *partie carrée*. It could be managed, Francis? Beautiful—beautiful—beautiful! There. That is settled."

"I'm most awfully sorry; we'd love to," Eva said. "But we couldn't possibly. Supper's at seven and Mum's expecting us."

"Thank you very much, though," said Don, who was still staring at her. "Could we do it another time?"

"But of course! Tomorrow; what could be better? Except tonight," said the Duchess. "I was looking to Penelope to bring me good luck. Do you remember last year, how I took you to dine at the Carlton and won a fortune afterwards?"

"And lost it on the following afternoon," said Francis. The Duchess said an incomprehensible Italian word that sounded like a snake hissing. She took a little ivory hand out of her bag and pointed it at him.

"I thought one never could win at roulette," said Don. "According to my father, the game is rigged in favour of the Casino."

"Ask your father why there are no taxes in Monaco," said the Duchess. "In a game of this mathematic there is no need for the Casino to cheat. The majority loses naturally, not artificially. And tell him further that all European Casinos are of the highest order of probity, with the possible exception of Estoril and Bucharest. Do you know the game?"

When the Bradleys said that they did not, she took from her bag one of the cards that had upon it a replica of the wheel and the cloth. She embarked upon a roulette lesson. The Bradleys were fascinated and of course we were late for supper. Francis delayed me further, holding me back to speak to me on the terrace: "Do you have to have supper with the Smugs?"

"Please don't call them that. Yes, I do."

"It would be reasonable, I should think, to send a message saying that an old friend of the family had arrived unexpectedly."

Of course it would have been reasonable; Mrs. Bradley had expected me to ask permission. But nothing would have made me stay.

"I'm extremely sorry, Francis; I can't do it."

"You should know how much it means to her. She has ordered your favourite dinner. All right," he said, "I see that it is useless to appeal to your better nature. Tonight you qualify for R.C.I." He went back to the bar, calling, "The verdict can always be withdrawn if the candidate shows compensating behaviour."

"Didn't you want to stay and dine with the Duchess?" asked Don, as we raced through the twilit garden.

"I did not. She embarrasses me greatly."

"I thought she was terrific. I do hope Mum and Dad will let us have dinner with her tomorrow."

"But *don't* say it's *écrevisses*, Don, whatever you do. There's always a row about shell-fish," Eva reminded him.

"I wouldn't be such an ass," Don said. "And the only thing that would give it away would be if you were ill afterwards."

"Why should it be me?"

"Because it usually is," said Don.

I awoke with a sense of doom. I lay under my mosquito-net, playing the scenes of last evening through in my mind. A slight chill upon the Viking parents, due to our being late; smiles pressed down over crossness, because of the visitor. Don and Eva pouring forth a miscellany of information about the Duchess and the signed photographs; myself making mental notes, a devoted sociologist studying a favourite tribe: grace before supper; no garlic in anything; copies of *Punch* and the English newspapers; silver napkin rings; apple pie. The secret that I found in the Cotswold house was here, I told myself; the house in Devonshire took shape; on the walls there were photographs of it; a stream ran through the garden; they rode their ponies on Dartmoor; they had two wire-haired terriers called Snip and Snap. I collected more evidence of Bradley organisation: an expedition tomorrow to the Saracen village near Brignoles; a Current-Affairs Quiz that was given to the family by their father once a month.

No, I said to myself, brooding under my mosquito-net, nothing went wrong until after the apple pie. That was when Eva had said, "The Duchess told all our fortunes." The lines spoken were still in my head:

Don saying, "Penelope's was an absolute fizzer; the Duchess says she will have genius, fame, and passion." Mr. Bradley's Viking profile becoming stony; Mrs. Bradley's smooth white forehead puckering a little as she asked me gently, "Who is this wonderful lady?"

Myself replying, "The Duchessa de Terracini," and Mrs. Bradley remarking that this was a beautiful name. But Mr. Bradley's stony face growing stonier and his officer-to-men voice saying, "Have we all finished?"; then rising so that we rose too and pushed in our chairs and bowed our heads while he said grace.

After that there was a spirited game of Monopoly. 'But the atmosphere,' I said to myself, 'went on being peculiar.' I had waited for Don and Eva to comment on it when they walked me home, but they were in a rollicking mood and appeared to have noticed nothing.

'Indubitably there is a doom,' I thought while I put on my swimming suit, 'and since I shall not see them until this evening, because of the Saracen village, I shall not know what it is.'

As I crossed the terrace, the Duchess popped her head out of the corner window above me; she leaned like a little gargoyle above the bougainvillæa; she wore a lace veil fastened under her chin with a large diamond.

"Good morning, Duchessa. Did you win?"

"I lost consistently, and your friends cannot come to dine tonight, as you may know; so disappointing, though the note itself is courteous." She dropped it into my hands. It was written by Mrs. Bradley; fat, curly handwriting on paper headed

CROSSWAYS

CHAGFORD

DEVON

It thanked the Duchess and regretted that owing to the expedition, Don and Eva would not be able to accept her kind invitation to supper.

I knew that the Bradleys would be back by six.

IV

I SPENT most of the day alone working on the Anthology. I had found quite a new Hate, which was headed 'Characters'. People called the Duchess a character and this was said of others who came here. I made a brief description of each and included some of their sayings and habits.

There was the usual paragraph about the Duchess in the *Continental Daily Mail*; it referred to her gambling and her emeralds and her *joie-de-vivre*. *Joie-de-vivre* seemed to be a worthy subject for Hate and I entered it on a separate page, as a subsection of Jokes.

At half-past four, to my surprise, I looked up from my rock writing-desk and saw the Bradleys' car sweeping in from the road. Presently Eva came running down the tiers of terrace alone. When she saw me she waved, put her finger to her lips, and signalled to me to stay where I was. She came scrambling up.

"I'm so glad to see you. There's a row. I can't stay long. Don has been sent to bed."

"Oh, dear. I was conscious of an unfavourable aura," I said. "What happened?"

Eva looked miserable. "It isn't anything against you, of course. They like you terribly. Mum says you have beautiful manners. When Don and I said we wanted you to come and stop a few days with us at Crossways in September, it went down quite *well*. Would you like to?" she asked, gazing at me, "or would it be awfully boring?"

I was momentarily deflected from the doom and the row. "I cannot imagine anything that would give me greater pleasure," I said. She wriggled her eyebrows, as usual, at my phrases.

"That isn't just being polite?"

"I swear by yonder hornèd moon it isn't."

"But, of course, it may not happen now," she said in melancholy, "although it wasn't *your* fault. After all you didn't make us meet the Duchess on purpose."

"Was the row about the Duchess?"

"Mm-m."

"Because of her telling your fortunes and teaching you to play roulette? I did have my doubts, I admit."

"Apparently they were quite cross about that, but of course they couldn't say so in front of you. Daddy had *heard* of the Duchess, anyway. And they cracked down on the dinner party and sent a note. And Don kept on asking why until he made Daddy furious; and there seems to have been something in the *Continental Mail*, which we are not allowed to read."

"Here it is," I said helpfully. She glanced upward over her shoulder. I said, "Have no fear. We are invisible from the villa at this angle."

She raised her head from the paper and her eyes shone; she said, "Isn't it wonderful?" I had thought it a pedestrian little paragraph, but I hid my views.

"Mummy said that the Duchess wasn't at all the sort of person she liked us to mix with, and that no lady would sit in a bar drinking champagne when there were children present, and that we shouldn't have gone into the bar again anyway. And Don lost his temper and was quite rude. So that we came home early instead of having tea out; and Dad said that Don had spoiled the day and asked him to apologise. And Don said a word that we aren't allowed to use and now he's gone to bed. Which is awful for him because he's too big to be sent to bed. And I'll have to go back. I'm terribly sorry."

"So am I," I said. "Please tell your mother that I deplore the Duchess deeply, and that I always have."

As soon as I had spoken, I became leaden inside with remorse. It was true that I deplored the Duchess because she was possessive, overpowering, and embarrassing, but I did not disapprove of her in the way that the Bradleys did. I was making a desperate effort to salvage the thing that mattered most to me.

In other words, I was assuming a virtue though I had it not, and while Shakespeare seemed to approve of this practice, I was certain that it was wrong. (And I went on with it. I added that Francis would not have dreamed of bringing the Duchess into the bar if he had known that we were there. This was an outrageous lie. Francis would have brought the Duchess into the bar had the Archbishop of Canterbury been there— admittedly an unlikely contingency.)

When Eva said that this might improve matters and might also make it easier for Don to apologise, because he had stuck up for the Duchess, I felt lower than the worms.

Which is why I quarrelled with Francis. And I knew that that was why. I had discovered that if one were feeling guilty one's instinct was to put the blame on somebody else as soon as possible.

Francis called to me from the bar door as I came up on to the terrace. I had been freed from R.C.I. on the grounds of having replaced Laurent before lunch at short notice. He grinned at me. "Be an angel and take these cigarettes to Violetta's room, will you, please? I swear that woman smokes two at a time."

"I am sorry," I said. "I have no wish to run errands for the Duchess just now."

Francis, as usual, was reasonable. "How has she offended you?" he asked.

I told him about the Bradleys, about the possible invitation to Devonshire; I said that, thanks to the Duchess cutting such a pretty figure in the bar, not to mention the *Continental Mail*, my future was being seriously jeopardised. I saw Francis' eyebrows twitching.

He said, "Penelope, you are a thundering ass. These people are tedious *petits bourgeois*, and there is no reason to put on their act just because you happen to like their children. And I see no cause to protect anybody, whether aged seven or seventy, from the sight of Violetta drinking champagne."

"Mrs. Bradley said that no lady would behave in such a way."

"Tell Mrs. Bradley with my love and a kiss that if she were a tenth as much of a lady as Violetta she would have cause for pride. And I am not at all sure," he said, "that

I like the idea of your staying with them in Devonshire."

This was, as the French said, the *comble*.

"Do you mean that you wouldn't let me go?" I asked, feeling as though I had been struck by lightning.

"I did not say that. I said I wasn't sure that I liked the idea."

"My God, why not?"

"Do not imagine when you say, 'My God'," said Francis, "that you add strength to your protest. You merely add violence."

He could always make me feel a fool when he wanted to. And I could see that he was angry; less with me than with the Bradleys. He said, "I don't think much of the Smugs, darling, as you know. And I think less after this. Violetta is a very remarkable old girl, and if they knew what she went through in Rome when the Germans were there, some of that heroism might penetrate even their thick heads. Run along with those cigarettes now, will you please?"

I was trembling with rage; the worst kind of rage, hating me as well as everything else. I took the cigarettes with what I hoped was a dignified gesture, and went.

The Duchess was lying on the chaise-longue under her window; she was swathed like a mummy in yards of cyclamen chiffon trimmed with marabout. She appeared to be reading three books at once: a novel by Ignazio Silone, Brewer's *Dictionary of Phrase and Fable*, and a *Handbook of Carpentry for Beginners*.

The room, the best of the rooms, having two balconies, had become unrecognisable. It worried me with its rampaging disorder. Three wardrobe trunks crowded it: many dresses, scarves, and pairs of small pointed shoes had escaped from the wardrobe trunks. The Duchess always brought with her large unexplained pieces of material; squares of velvet, *crêpe de Chine*, and damask, which she spread over the furniture. The writing-table had been made to look like a table in a museum; she had put upon it a black crucifix and two iron candlesticks, a group of ivory figures, and a velvet book with metal clasps.

Despite the heat of the afternoon the windows were shut; the room smelled of smoke and scent.

"Beautiful—beautiful—beautiful!" said the Duchess, holding out her hand for the cigarettes. "There are the *bonbons au miel* on the bedside table. Help yourself liberally, and sit down and talk to me."

"No, thank you very much. If you will excuse me, Duchessa, I have to do some work now."

"I will not excuse you, darling. Sit down here. Do you know why I will not excuse you?"

I shook my head.

"Because I can see that you are unhappy, frustrated, and restless." She joined her finger-tips and stared at me over the top of them. "Some of it I can guess," she said, "and some of it I should dearly like to know. Your mother would have known."

I was silent; she was hypnotic when she spoke of my mother, but I could not make myself ask her questions.

"Genius is not a comfortable possession. What do you want to do most in the world, Penelope?"

The truthful reply would have been, "To be like other people. To live in England; with an ordinary father and mother who do not keep an hotel. To stop having dooms; never to be told that I am a genius, and to have people of my own age to play with so that I need not spend my life listening to grown-ups."

I said, "I don't know."

The Duchess sighed and beat a tattoo with her little feet inside the marabout; they looked like clockwork feet.

"You are, beyond doubt, crying for the moon. Everybody at your age cries for the moon. But if you will not tell me which moon, I cannot be of assistance. What is the book that you are writing?"

"It is an Anthology of Hates," I said, and was much surprised that I had told her, because I had not told anybody.

"Oho!" said the Duchess. "Have you enough Hates to make an anthology?"

I nodded.

"Is freedom one of your Hates?"

I frowned; I did not want to discuss the book with her at all and I could not understand her question. She was smiling in a maddening way that implied more knowledge of me than I myself had.

"Freedom is the most important thing that there is. You have more freedom than the average child knows. One day you will learn to value this and be grateful for it. I will tell you why." Her voice had taken on the sing-song, lecturing note that preceded a fifteen-minute monologue. I stared at the figures on the writing-table. She had let her cigarette lie burning in the ash-tray, and a small spiral of smoke went up like incense before the crucifix; there was this, there was the hot scented room and the sound of her voice: "It is necessary to imprison children to a certain degree, for their discipline and their protection. In schools, they are largely hidden away from life, like bees in a hive. This means that they learn a measure of pleasant untruth; a scale of simple inadequate values that resemble the true values in life only as much as a plain coloured poster of the Riviera resembles the actual coastline.

"When they emerge from the kindly-seeming prisons, they meet the world of true dimensions and true values. These are unexpectedly painful and irregular. Reality is always irregular and generally painful. To be unprepared for its shocks and to receive the shocks upon a foundation of innocence is the process of growing up. In your case, Penelope, you will be spared many of those pains. Not only do you have now a wealth of freedom which you cannot value because you have not experienced the opposite, but you are also endowing yourself with a future freedom; freedom from the fear and shock and shyness which make the transition from youth to maturity more uncomfortable than any other period of existence. Francis is bringing you up through the looking-glass, back-to-front. You are learning what the adult learns, and walking through these lessons towards the light-heartedness that is usually to be found in childhood but later lost. I wonder how

long it will take you to find that out." She sat up on her
elbows and stared at me again. "Do you know what I think
will happen to your Anthology of Hates when you do find it
out? You will read it through and find that these are not
Hates any more."

By this last remark she had annoyed me profoundly, and
now she clapped her hands and cried, "If young people were
only allowed to gamble! It takes the mind off every anxiety.
If I could take you to the Casino with me tonight, Penelope!
Wouldn't that be splendid? Disguised as a young lady of
fashion!" She sprang off the chaise-longue, snatched the
square of velvet from the bed and flung it over my shoulders.
Its weight almost bore me to the ground; it was heavy as a
tent and it smelled musty. "Look at yourself in the mirror!"
cried the Duchess. "Beautiful—beautiful—beautiful! A
Principessa!" She scuttled past me. "We will place this silver
girdle here." She lashed it so tightly that it hurt my stomach;
I was stifled; it felt like being dressed in a carpet. "Take this
fan and these gloves." They were long white kid gloves, as
hard as biscuits; she forced my fingers in and cajoled the gloves
up my arms as far as the shoulders.

"The little amethyst circlet for your head."

She caught some single hairs as she adjusted it and put one
finger in my eye. Sweat was trickling all over me.

"Now you have a very distinct resemblance to your mother,"
said the Duchess, standing before me and regarding me with
her head on one side.

"This is the forecast of your womanhood. Will you please
go downstairs at once and show yourself to Jeanne?"

I said that I would rather not. She was peevishly disappointed. I struggled out of the ridiculous costume; hot
dispirited, no fonder of myself than before, I got away.

V

My bedroom was on the ground floor, with a window that opened on to the far end of the terrace. It was late, but I was still awake and I heard Francis and Jeanne talking outside. I did not mean to listen, but their voices were clear and when I heard the name 'Bradley' I could not help listening.

"I agree with you," Jeanne said, "that it is all an outrageous fuss. But these Bradleys mean a great deal to Penelope."

"Wish I knew why," said Francis. "They represent the worst and dullest aspect of English 'county'; a breed that may soon become extinct, and no loss, either."

"They are the kind of friends that she has never had; English children of her own age."

Their footsteps ceased directly outside my window. I heard Francis sigh. "*Ought* we to send her to school in England, do you think?"

"Perhaps next year."

"That will be too late, beloved."

I had heard him call Jeanne 'beloved' before, but tonight the word touched my heart, perhaps because I was already unhappy; it made me want to cry. "She will be fifteen," Francis said. "First she'll kill herself trying to fit into the pattern, and if she succeeds in the task, we shall never see her again. God knows what we'll get but it won't be Penelope."

"She will change in any case, whether she stays or goes, darling; they always do."

"Perhaps I've done a poor job with her from the beginning," Francis said; he spoke my mother's name. And then I was so sure I must listen no more that I covered my ears with my hands. When I took them away Jeanne was saying, "You are always sad when your back is hurting you. Come to bed. Tomorrow I'll invite the Bradley children for lunch again; on Thursday when Violetta's in Monte Carlo."

"Why should we suck up to the Smugs?" Francis grumbled,

and Jeanne replied, "Only because of Penelope, *tu le sais*," and they walked away down the terrace.

I wept because they destroyed my defences; my conscience still troubled me for the speeches of humbug that I had made to Eva, for quarrelling with Francis, and for being uncivil to the Duchess. It was a weary load. If the Bradleys accepted the invitation to lunch, it would seem that God was not intending to punish me for it, but exactly the reverse, and that was a bewildering state of affairs.

By morning, however, God's plan became clear. Jeanne brought me my breakfast on the terrace. She sat with me while I ate it. I thought, as I had thought before, that she looked very young; more an elder sister than a stepmother, with her short, flying dark hair, the blue eyes in the brown face, the long slim brown legs. She smoked a Caporal cigarette.

I could hardly wait for her to tell me whether she had healed the breach with the Bradleys. But I dared not ask. Their talk on the terrace had been too intimate for me to admit that I had heard it. She said, "Penelope, the situation with your friends at La Lézardière has become a little complex."

My heart beat downward heavily and I did not want to eat any more.

"I thought that it would give you pleasure if I asked them to lunch and would perhaps clear up any misunderstanding. But I have been talking to Mrs. Bradley and apparently she would prefer them not to visit the hotel."

I did not know whether I was blushing for the hotel, for my own disappointment, or for the Bradleys; I was only aware of the blush, flaming all over my skin, most uncomfortably.

"Mrs. Bradley was friendly and polite, you must not think otherwise. She wants you to swim with them as much as you like; she said that she hoped you would go out in the speedboat again. But her exact phrase was, 'We feel that the hotel surroundings are just a little too grown-up for Don and Eva.' "

I was silent.

"So I thought that I would tell you. And ask you not to

be unhappy about it. People are entitled to their views, you know, even when one does not oneself agree with them."

"Thank you, Jeanne: I am not at all unhappy," I said, wishing that my voice would not shake. "And if the Bradleys will not come to me, I am damned if I am going to them." And I rose from the table. She came after me, but when she saw that I was near to tears she gave me a pat on the back and left me alone.

This was the point at which I discovered that hate did not cast out love, but that it was, on the contrary, possible to hate and love at the same time. I could not turn off my infatuation for the Bradleys, much as I longed to do so. They were still the desirable Vikings. The stately pink villa above the orange trees, the grey rocks where the diving-board jutted and the speedboat lay at anchor, remained the site of romance, the target of forlorn hopes. It hurt me to shake my head and retire from the flat rock when Don and Eva beckoned me. They seemed to understand quickly enough, more quickly than their parents did. Mr. Bradley still called, "Coming aboard?" and Mrs. Bradley waved to me elaborately on every possible occasion. The children turned their heads away. For two days I saw them all like figures set behind a glass screen; only the echo of their voices reached me; I gave up haunting the beach and worked in a corner of the garden; the regularity of their time-table made it easy to avoid the sight of them. I told myself that they were loathsome, that they were the Smugs, that Don and Eva were both candidates for R.C.I. I even considered including them in the Anthology of Hates, but I found it too difficult. Now they had indeed become the moon that the Duchess told me I cried for. I cherished dreams of saving Don's life or Eva's at great risk to myself, and being humbly thanked and praised by their parents. Then I hoped that they would all die in a fire, or better still that I would die and they would come to my funeral.

In these two days I found myself looking at my home differently; seeing it in Bradley perspective. I had been plagued

by the crises and irregularities but never ashamed of them.
Was I ashamed now? I could not be sure; the feeling was one
of extra detachment and perception; I was more than ever
aware of the garden's bright colours, of the garlic smells from
the kitchen, of the dusky coolness in the bar; every time that I
walked through the *salon* I looked at it with startled visitors'
eyes; Bradleys' eyes.

"It's pretty, of course; it's like a little room in a museum,
but it isn't the sort of place where one wants to *sit*." The
terrace with the blue and white umbrellas above the tables,
the stone jars on the balustrade, the lizards flickering along
the wall, seemed as temporary as the deck of a ship on a short
voyage. I felt as though I were staying here, not living here.
And there was no consolation in my own room with my own
books because here the saddest thoughts came and they seemed
to hang in the room waiting for me, as palpable as the tented
mosquito-net above the bed.

I found that I was seeing Francis, Jeanne, and the Duchess
through a grotesque lens; they were at once complete strangers
and people whom I knew intimately. I could place them in a
Bradley context, thinking, 'That is Francis Wells, the poet,
the poet who keeps the mad hotel. He always seems to wear
the same red shirt. He looks like Mephistopheles when he
laughs. And that is his wife, his *second* wife; younger than he
is; very gay always, isn't she? What very *short* shorts. And
there goes the Duchessa di Terracini, rather a terrible old lady
who gambles at the Casino and drinks champagne; doesn't she
look ridiculous in all that make-up and chiffon?' And then I
would be talking to them in my own voice and with my own
thoughts and feeling like a traitor.

I knew that they were sorry for me; that Francis above all
approved my defiant refusal. I was aware of their hands held
back from consoling gestures, to spare me too much overt
sympathy. Even the Duchess did not speak to me of the
Bradleys.

For once I welcomed the crises as diversion. And these two
days naturally were not free from crisis; a British ambassador

and his wife found themselves *en panne* at our gates. All the entrails of their car fell out upon the road and we were obliged to give them rooms for the night.

This would not of itself have been other than a mechanical crisis, because the ambassador and Francis were old friends. Unfortunately the ambassador and the press baron from Menton, who was dining with the Duchess, were old enemies. So a fierce political fight was waged in the bar, with both elderly gentlemen calling each other poltroon, and they would have fought a duel had not the electric current failed and the hotel been plunged in darkness till morning. (My only grief was that Don and Eva had missed it. All roads led to the Bradleys.)

On the third morning, which was Thursday, doom accelerated. I woke to find Francis standing beside my bed.

"Sorry, darling; trouble," he said. "A telephone call just came through from Aix; Jeanne's mother is very ill and I'm going to drive her over there now. Can you take care of you for today?"

He never asked me such questions: this was like a secret signal saying, "I know you are miserable and I am sorry."

"But of course. Please don't worry."

"There are no guests, thank God. Violetta's going over to Monte Carlo; Laurent will be in charge tonight. You might see that he locks up, if I'm not back."

"I will do that."

"But don't let him lock Violetta out, for Heaven's sake."

"I will see that he does not. Can I help Jeanne or do anything for you?"

"No, my love. We are off now. I'll telephone you later." He ducked under the mosquito-net to kiss me.

"You must pray rather than worry," the Duchess said to me, standing on the doorstep. For her expedition to Monte Carlo, she wore a coat and skirt of white shantung, a bottle-green frilly blouse, and the usual chiffon scarf. She was topped by a bottle-green tricorne hat with a green veil descending from it. "Death is a part of life," she added, pulling on her white gloves.

I could feel little emotion for my step-grandmother who lived in seclusion near Aix-en-Provence, but I was sorry for Jeanne.

"The best thing that you could do, Penelope," said the Duchess, grasping her parasol like a spear, "would be to come over with me to Monte Carlo. We will lunch delightfully on the balcony of the Hotel de Paris; then you shall eat ices while I am at the tables; then a little stroll and a little glass and we could dine on the port at Villefranche and drive home under the moon. The moon is at the full tonight and I look forward to it. *Viens, chérie, ça te changera les idées*," she added, holding out her hand.

I thanked her very much and said that I would rather stay here.

When she was placed inside the high purple Isotta-Fraschini, I thought that she and her old hooky chauffeur looked like a Punch-and-Judy show. The car was box-shaped with a fringed canopy under the roof and they swayed as it moved off. I waved good-bye.

The first part of the day seemed endless. I sat in the garden on a stone bench under the largest of the umbrella pines. That way I had my back to La Lézardière. I could hear their voices and that was all. When the bell rang for their lunch, I went down to the pool and swam. I swam for longer than usual; then I climbed to the flat rock and lay in the sun. I was almost asleep when I heard Eva's voice. "Penelope!"

She was half-way up the rock; she said, "Look; we are so miserable we've written you this note. I have to go back and rest now." She was like a vision out of the long past; the freckles, the sunburn, and the wet hair. I watched her scuttle down and she turned to wave to me from the lowest tier of the terrace. I gave her a half-wave and opened the note.

It said:

'DEAR PENELOPE,

'Please don't be cross with us. Mum and Dad are going out to supper tonight. Don't you think that you could come? They have asked us to ask you.

'Always your friends,
'DON and EVA.'

I wrote my reply at the *écritoire* in the *salon*. I wrote:

'Much as I appreciate the invitation, I am unable to accept it. Owing to severe illness in the family my father and step-mother have left for Aix. I feel it necessary to stay here and keep an eye on things.

'PENELOPE.'

To run no risk of meeting them, I went into the bar and asked Laurent if he would be so kind as to leave this note at La Lézardière.

Laurent was in one of his moods; he replied sarcastically that it gave him great pleasure to run errands and do favours for young ladies who had not the energy to perform these for themselves. I echoed the former cook's husband, the assassin, and said, "*Salaud*," but not until he was gone.

After I had answered the note, I alternated between wishing that I had accepted and wishing that I had given them more truthful reasons for my refusal.

Later, I sought comfort by writing to my Aunt Anne in England; I sat there conjuring the fortnight as it would be and putting in the letter long descriptions of the things that I wanted to see and do again. It helped. I had covered twelve pages when the telephone rang.

Francis' voice spoke over a bad line: "Hullo, Child of Confusion. Everything all right?"

"Yes, indeed. Nothing is happening at all. What is the news?"

"Better," he said, "but Jeanne will have to stay. I may be very late getting back. See that Laurent gives you the cold lobster. Jeanne sends her love."

Nothing would have induced me to ask Laurent for my
dinner, but I was perfectly capable of getting it myself and the
reference to cold lobster had made me hungry. No reason
why I should not eat my dinner at six o'clock. I was on my
way to the kitchen by way of the terrace when I heard a voice
calling me:

"Penelope!"

I turned, feeling that horrible all-over blush begin. Mrs.
Bradley stood at the doorway from the *salon* on to the terrace.
She looked golden and statuesque in a white dress with a
scarlet belt. The sight of her was painful. It seemed as though
I had forgotten how lovely she was.

"May I talk to you a moment, my dear?"

"Please do," I said, growing hotter and hotter.

"Shall we sit here?" She took a chair beneath one of the
blue and white umbrellas. She motioned to me to take the
other chair. I said, "Thank you, but I prefer to stand."

She smiled at me. I could feel in my heart the alarming
collision of love and hate and now I could see her in two con-
texts: as a separate symbol, the enemy; as a beloved haunting
of my own mind, the Mrs. Bradley of the first days, whom I
had made my private possession. Her arms and hands were
beautifully shaped, pale brown against the white of her dress.

"Can't we be friends, Penelope? I think we can, you know,
if we try. Don and Eva are so sad and it all seems such a
pity."

I said, "But, Mrs. Bradley, you made it happen."

"No, dear. That is what I want to put right. When I talked
to your stepmother, I made it quite clear that we all hoped to
see much more of you."

"But," I said, "that Don and Eva couldn't come here. As
though it were an awful place."

She put her hand on mine; she gave a soft low laugh.
"Penelope, how foolish of you. Of course it isn't an awful
place. You have just imagined our thinking that, you silly
child."

"Did I imagine what you said about the Duchess?"

Still she smiled and kept her hand on mine. "I expect that what I said about the Duchess was quite a little exaggerated to you by Eva and Don. That was an uncomfortable day for all of us. We don't often quarrel in our family; I don't suppose that you do, either. Quarrels are upsetting to everybody and nobody likes them."

"Certainly," I said, "I don't like them."

"Let's try to end this one, Penelope."

Did she guess how badly I wanted to end it? I could not tell.

"Supposing," she said, "that you let me put my point of view to you, as one grown-up person to another. You are very grown-up for your age, you know."

"I do know, and I deplore it."

She gave another little low laugh. "Well, I shouldn't go on deploring it if I were you. Think what a dull world it would be if we were all made alike."

I winced at the cliché because Francis had taught me to wince at clichés. But I pretended that she had not said it. She went on, "Listen, dear. Just because you are so grown-up and this place is your home, you have a very different life from the life that Don and Eva have. I'm not saying that one sort of life is right and the other wrong. They just happen to be different. Now, my husband and I have to judge what is good for Don and Eva, don't we? You'll agree? Just as your father and stepmother have to judge what is good for you."

"Yes. I agree to that." It sounded reasonable; the persuasion of her manner was beginning to work.

"Well, we think that they aren't quite grown-up enough yet to understand and appreciate all the things that you understand and appreciate. That's all. It's as though you had a stronger digestion and could eat foods that might upset them. Do you see?"

When I was still silent, she added, "I think you should. Your stepmother saw perfectly."

"I suppose I see."

"Do try."

In fact I was trying hard; but the struggle was different from

the struggle that she imagined. I felt as though I were being
pulled over the line in a tug-of-war. Inside me there was a
voice saying, "No, no. This is wrong. Nothing that she says
can make it right. It is not a matter of seeing her point of view;
you *can* see it; she has sold it to you. But you mustn't surrender." Oddly, the voice seemed to be the voice of the
Duchess. I felt as though the Duchess were inside me,
arguing.

I looked into the lovely, smiling face. "Do try," Mrs.
Bradley repeated. "And do please come and have supper with
the children tonight. Let's start all over again; shall we?"

When she held out both hands to me, she had won. I found
myself in her arms and she was kissing my hair. I heard her
say, "Poor little girl."

VI

ONLY the smallest shadow stayed in my heart and I forgot it
for long minutes. We talked our heads off. It was like meeting
them again after years. I found myself quoting in my head,
'And among the grass shall find the golden dice wherewith we
played of yore.' They still loved me; they still laughed at
everything I said. When I ended the description of the
ambassador fighting the press baron and the failure of the
electric lights, they were sobbing in separate corners of the
sofa.

"Go on; go on. What did the Duchess do?"

"I think she enjoyed it mightily. She had an electric torch
in her bag and she flashed it over them both like a searchlight."

"You do have the loveliest time," said Eva.

"Where is the Duchess tonight?" asked Don.

"In fact I think I heard her car come back about ten minutes
ago." I began to describe the car and the chauffeur.

"*Older* than the Duchess? He can't be. I'd love to see them
bouncing away under the fringe. Let's go out and look."

"Too late," I said. "At night he takes the car to the garage in Théoule."

"Hark, though," Don said. "There's a car now." He ran to the window; but I knew that it wasn't the Isotta-Fraschini. It was the putt-putt noise of Laurent's little Peugeot.

"How exactly like Laurent," I said. "As soon as the Duchess gets home, he goes out for the evening. And Francis has left him in charge."

It occurred to me now that I should go back. I reminded myself that Charlemagne was an effective watchdog. But I was not comfortable about it.

"D'you mean you ought to go and put the Duchess to bed? Undo her stays; help her off with her wig?"

"It isn't a wig; it's her own hair, and she requires no help. But I do think I should go back. The telephone may ring."

"Well then, the Duchess will answer it."

"She will not. She claims that she has never answered a telephone in her life. She regards them as an intrusion upon privacy."

"Isn't there anybody else in the hotel?"

"No."

"Oh you *can't* go yet," said Eva.

I sat on a little longer. Then I knew that it was no good. "I shall have remorse if I don't," I said, "and that is the worst thing."

"All right, then. We'll go with you."

"Oh, Don——" said Eva.

"Mum and Dad won't be back yet awhile," said Don, "and we'll only stay ten minutes."

"They'll be furious."

"We won't tell them."

Eva looked at me. I said, "I cannot decide for you. I only know I must go."

"Of course, if you want to stay behind," Don said to Eva.

"Of course I don't. What shall we say to Nanny?"

"We can say we went down to the beach."

.   .   .   .   .

We crept out, silent in the spirit of adventure. The moon had risen, the full moon, promised by the Duchess, enormous and silver and sad; its light made a splendid path over the sea; the palms and the orange trees, the rock shapes on the water, were all sharp and black.

"Here we go on Tom Tiddler's ground," Eva sang. We took the short cut, scrambling through the oleander hedge instead of going round by the gate, I could hear Don panting with excitement beside me. Almost, their mood could persuade me that the hotel was an enchanted place. We came on to the terrace and darted into the empty bar; Laurent had turned off the lights; I turned them up for the Bradleys to look at the photographs.

"What'll we drink?" said Don facetiously, hopping on to a stool.

"Champagne," said Eva.

"If the Duchess was still awake, she'd give us some champagne."

"You wouldn't drink it," said Eva.

"I would."

"You wouldn't."

"I jolly well would."

"She's probably in the *salon*," I said. "She never goes to bed early."

I put out the lights again and led them to the *salon* by way of the terrace. The *salon* lights were lit. We looked through the windows.

"There she is," said Don. "She's lying on the sofa."

They bounded in ahead of me. I heard Don say, "Good evening, Duchessa," and Eva echoed it. There was no reply from the Duchess. With the Bradleys, I stood still, staring at her. She was propped on the Empire sofa; her red head had fallen sideways on the stiff satin cushion. Her little pointed shoes and thin ankles stuck out from the hem of her shantung skirt and the skirt, which was of great width, drooped down over the edge of the sofa to the floor. On the table beside her she had placed the green tricorne hat, the green scarf, and her green velvet bag. A bottle of champagne stood in an ice pail; the glass had fallen to the floor; since one of her arms dangled limply, I thought that she must have dropped the glass as she went off to sleep.

"Please wake up, Duchessa; we want some champagne," said Don.

He took a step forward and peered into her face, which was turned away from us.

"She looks sort of horrid," he said; "I think she's ill."

For no reason that I could understand I felt that it was impertinent of him to be leaning there so close to her. When he turned back to us, I saw that his face was pale; the freckles were standing out distinctly on the bridge of his nose.

"She is ill, I'm sure," he said. "She's unconscious." He looked at the bottle of champagne. "She must be——" He stopped. I saw that he thought that the Duchess was intoxicated and that he could not bring himself to say so.

"Let's go," Eva said in a thin, scared voice. She grabbed Don's hand. "Come on, Penelope. Quick."

"But of course I'm not coming."

They halted. "You can't stay here," Don said. Eva was shivering. There was no sound nor movement from the figure on the sofa. I said, "Certainly I can stay here. What else can I do? If she is ill, I must look after her."

I saw them straining against their own panic. Suddenly they seemed like puppies, very young indeed.

"But *we* can't stay here," Eva said. "Oh, please, Penelope, come with us."

"No indeed. But you go," I said. "It's what you want to do, isn't it?"

"It's what we ought to do," Eva stammered through chattering teeth. Don looked a little more doubtful. "Look here, Penelope, you needn't stay with her. When they—they get like that, they sleep it off."

Now I was angry with him. "Please go at once," I said. "This is my affair. And I know what you mean and it isn't true." I found that I had clapped my hands to shoo them off;

they went; I heard the panic rush of their feet on the terrace. I was alone with the Duchess.

Now that they were gone, I had no hesitation in approaching her. I said softly, "Hullo, Duchessa. It's only me," and I bent above her as Don had done. I saw what he had seen; the shrunken look of the white face with the false eyelashes. Indeed she looked shrunken all over, like a very old doll.

I lowered my head until my ear touched the green frilled chiffon at her breast. I listened for the beat of her heart. When I could not hear it, I lifted the little pointed hand and felt the wrist. There was no pulse here that I could find.

I despised myself because I began to shiver as Eva Bradley had shivered. My fingers would not stay still; it was difficult to unfasten the clasp of the green velvet bag. I thought that there would be a pocket mirror inside and that I must hold this to her lips. Searching for the mirror I found other treasures; the ivory hand that she had aimed at Francis, a cut glass smelling-bottle, some coloured plaques from the Casino, a chain holding a watch, and a cluster of seals.

The mirror, when I found it, was in a folding morocco case with visiting-cards in the pocket on the other side. I said, "Excuse me, please, Duchessa," as I held it in front of her face. I held it there a long time; when I took it away the bright surface was unclouded. I knew that the Duchess was dead.

A profound curiosity took away my fear. I had never seen a person lying dead before. It was so strange to think of someone I knew well, as having stopped. But the more I stared at her, the less she looked as though she had stopped; rather, she had gone. This was not the Duchess lying here; it was a little old doll, a toy thing of which the Duchess had now no need. Where, I wondered, had she gone? What had happened to all the things that she remembered, the fencing lessons, and the child's dreams, and the Emperor? What happened, I wondered, to the memories that you carried around in your head? Did they go on with your soul or would a soul not want them? What did a soul want? Did the Duchess's soul like roulette?

Theology had never been my strongest subject and I found myself baffled by the rush of abstract questions flowing through my mind.

Then I became aware of her in relation to me. It was impossible to believe that I would not talk to her again. I was suddenly deeply sorry that I had not dined with her on the first evening, that I had not gone down in the fancy-dress to show myself to Jeanne. She had asked me to do this; she had asked me to come to Monte Carlo with her. '*Viens, chérie, ça te changera les idées.*' Always she had been kind. I had not. I had never been nice to her, because she embarrassed me, and now I should never have another chance to be nice to her.

Automatically I began to perform small meaningless services. I covered her face with the green scarf, drawing it round her head so that it made a dignified veil. I fetched a rug and laid it across her feet; I did not want to see the little shoes. I carried the untouched champagne back to the bar. I lifted her hat, her bag and gloves off the table; I took them up to her room. It was more difficult to be in her room, with the bed turned down and the night-clothes laid there, than it was to be in the *salon* with her body. I put the hat, bag, and gloves down on the nearest chair and I was running out when I saw the crucifix on the table. I thought that she might be pleased to have this near her ('Although,' I said to myself, 'she isn't there any more, one still goes on behaving as if she is'), and I carried it down; I set it on the table beside her. There seemed to be too many lights here now. I turned off all but one lamp; this room became a suitable place for her to lie in state, the elegant little shell of a room with the Empire furnishings. I pulled a high-backed chair from the wall, set it at the foot of the sofa, and sat down to watch with her.

Outside the windows the moonlight lay in the garden. I heard her saying, "The moon is at the full tonight. I look forward to it." I heard her saying, "Naturally, you cry for the moon." I heard her saying, "Death is a part of life," as she pulled on her white gloves.

At intervals I was afraid again; the fear came and went like intermittent seasickness. I did not know what brought it. She was so small and still and gone that I could not fear her. But I felt as though I were waiting for a dreadful thing to walk upon the terrace, and the only poem that would stay in my head was one that had always frightened me a little, 'The Lykewake Dirge':

> 'This ae nighte, this ae nighte,
> Everye nighte and alle,
> Fire and sleet and candlelyte,
> And Christe receive thy saule.'

It made shivers down my back. I would have liked to fetch Charlemagne from his kennel, but I had heard that dogs howled in the presence of the dead and this I did not want.

Sitting there so stiffly I became terribly tired: 'But it is a vigil,' I said to myself, 'and it is all that I can do for her.' It was not much. It was no true atonement for having failed her in kindness; it could not remit my having betrayed her to the Bradleys. It seemed hours since I had thought of the Bradleys. Now I wondered whether the parents had returned, and with the question there came incredulity that Don and Eva should not have come back. They had simply run off and left me, because they were afraid. The memory of their scared faces made them small and silly in my mind. Beside it, I uncovered the memory of my talk with Mrs. Bradley: the talk that had left a shadow. I admitted the shadow now: it was the note of patronage at the end of all the spellbinding. She had called me 'poor little girl'.

'You never called me poor little girl,' I said in my thoughts to the Duchess. She had called me fortunate and a genius. She had spoken to me of the world, of freedom and maturity. That was truly grown-up conversation. In comparison the echo of Mrs. Bradley saying, "As one grown-up person to another," sounded fraudulent. Some of the magic had left the Bradleys tonight.

I was so tired. I did not mean to sleep, because this was

vigil. But I found my head falling forward and the moonlight kept vanishing and the Duchess's voice was quite loud in my ears. "Of death," she said, "I remember three things; being tired, being quiet, and being gone. That's how it is, Penelope." She seemed to think that I could not hear her. She went on calling, "Penelope! Penelope!"

I sat up with a start. Somebody was in fact calling "Penelope": a man's voice from the terrace. I climbed down stiffly from the chair. "Who's that?" I asked, my voice sounding cracked and dry. Mr. Bradley stood against the moonlight.

"Are you there, child? Yes, you are. Come along out of this at once." He looked large and golden and worried; he seized my hand; then he saw the Duchess on the sofa.

"Lord," he said. "She's still out, is she?" He started again. "Did you cover her up like that?"

"Yes. Please talk quietly," I said. "She is dead."

He dropped my hand, lifted the scarf a little way from her face, and put it back. I saw him looking at the crucifix.

"I put it there. I thought that she would like it. I am watching by her," I said.

He looked pale, ruffled, not the way, I thought, that grown-up people should look. "I'm terribly sorry," he said in a subdued voice. "Terribly sorry. Young Don came along to our room, said he couldn't sleep for knowing you were over here with her. Of course he didn't think——"

"I know what he thought, Mr. Bradley," I said coldly. "Don and Eva are only babies really. Thank you for coming, just the same."

He said, in his officer-to-men voice, "Out of here now. There's a good girl."

"I beg your pardon?"

"You're coming to our house. I'll telephone the doctor from there." He took my hand again; I pulled it free.

"I'll stay with her, please. You telephone the doctor."

He looked down at me, amazed, almost smiling. He dropped his voice again. "No, no, no, Penelope. You mustn't stay."

I said, "I must."

"No, you mustn't. You can't do her any good."

"It is a vigil."

"That's just morbid and foolish. You're coming over to our house now."

"I am not."

"Yes, you are," he said, and he picked me up in his arms. To struggle in the presence of the Duchess would have been unseemly. I remained tractable, staying in his arms until he had carried me on to the terrace. He began to put me down and at once I twisted free.

"I'm not coming with you. I'm staying with her. She is my friend and she is not your friend. You were rude about her, and stupid," I said to him.

He grabbed me again and I fought: he imprisoned me with my arms to my sides. For the moment he did not try to lift me. He simply held me there.

"Listen, Penelope, don't be hysterical. I'm doing what's best for you. That's all. You can't possibly sit up all night alone with the poor old lady; it's nearly three o'clock now."

"I shall stay with her till dawn; and she is not a poor old lady, just because she is dead. That is a ridiculous cliché."

I was aware of his face close to mine, the stony, regular features, the blue eyes and clipped moustache in the moonlight. The face seemed to struggle for speech. Then it said, "I don't want insolence any more than I want hysteria. You just pipe down and come along. This is no place for you."

"It is my home," I said.

He shook me gently. "Have some sense, will you? I wouldn't let my kids do what you're doing and I won't let you do it."

"Your children," I said, "wouldn't want to do it anyway; they are, in vulgar parlance, a couple of sissies."

At this he lifted me off my feet again and I struck at his face. I had the absurd idea that the Duchess had come to stand in the doorway and was cheering me on. And at this moment there came the miracle. The noise of the car sweeping in from the road was not the little noise of Laurent's car, but the roaring powerful engine that meant that Francis had come home.

The headlights swung yellow upon the moonlit garden. Still aloft in Mr. Bradley's clutch I said, "That is my father, who will be able to handle the situation with dignity."

He set me down as Francis braked the car and jumped out.

"That you, Bradley?" said Francis. "What, precisely, are you doing?"

Mr. Bradley said, "I am trying to make your daughter behave in a sensible manner. I'm very glad to see you."

Francis came up the steps on to the terrace. He sounded so weary that I knew his back hurt him: "Why should it be your concern to make my daughter behave in any manner whatsoever?"

"Really, Wells, you'll have to know the story. There's been a tragedy here tonight, I'm afraid. Just doing what I could to help."

"I will tell him," I said. I was grateful for Francis' arm holding me; my legs had begun to feel as though they were made of spaghetti.

"You let me do the talking, young woman," said Mr. Bradley.

"If you don't mind, I'd prefer to hear it from Penelope," said Francis.

I told him. I told him slowly, leaving out none of it; there seemed less and less breath in my lungs as I continued. "And Mr. Bradley called it morbid and foolish and removed me by force," I ended.

"Very silly of you, Bradley," said Francis.

"Damn it, look at the state she's in!"

"Part of which might be due to your methods of persuasion, don't you think? All right, Penelope, easy now." I could not stop shivering.

"Leaving her alone like that in a place like this. You ought to be ashamed of yourself," Mr. Bradley boomed.

"Quiet, please," said Francis in his most icy voice.

"Damned if I'll be quiet. It's a disgrace and I don't want any part of it."

"Nobody," I said, "asked you to take any part in it, Mr. Bradley."

"Hush," said Francis. "Mr. Bradley meant to be kind and you must be grateful."

"I am not in the least."

"Fine manners you teach her," said Mr. Bradley.

"Quiet, please," said Francis again. "Penelope has perfect manners, mitigated at the moment by perfect integrity and a certain amount of overstrain." Looking up at him, I could see the neat Mephistophelean profile, the delicate shape of his head. I loved him more than I had ever loved him. Mr. Bradley, large and blowing like a bull, was outside this picture, nothing to do with either of us.

Suddenly he looked as though he realised this. He said, "I don't want my wife or my kids mixed up in it either."

"Mixed up in what, precisely?" Francis asked.

I said, "It is possible that he is referring to the inquest. Or do you mean mixed up with me? Because if you do, no problem should arise. After tonight I have not the slightest wish to be mixed up with them or you."

It would have been more effective had I been able to stop shivering; I was also feeling rather sick, never a help when attempting to make dignified speeches.

Mr. Bradley faded away in the moonlight.

Francis said gently, "Did you mean it? It is easy to say those things in anger."

"I think I meant it. Was the vigil, in your opinion, the right thing to do?"

"It was. I am very pleased with you."

I said, "But I am not sure that I can continue with it for a moment. I feel funny."

Francis took me into the bar; he poured out a glass of brandy and a glass of water, making me drink them in alternate swallows.

"Of course," he said gloomily, "it may make you sick.

In which event the last state will be worse than the first."

But it did not; it made me warm.

"They can't *help* being the Smugs, can they?" I said suddenly, and then for the first time I wanted to cry.

"They're all right," said Francis. "They are merely lacking in imagination."

I managed to say, "Sorry," and no more. I knew that he disliked me to cry. This time he said, watching me, "On some occasions it is better to weep."

I put my head down on the table and sobbed, "If only she could come back; I would be nice."

Francis said, "You gave her great pleasure always."

"Oh, not enough."

"Nobody can give anybody enough."

"Not ever?"

"No, not ever. But one must go on trying."

"And doesn't one ever value people until they are gone?"

"Rarely," said Francis.

I went on weeping; I saw how little I had valued him; how little I had valued anything that was mine. Presently he said, "Do you think that you can cry quite comfortably by yourself for a few minutes, because I must telephone the doctor?"

Though I said, "Yes, indeed," I stopped crying immediately. As I sat waiting for him, I was saying good-bye, to my first dead, to a love that was ended, and to my dream of being like other people.

The next day I tore the Anthology of Hates into pieces and cast the pieces into the sea. I did not read through the pages first, so certain was I that I had done with hating.

II

SMUG'S-EYE VIEW

Told by Don Bradley

I

WHEN I heard that my sister Eva had mumps, I was absolutely delighted. It meant that I couldn't go home for the half-term week-end. Penleith, my house master, broke it to me gently and suggested various local entertainments that might be found palatable. There was a good picture showing at the Playhouse. Would I care to join Mrs. Penleith and himself on an expedition to Tewkesbury? One or two other 'unfortunates similarly placed' were making up the party.

I thanked him and refused as politely as I could, explaining that I could easily fill the time. I said, "I want to get my McColl essay into shape. And there's a new colt over at Whiteford, so it's a good opportunity to put in some work on him."

Penleith had no objection to my exercising Crusoe's horses. For a moment I was tempted to ask if I might spend the week-end at Whiteford. It would, I knew, be all right with Crusoe. The temptation glittered.

Reluctantly I pushed it down. There would be trouble if my parents heard about it and they would have to hear because I was no good at telling lies. I couldn't face telephoning them today to ask permission. It was highly unlikely that I would get it. Invitations from friends were carefully studied; formal exchanges of letters were the rule. Although they had not met Crusoe, and although I took pains to soft-pedal him, I had already detected their reservations. They would never say Yes and I should hate them for saying No.

Still, I walked out of Penleith's study to stand grinning at a world grown huge with freedom.

It was almost too good. The explosions of joy went on like fireworks in my head until I could digest and believe my fortune. Then there came a sudden peace of mind that made me almost sleepy. I walked and blinked. There were two gifts

53

here: the bad thing taken away and the good thing given. I was so placidly grateful that I didn't even hammer at my conscience with the question: 'Why is going home the bad thing? It never used to be.' There was no room for guilt in this dazzle of reprieve.

The free time began after lunch on Friday. I put the McColl essay into a folder and wondered if my nerve would fail me when the time came to show it to Crusoe.

From Laxton I used to approach Whiteford in a little leisured bus that took nearly half an hour on its four-mile journey. The short cut to the Whiteford Road lay across the playgrounds, over the wall and down through the river-field. This had become the path into escape. I began to run as soon as I was over the wall; run and wish that I had four legs; I wanted my head down and my heels up, like a frisking pony. I might have turned a cartwheel; but at seventeen I was invested with a natural solemnity. I could only be undignified within. Even to run for joy was a weakness, a give-away and would be explained, should I meet anybody, by the lie that I was late for the bus.

There were cows in the river-field; friendly cows who trod the soft ground on either side of the water into marsh. There was a narrowing of the river, where I used to jump. I jumped now and scared the cows; I climbed the steep bank under the trees, vaulted the low fence and was out on the Whiteford Road. I stood wiping off my muddy shoes in the grass, looking down the road until the dawdling bus came into sight.

Sometimes I borrowed a bicycle for the journey; sometimes in extravagance I took a taxi; Crusoe would on occasion send the car for me. But I liked the bus ride the best; jogging through the Cotswold country, alone. School gave little opportunity to be alone and at home the wish for solitude was incomprehensible; the signal for investigation: "What's the matter? Don't you feel well? Alone . . . aren't you funny?"

I sat in the bus, content as a king. Crusoe wasn't expecting me. I wondered what sort of mood I would find. A grey afternoon, so his eyes would not be hurting him. Automatically now I was glad of a dull day; just one minute example of the many differences that he had made in my way of thinking. The time before Crusoe and the time since Crusoe were sharply divided. The older time looked dull and far.

I went back in my mind to the afternoon of last term when I met him. It was a Saturday, the day of the Laxton Governors' Meeting. Penleith and his wife used to give a rather depressing tea and sherry party for the members of the Governing Body. As a prefect, I had to be there, desperately handing cups and glasses. Nobody talked to us much.

This was a mild day of April and they were all in the garden. Crusoe was not a Governor; he had been brought by Colonel French, who was. When I saw him, my heart sank. It was queer to recall that now. But then he wasn't yet Crusoe; he was a demand on pity and horror; he was poor Raines in his black invalid-chair.

There was, to me, a peculiar horror about the chair itself. Not an ordinary invalid-chair that somebody pushed, but a motor-chair, a kind of black torpedo with a steering-gear; he could shoot about in it very fast. It worried me when I saw him on the cricket-field; he would come there quite often, even to watch the practice games; I would look up and see the sinister little black carriage parked beside the empty benches. When the game was over, it shot away like a beetle. I had only had to speak to him once before the day of the Governors' tea.

And here he was, with the group in Penleith's garden, parked beside the golden willow. I remembered the shower of leaves, pointed patterns of light themselves, with the other lights of the sunshine winking through. And the black machine, separating him horribly from everybody else; a magnet to which eyes were drawn, and I could see that some people looked away quickly, as I wanted to do; I wondered if he saw this.

He was talking to Colonel French when I came up with a tray of glasses and sandwiches. He was extremely audible. His voice had a clearer, higher note in it than most men's voices had; not piercing nor effeminate, but lightly loud:

"The abomination of field-sports," were the words.

"Sherry, sir?"

"Certainly, sherry."

I forced myself to look him in the face. He wore thick dark spectacles, solid and straight-bridged, almost a mask, blinkered at the sides. I noticed his hair, fair, wavy hair with a reddish gleam. It looked unreal, not like a wig, but frozen or lacquered, growing in whorls that came up to a crest. The small moustache and beard were lighter than the hair. I could see a straight nose and a mouth that curved, a smiling mouth, but the face was still unknown because of the hidden eyes.

"Would you by any chance know what is in these sandwiches?" he asked me.

"They're sardine, sir."

"French, Portuguese or Norwegian?"

"I'm afraid I don't know, sir."

He appeared to be staring at me through the lightless mask. "Wasn't it you who hauled me out of the mud last winter?"

"Yes, it was." The memory still embarrassed me. The wheels of the black torpedo had stuck at the gateway to the playing-field. There wasn't a soul in sight. I hadn't been playing football; I'd just walked that way, and I cursed my luck in choosing it. He had laughed uproariously all the time that I was tugging and pushing.

"Terrible for you," he now said blithely. I couldn't think of any adequate reply. I mumbled, "Oh no, not a bit," and handed the tray to Colonel French.

"Do they get paid for performing these menial tasks, French?" the light, loud voice demanded.

"Handsomely," said the tufted pink Colonel, whom I liked; "they miss an hour or more of private study."

"I should, on the whole, prefer the private study," said Raines.

So would I; it was sympathetic of Raines to understand that this was no fun. He was singing softly, "*Oh, I didn't raise my boy to be a butler*," when Penleith and his wife came into reverent attendance. Penleith was a benign silly with a walrus moustache; the wife was unexpectedly pretty. How he got her was one of our sources of speculation. They introduced a Mr. and Mrs. Stephens, who reminded me a little of my own parents; fair and tall and tucked-up.

I realised that Raines was losing his horror. When I had done my tour of duty, I helped myself to a glass of lemonade and drifted back within earshot of the chair. The group still held; Mrs. Penleith and Mrs. Stephens perched precariously on a bench brought out from the dining-room, the others standing.

"Hideous fate," the clear voice was saying; "I refer to being young. Doesn't last, of course; has that in common with love and seasickness; but how infinitely worse than either. What is the precise nature of the arsenical-looking liquid that you are consuming?" he fired at me.

"Lemonade, sir."

"Dear God . . ." said Raines and lapsed into silence before adding, "Simply goes to illustrate my point."

"Another sherry?" Penleith said quickly.

"*A* sherry, if you please."

Penleith beckoned a tray-bearer and said with heavy waggishness, "You *don't* subscribe to the theory that school days are the happiest days of one's life?"

Raines turned his head; slowly, all around once, like a hawk; or was that merely the effect of the black bar across the eyes— effect of a hawk, hooded?

"Theory, did you say? Theory? My dear Entwistle, that's not a theory; it's pedagogue's propaganda. Bah!" The 'Bah!' was a shout of laughter and he waved his hands; fragile, well-shaped hands that looked as though they had once been strong. "Wordsworth was a numskull, naturally," he added.

Something clicked in my mind; a neat thrill of familiarity, as when you feel: 'But we've done this before.' That feeling, I had been told, was caused by an unequal movement of the two lobes of the brain. It wasn't now. I was reminded of a small, lost adventure, an odd magic that I had once met. It gave me especial pleasure that he called Penleith 'Entwistle'.

"Wordsworth?" Colonel French repeated. "What's Wordsworth got to do with it?"

"I was thinking," said Raines, "of that fat-headed misconception: 'Shades of the prison-house begin to close upon the growing boy.' See what I mean, Enderby?"

"Can't say I do," said Penleith, grinning.

" '*Begin* to close' . . . oh my God!" said Raines, "suggesting that to grow up is to move into prison instead of out."

Mr. and Mrs. Stephens looked, I thought, as my parents would have looked, afloat and disturbed. Colonel French mumbled, "Responsibilities, after all; decisions."

"Bah! The whole of literature is an infantilist conspiracy. Not only literature—life! Youth is torture. Anybody who doesn't acknowledge it is a thug and a cheat. I don't mean people like yourself, Prendergast. You couldn't keep your employment for a minute if you allowed yourself to admit that what you're in charge of is a parcel of human misery."

It was the 'Prendergast' that made me do what is vulgarly called the nose-trick with my lemonade. I tried to thump myself on the back. Mrs. Penleith took pity and thumped vigorously. I came out of it with streaming eyes, to see the hooded head pointing towards Mr. Stephens.

"You really think so, sir? You do indeed? You aren't just saying so for the benefit of the young man, who, incidentally, appears to be strangling?"

"No," said Mr. Stephens, "certainly not."

"You avow that your youth was a happy one? My dear Mr. Strachey, you ought to be in a museum."

"Er, Stephens," said Mr. Stephens.

"Stephens?" asked Raines, sounding puzzled.

"Stephens is my name."

"A good, serviceable name," said Raines. "Might I trouble you for a glass of sherry, Penshurst?"

"Excuse me, does anybody know the time?" Mrs. Stephens asked, a little agitatedly.

"Never use it," said Raines, "a man-made institution of singular inconvenience to all."

His effect, I saw, was various. The Penleiths appeared to take him for granted. Colonel French was comfortably giggly.

Mr. and Mrs. Stephens were no longer floating, but drowning.

"We should go, dear," Mrs. Stephens said, and it was just what my mother would have said to my father at this point.

I looked at my watch. (One of the major exhaustions of school: it was always time to stop doing something and begin doing something else.) I said my good-byes. When I came to Raines, halting beside the chair that had ceased to be a menace, I asked after the health of his steeplechasers.

He leaned back his head to look up at me. I saw his skin, smooth, transparent, artificial somehow, like the hair. Not a line on the forehead above the solid black bar that the glasses made. They were wrong about his age, I thought; he was young; he must be young.

"They are beautiful," he said. "And fond and foolish. Like all horses. Do you care for horses?"

"Yes, I do. My father breeds hunters. I exercise them for him in the holidays. I've never thought that they were foolish animals," I said.

"Think again. And come over and ride mine for me, some time, if you'd like. Have you a name?"

"Yes, sir. Bradley. Don Bradley."

I expected him to call me Hutchins or Wotherspoon, but he said, "All right, Bradley. Don't forget. By the way, those were not sardines but brisling; not really a disappointment; I was confidently expecting them to be."

I said, "Good-bye, sir: I'd love to come and ride; I really would."

"All right. Any time." He called after me as I left, "I don't live in the big house, you know. In the little Palladian monstrosity by the lake; the Dower House."

Today, as the bus jogged along, I reviewed that first minute when my mind had clicked and responded, back in Penleith's garden. Why? What was it that had turned him so quickly from horror and pathos into a source of fun? Now that I knew him it was easy to value him. But then? I knew nothing. What was the glimpse that I had got, the clue?

It wasn't in his words. (I didn't take the indictment of youth seriously; nor ponder it; my age was a thing that I took for granted, with my lankiness and my fair hair and my face that looked, Eva said, like the face of a puzzled dog.) Neither the exuberant noisiness nor the nonsense gave the clue. There was an overtone, an echo sounding.

Wasn't it the overtone of a person who was free? Queer to think of a man paralysed in a wheel-chair as free. I meant that he had his own rules and that these were not like other people's rules. He had shone for me as the possessor of a sort of outrageous wisdom. It was the sort that I was always looking for in grown-ups and failing to find. I had had one such glimpse before and only one.

Adults perplexed me. I was for ever expecting them to riot in the freedom of having grown-up, having got away, and they never rioted. I was not unhappy, but I awaited with impatience the exciting end of minor tasks and tyrannies. Yet when I saw grown-ups living the sequel, it didn't look as though it were exciting. Horses, I was convinced, had more fun than people had.

The bus was jogging the last mile into Whiteford now. Crusoe alone, I thought, possessed that quality, that flourish; though it was only his mind that could kick up its heels; I saw the comet-streak of it, dashing from one idea to another.

At home we never talked ideas; we only talked about things. Abstract argument and discussion were quenched sooner or later by an uneasy glance travelling from parent to parent; signal for the veto—'Let's change the subject, shall we?', my least favourite way of ending a conversation, the axe coming down. Eva and I liked to argue when we were alone. We never reached conclusions; there was little common ground between us in those days. She was essentially light-hearted, a non-worrier; she sailed where I floundered. But we enjoyed a statement of the problem—any problem. And to the parents the only thing more indecent than a problem was the stating of it. We had learned to submit, to spend the evenings as they liked us to spend them, listening to the wireless and playing card games.

We believed that, if challenged, they would diagnose the art of conversation as 'unhealthy', the adjective most mysteriously applicable to other arts, to introspection, to religions that showed and to extremes of all kinds.

It was difficult not to compare Crusoe's tang with the aridity of home; not to compare the freedom of his company with the cramping restrictions that were becoming yearly more recognisable, and less bearable. The disloyalty worried me. Hints of a disturbing pattern had begun to emerge. I saw it when I looked back on my earlier friends. Every parental reaction had been the same. "Rather an odd chap, isn't he?" "Why do you have to pick these queer fish?" . . . "Nice fellow, but a bit nutty."

Those friends were small pointers on the way to Crusoe. My admiration for the oddity, the rebel, the clown and the eccentric never faltered. I couldn't hope to imitate them; I simply needed them. It was natural, in the sad struggle whose importance my mind would not confess, to leap at the antithesis of Bradley-ism. But I couldn't settle for it yet.

And the issue was, for the moment, kept small. Because life at home was only 'The Holidays', that series of half-true intervals between the long stretches of real life. School was real life. There was no disloyalty in this feeling; it came naturally. Eight months out of every twelve were lived here.

Real life was life in the crowd; life in a line; a line of desks in the classroom, a line of narrow beds in the dormitory. The smells of real life were floor-polish and blackboard-chalk, carbolic soap, hot tea-urns, other people's socks and hair-oil. Its sounds were the clatter of the crowd's heavy boots, the shapeless roar of the crowd-voice, the rattling of the crowd's knives and forks at table.

It was, I suppose, a life of limited adventure. I was at my most alive when I played games. Adventures in learning were spasmodic; sudden responses of affection and understanding; most often the response of my ear to words. Occasionally a sense of the past gave me mysterious pleasure (flint arrows, Roman roads, Hadrian's Wall; 'the barrow and the camp

abide'). Sometimes the noise of battle sounded clear through
the Greek or Latin embalming it, so that you saw the walls of
Troy.

But those moments had come seldom, before this term. I
had perhaps owned an inquiring mind that wasn't sure where
its inquiries should begin. Now they were in full cry. Crusoe's
knowledge illuminated alike the classics and the crowd. Dead
languages spoke with a new liveliness; music stopped being
dull as he taught me how to listen; religion was widening
beyond the boundaries of 'O.T.', 'N.T.' and attendance at
chapel. His wild explorations of human behaviour set me to
watching my masters and my fellows with keen eyes. I was
conscious of doors opening in all directions; they opened and
I walked through them. Was I changing as I walked? Some
people seemed to think so; Levy, my acidly highbrow friend,
Gort, the instructor in Greek, Burrowes, who gave us English
literature.

(Levy: "What *is* this Brighter-Bradley Movement, I'd like
to know?"

Gort: "Something of an authority on the *Crito*, this week,
aren't you?"

Burrowes: "How did *you* happen to arrive at a likeness
between the hates of Swift and the hates of Aldous Huxley?")

Here was the village of Whiteford; the uphill street whose
pavements were banked on cobbles, with narrow gutters of
water running beside them; the golden-grey almshouses, the
small, curved shop-windows, the tenth-century church at the
top of the hill.

I knew it by heart. There wasn't much to know, and I had
taken possession easily. From the pale, heraldic colours stain-
ing the Crusader's tomb in the church, to the wet black spokes
of the mill-wheel, Whiteford belonged to me.

The bus stopped at the top of the hill; here it turned round
and went back; I had to walk the rest of the way. I passed
under the shadow of the church, with the grey-timbered inn
fronting it across the street. I walked down the other hill, past
the grain-merchant's, past the cottages that would soon come

to an end, towards the bridge. There were gutters at the edges of these pavements too. I had made it a superstition that when they were full and fast-flowing, all would go well for me; when the water was dried to a thread or less, trouble would come. They were full today; rain had fallen; the water ran fast and brown.

I came to the bridge and halted, leaning over for a moment's ritual stare at the river. I did it every time I crossed, leaning out over the low, lichened coping, looking down. Then I walked on.

From the road now I saw the parklands of Whiteford Manor, the trees growing out of the grass and the spear-point of the lake. The parkland sloped up to the big house, with its grey Inigo Jones façade. It had a bleached look, the look of a grim, solid temple, far away, eternally shuttered, nobody there. The Dower House was still invisible, but you saw it before you got to the gates. The trees were cut; you looked down a green ride to the garden, the water, and the stone pavilion.

Now the gates, mossy stone pillars with wrought-ironwork between, a stone stag couchant behind a battered stone shield on the top of each pillar. I pushed the gates and walked in. Crusoe might be up at the stables, but it was a two-mile walk, so I thought I'd call at the house first. I went down the ride.

The garden came suddenly, between the trees and the water; lawns and low hedges, herbaceous border and rockery; beautifully tended, a model garden, with the pavilion at its end. I had not Crusoe's quarrel with Palladian architecture. I liked the portico and the shallow stone steps; pompous, but not offensive, I said to myself. The middle part of the steps was covered by a wide, sloping board; this for Crusoe's chair.

I saw the tabby cat sitting upright in a flower-bed; a well-rounded cat with magnificent whiskers. I chirruped at him and he gave a pink yawn.

Crusoe's manservant Joel opened the door; he was quite old, not doddering, but erect and grey-headed. The secretary, Miss Wood, was as usual scuttling across the hall with papers. I never saw a woman so often in transit. She was middle-aged and bashful. Crusoe swore that her real name was Woodpecker and that even the dropping of the last two syllables had not helped her sense of inferiority. She was given to cliché-quotations, incompletely mastered. Crusoe likewise swore that she had once approached him with a teapot, saying, "How about a cup of the Harmless Necessary?" The period of waiting for her to follow this up with 'The cat that cheers', lengthened, but he did not, he said, despair.

Miss Wood gave me a whicker of greeting and vanished. Joel said that Crusoe had just finished luncheon; he was having coffee on the terrace with Mrs. Irvine.

"You'd better announce me, I think. I'm not expected."

("The monstrous effrontery of those who drop in without warning," his voice echoed.)

Through the glass doors at the end of the hall I could see the terrace. Crusoe was in the ordinary wheel-chair, not the black torpedo; I could see Mrs. Irvine leaning towards him, her neck extended; he had called her 'the prim swan'. All his people were identified with animals or birds and this had begun to be my own habit.

Mrs. Irvine was a neighbour, a widow and a horsewoman. You never could tell with Crusoe's guests. He knew everybody in the world. Between his trickiness with names and his casual indifference, you were likely to find, after some quiet little man had left, that you'd been talking to a Nobel Prize poet or the First Lord of the Admiralty.

I heard a bellow, "What the devil's *he* doing here?" Then, "Don! That you?"

I left the essay in its folder on the table and loomed at the glass doors. He spun the chair half-way round to meet me.

"Hullo. Are you in trouble?"

"No."

"No trouble?"

"No, really not."

"How disappointing. Is it—for some reason that escapes me—a half-holiday?"

"It's the half-term week-end. My sister's got mumps, so I can't go home."

"Good."

Mrs. Irvine said gently, "Really, Crusoe—isn't that the wrong way round? I should have thought that when Mr. Bradley tells you he isn't in trouble you would say 'Good'; and when he tells you he can't go home, you would say 'How disappointing'."

Crusoe brooded, twitching his chin sideways, so that he seemed to be seeing how far he could move his beard. I perched on the balustrade.

"The first observation was dictated by honesty and the second by selfishness," he said at last. "Ever noticed the dust of disappointment settling on the company at the news that the dying man is going to recover? Trouble is drama; and I, in common with the rest of the world, have an appetite for drama. As far as Don's sister's mumps are concerned, I'm delighted that he can put in some work on my horses." He spun the chair-wheels.

"What's happening to your essay?" he asked me. He had an odd wave-length, a way of picking up your thoughts out of the air. We hadn't talked of the essay for weeks.

"I've got it. I've done a sort of end."

"Sort of?" The qualification was one of his phobias. I could see Mrs. Irvine wanting to say, 'Really, Crusoe'—again. She couldn't know that I was used to his heckling and that when he wasn't wholly unreasonable I liked to argue back.

"Surely there can be more than one sort of end," I said mildly. "I've done one sort, that's all."

"Hedging," said Crusoe.

"Tell me about the essay," said Mrs. Irvine.

I was still shy with the subject because it wasn't in a field where my sort of (sorry, Crusoe) person ventured. It was the target of the intellectuals; of Hemingway with his black lock of hair and fluting voice, Hemingway who listened to the Third Programme; of Gunn, who liked Bartok and the free-verse poets and Jean-Paul Sartre; of Levy who wrote school satires and made Latin puns. Not a natural goal for Bradley (D.), horseman and cricketer. But then nobody knew that Bradley (D.) now wanted to be a writer. Anyway I would never have put my name down for it except for one most humiliating conversation with Crusoe.

"The McColl Gold Medal," he was saying to Mrs. Irvine, "is a yearly prize endowed by some Victorian with a taste for genteel philosophising. It is awarded for the best essay on any abstract subject that the writer cares to choose. Love, Death, Happiness, Hatred, Pox, Porridge——"

—"I shouldn't have thought," Mrs. Irvine began.

"No, but you get the idea," said Crusoe impatiently.

"What subject did you choose?" she asked, looking at me. The turn of her neck made the 'prim swan', but there was something pointed and Spanish in the face; a medallion's look. I explored for a moment the thought of people who looked more interesting than they were.

I said, "It's on Penitence."

She was surprised: "Penitence? What made you choose that?"

The memory of the humiliating talk disturbed me still. "Well, Crusoe did, really," I mumbled. "We were discussing what one was sorry for, and who one was sorry to." At the grammar he put his hands over his ears.

Mrs. Irvine continued to look puzzled and interested. But I was playing the conversation back. It had happened in the circular panelled room with the books; a bright day and his eyes were hurting him, so the curtains were drawn at the windows. I had just finished eating an enormous tea. I was enlarging upon a row at home.

"And every time I fight, I feel mean to them afterwards. I'm eaten with remorse."

"You needn't niggle around with remorse," said Crusoe.

"Don't all decent sinners suffer from it?"

"On the contrary. Decent sinners, given time, become penitent. From penitence you can at least learn something. Remorse is sheer indulgence; threshing about in a self-made trap. Going back over it all, trying to pretend that it didn't happen; or that it happened quite differently; excusing yourself and cursing yourself by turns. All going *in*, d'you see?—instead of out. Just battering up against the walls of your own ego."

He interested me. "I know that one," I said, "I've done it. I remember pretending that it all happened differently. That went on for ages. I reconstructed the whole scene as it *should* have happened."

"What was this?"

"Not sure I can tell you, even now."

"Really? Why not?" His voice was gentle.

I hesitated: "Well, it was an awfully long time ago. I was a kid. But it made me squirm for years."

"You can't shock me, you know," said Crusoe.

In fact, I wasn't afraid of shocking him. Rather I was afraid that he would find it childishly innocent and dull. He would, I thought, roar me down with ridicule.

"Well," I said uncertainly, "ages ago—I was thirteen; we were in France. And I left a girl alone with—hell, it does sound silly—with an old lady who I thought was drunk."

Here I expected an acid comment. '*You have yet to catch my attention,*' was one of his worst. He didn't make it.

"How d'you mean, you left her alone?"

"In an hotel. Her father owned the hotel; we had the villa next door to it. She came to supper with us, and my sister and I went back there with her and we found the old lady lying on a sofa. We were scared. She did look—sort of horrible, and we ran away."

His head and shoulders, silhouetted, were rigidly attentive.

"This was at night?"

"Yes."

"But there was somebody else in the hotel besides the girl, surely—somebody in charge?"

"Well, no, there wasn't."

"The girl was quite alone there?"

"Yes."

"You knew that?"

"Yes."

"How old was the girl?"

"About fourteen."

"And you just ran off and left her?"

It had become an inquisition. I nodded my head.

"Why did you do that? What was so frightening about the old lady? Was she ill—or violent—or both?"

"I only saw her for a minute. She looked queer."

"Was the girl frightened of her?"

"I don't know if she was or not. Look, Crusoe—mind if we don't go on talking about it?"

"Of course I don't mind . . . but why not?"

I couldn't give him all the reasons. I said, plunging deeper, "Because it was worse than we thought. The old lady wasn't drunk at all; she was dead. We didn't know till the next day."

I expected some sympathy here. I didn't get it. After a pause he said, "Yes. I damned well would be ashamed of that if I were you."

He had dropped the old cloak of misery down upon my head. I said angrily, "I've told you. I was. It bothered me for ages afterwards."

He was silent, resting the tips of his fingers together. There were moments when I felt that I could hear him thinking.

"Thirteen, you were?"

"Yes."

"Didn't it occur to you to try and get help? Call your father or somebody?"

"He and my mother were out. But I'm not sure I would have called them. We'd been forbidden to go to the hotel. It was an odd sort of place."

"Ha!"

"What do you mean, 'Ha'?"

He was silent again.

"I did go along and wake Daddy at about two in the morning," I said, "because it was on my conscience."

"So it might be."

I mumbled, "Why d'you think it was so bad?"

"For the same reason that you yourself think so. Because it was cowardly."

Now I was entirely wretched. I couldn't tell him how important the old lady had been to me. Nor could I tell him of the furious vow that came afterwards; a secret vow, made and kept. That never would I again desert in time of trouble. Not a person, not an animal, nor show fear of any ugly thing. I had sworn this at my prayers, pressing my knuckles into my eyes. No matter what the subject of affliction was, I would stay with it, never leave it. And oddly, once the vow was made, the things had come; or so it looked now. There was the glorious yearling, the chestnut who broke his leg the first time that we had him out with a bridle. They shot him. My father was there and the groom and they didn't want me to stay. I stayed beside him. I had to be sick in the field when it was over, and I was ashamed. There was the shouting, lurching old woman with the bottle in her hand; I had met her in the lane two miles from my home and somehow I got her as far as her cottage, towing her like a tug. There was the dog hit by a car that broke his back and left him with half his inside spilling out on the road; it was forcing myself through a steel wall to go to him and take his head in my lap. I sat with him while somebody fetched the vet; it took him an hour to die. These things, and others like the trapped rabbit, or the bawling child who'd cut off the top of its finger, were they, I wondered, challenges to my valiant boast? You wouldn't think that God would take so much trouble, would you? But I couldn't tell any of this to Crusoe. I sat there steeped in the sense of his injustice.

Presently I heard my voice asking sulkily, "How would penitence operate?"

"Operate?"

"In that situation——"

"My dear Don, I've no objection to educating you in Christian knowledge, but I should have thought that it was adequately handled by your teachers. No, of course, it isn't," he added with the gentler note in his voice. And for the rest of the time he had sketched the principles of penance and atonement until I grew interested and forgot my sorrows. The vow seemed to square with the idea of atonement; I should have liked his reassurance about this, but I could not bring myself to ask it.

That was how the essay began.

To Mrs. Irvine I was saying vaguely, "I've always admired natural impenitents; the people who don't worry and get away with murder. Like my sister Eva. Crusoe says there's nothing to admire—that it's constitutional and——"

"Time we were going up to the stables," Crusoe interrupted. "Want to come, Anne?"

"No, I'm off." She shook hands with me. "I'd love to read the finished product," she said.

II

THE stables were behind the big house. When Crusoe was having a good day, he got his irons on and we went up in the car. This was always more worrying to me than the régime of the black torpedo. Even with the irons he could only hobble and totter, supported on two sticks. In the stable-yard he went too near the horses' heels; he could never have moved away quickly out of trouble. The head-groom used to yell at him and so did I. It was the same in the field. He would fix himself up beside a jump and give me heart attacks lest we fell at the jump and knocked him over. I think he liked to worry us.

Today was a good day, a day for the irons. The car took us up the drive, past the sad façade of the big house, Crusoe remarking, "Dead Man's Hall," and adding, "If my brother Livesey weren't such a feudal chump, I'd sell it."

"Who'd you sell it to?"

"To *whom* . . ."

"Sorry. To whom? I mean you'd hate to have strangers living on your grounds. And it couldn't be a family; nobody could afford it. Probably it would have to be nuns."

"I've nothing against nuns," said Crusoe.

Brother Livesey was a mysterious figure. He was younger than Crusoe; he was married "To a madwoman. Dear God, I should know; I was in love with her myself." The marriage was, according to Crusoe, in suspension and Livesey in America. "He is, unhappily for him, possessed of remarkable business talents. A bullock, equipped with a dynamo of energy. Lapped in lead as I am, I find infinite peace in contemplating the strenuousness of Brother Livesey."

But that was all I knew. I'd have liked to know more of the 'madwoman' and the love-affair. And I thought that a good business-man would certainly prefer to sell Whiteford. Crusoe had a genius for leaving stories half-told, tantalising references hanging in mid-air.

I had never heard the story of the accident that crippled him. Penleith had said, "Playing polo in the States"; the groom said that he got it hunting. Crusoe did not speak of it, though he talked blithely of the terrors that came afterwards. At one stage the paralysis had affected his speech: "My brain remained entirely clear. But nobody had any proof of that, so they all talked to me in baby-talk; to the pattern of those who automatically begin to whisper because the person they're addressing happens to have lost his voice. They felt obliged to make the sort of noises that I was making. It gave me an immense sympathy for babies, trapped with ideas in their heads and no vocabulary. How bloody silly their mothers must sound making noises like 'Goo Goo' and 'Woozer-woozer'. *Deepest* sympathy for babies, ever since," said Crusoe.

The car stopped at the gate of the stable-yard. We had to haul and hoist him. It still surprised me that he wasn't taller, standing up. He wasn't a small man; he was just short of six feet, but in the chair he was enormous, the head, the beard and the wide shoulders. Propped on these wavery, supported legs, he shrank down. His yellow waistcoat jutted over the beginning of a paunch. On sunny days I had sometimes seen him looking at his shadow.

(*"After middle-age, you'll find that you cultivate a certain pitying affection for your own body. Probably comes from realising that no one else is going to care for it again."*)

We came into the yard. "New cat, isn't it?" Crusoe said, peering across the cobblestones. "Always interesting, a new cat."

"It's just one of the grey cats, I think."

"Are you sure? It looks fuzzier. Good afternoon, Mallock. I bring you the unexpected benefits of Mr. Bradley."

Crusoe was his own trainer; he ruled over the head-groom, the under-groom, the stable-boy and me. There were times when his grasp, knowledge and instinct seemed to me supernatural. Half-blind and immobilised, he might well have had the power of mounting his spirit on a horse. He knew all that we knew of them and more; he could give us their tricks, their talents, their weaknesses before we had the chance to discover these for ourselves. Mallock told stories of his buying a stallion without appearing to look at him. "Weaves his head round and *listens* and then nods. He's half horse himself, if you ask me."

This part took a long time, as he staggered from stall to stall, using Mallock's shoulder or mine. Many of his talks with them were silent; I found it hypnotic to watch the black-barred profile and the caressing hand. I had argued his verdict, "Fond and foolish."

"Really, Crusoe, you can't say a horse is unintelligent. Look at the ways he'll take to avoid a hole. Look how he does his level best not to hurt you when he falls. He'll roll clear if he can. And he'll never trample you."

"Fond," Crusoe repeated. "Kind. Sensitive. Not clever."

"Well, but they aren't all kind. Take the mean ones; the ones who just don't like people."

"You would regard disliking people as a sign of intelligence?" Exasperating man.

The new colt hadn't been saddled yet. Mallock had taken him out on the exercising rein and I hoped that it would be my turn today. He was as pretty as a bronze. At first his head over the stall was gentle against Crusoe's hand; then the stable-boy clanged a pail down a little way off and he danced, jerking his velvet nose out of reach. I watched the hand pursuing him, soothing him, drawing him back.

Crusoe staggered on. We came to Rougemont's stall. Crusoe didn't caress Rougemont. He glanced first at Mallock, then at me. "Sorry, Don; the time's come. Breaks my heart, but there it is."

I knew what he meant. Of all the thoroughbred beauties in the stable, I liked Rougemont's looks the best. I looked him in the eyes now; he was jet-black, with a coppery glint; he had a twinkle; there was something about him that gave me hope, a kind of humour in his wickedness. Not unlike his owner, I thought, and wondered whether Crusoe's impatience might be due to a certainty that he himself, given back his body, could have found the clue to Rougemont before this.

"Please not," I said. "Please don't sell him yet."

I blamed Gill, the under-groom, for letting him get away with his fancies, so that now he had the habit of refusing or running out. But he had a sensitive mouth; he was physically perfect and he was fun; he could, I was sure, be made all right.

"Sorry," Crusoe said again.

"But——"

"No buts. He's a refuser and that's that."

Mallock stood silently switching his gaiters with a straight leather whip.

"Eh, Mallock?"

"Afraid you're right."

I looked despairingly upon him, at the curved beauty of his neck, and the disdainful, wicked head. I knew about being in love, I thought, looking at horses.

"Gill had him out again this morning," Crusoe said. "Same story."

"I tell you it's Gill's fault," I muttered.

Crusoe's mouth went thin. "You know better, do you?"

"I didn't say that. I've told you before, I believe we can get him right."

He snapped, "Very well. Go ahead. Try."

"Aren't we going to take the colt out?"

"No," he said crossly. "Since you're so obstinate you'd better prove your point."

"Now?"

"Now. Saddle him and bring him down. Mallock, give me a hand, will you?" He stumped away towards the car, with the groom.

"You're for it," said the stable-boy.

"What do *you* think?"

"I'm with them. He's a beauty, but he's a mean horse. He and Gill had a proper set-to this morning."

We had some trouble saddling him. My legs began to feel cold. I wasn't really afraid; I was just desperately anxious to save him. As clearly as though he spoke, I got the message, "I'm going to be as bloody as I possibly can. Fair warning. It's not every horse that gives you fair warning, is it?" And the black wink, the sideways toss of the head, the kick and the plunge; then a sudden moment of absolute stillness, before he lashed out again.

"Better take a whip," the stable-boy said.

"No. I can handle him without."

As an appeal to his better nature it had little effect. But I was up; the boy was leaping back out of reach of his heels. We clattered out of the yard.

I followed the dirt lane down under the trees. I could see Crusoe's car bouncing ahead. Between my knees and answering my hands, I got the feel of sly obstinacy that was more disturbing than mere sulks. Perhaps I'm all wrong about him, I thought, as I rode towards the challenge that was the field.

Before Crusoe, I had taken horses for granted as the best companions in the world, the easiest to understand, the most exciting. Their characters were clearer to me than people's characters; I never felt baffled by them nor worried by their behaviour; a mean horse gave you palpable clues to his meanness. "Half a horse myself, maybe," I echoed Mallock. There were moments at full gallop when I'd had that feeling, that we were not horse and rider, but one person. Solemnly at the age of twelve when asked what I would most like to be, I had replied "A Satyr." My parents' reaction was uncooperative until they realised that what I had in mind was a Centaur.

Since Crusoe, my love had sharpened with poignancy, because I was always seeing them through his eyes. How would it feel to be Crusoe, 'lapped in lead', exulting in the magic of movement that he could not share? I couldn't bear it, I thought and wondered often how he bore it, thinking that if I were crippled I'd never want to be near a horse again. I wouldn't want to smell the stables nor the leather in the harness-room; I would stop my ears to the hollow, thrilling noise of hooves on turf. I couldn't, I was sure, be one with it all as he was. Sometimes when he gave us orders, he could sound as though he gave them to himself; I could believe that he lived out the jump or the canter inside our bodies, that when we fell he fell.

Yet, on difficult days, he seemed to be all opposition, enjoying every triumph of the horse, every failure of the rider. Was he living inside the horse's brain and body then? You couldn't tell. He was easy to misinterpret. I had been quite wrong about his reasons for watching the cricket at school. In the old days, sighting the chair, I had been sure that he grieved and envied us. He had shot that one down: "I go for the simple pleasure of reminding myself that I need never compete again. The sweat of competition seen afar is a most wholesome horror; Grand Guignol in its effects."

When I came to the field I saw that the car had gone round to the biggest jump, the high turf wall. The chauffeur and Mallock were propping Crusoe in his place.

'Needn't think I'm going to put him at that one,' I said in my mind. I cantered Rougemont round the field. The beautifully easy movement lulled me. Lindsay Gordon's galloping verses came up in my head; it wasn't poetry, Crusoe said, but

I swore it was for me because it answered Housman's test of true poetry; it made my skin prickle:

> 'Where furrows looked lighter, I drew
>   the rein tighter,
> Her dark chest all dappled with flakes
>   of white foam,
> Her flanks mud-bespattered, a weak
>   rail she shattered.
> We landed on turf with our heads turned
>   for home.'

I said some of it to Rougemont. A faint shout from the top of the field was summoning me, I thought, to cut the canter and put him at the jump. "We're all right, aren't we?" I said to the black vignette of ears and mane.

I pulled him up gently; I patted him, turned him and rode him at the first hurdle. I took him at it confidently, lovingly, talking him on with 'How We Beat the Favourite'.

> *'She raced at the rasper, I felt my knees*
> *grasp her—'*

and I gripped with my knees, let my hands go forward. Then there was the exasperating anticlimax, the sideways swerve, and as he ran out I could feel the swing of the verse checked and silted up inside my head.

"Damn you, Rougemont, it isn't Gill now, it's me. You're just spoiling it for yourself. That's all. You know how it feels. It feels terrific; and you were set. You can't enjoy that piddling last-minute swerve, any more than I can. Make a little sense, will you, old boy?"

Did I imagine the jeering borne on the wind from where the high jump was? Whether I did or didn't, it wakened my temper. I didn't hate yet, but I might in a minute.

"Come on now—no more nonsense," I said to him. "You know what I want and it's what you want too. Let's have the laugh on Crusoe this time. Come on, Rougemont. Hell to Crusoe. Let's go."

Here, in one taunting moment, he went straight at it; the swallow-flight movement brought the verses back.

> 'She rose when I hit her, I saw the
> stream glitter
> A wide scarlet nostril flashed close
> at my knee.
> Between sky and water The Clown
> came and caught her—'

I'd mastered him, I thought; I was feeling us sail on and up and over. Then, damn his eyes, he pulled up hard. I shot forward on to his neck, his head came back and cracked my jaw; I don't know how I stayed on. I was rolling around, seeing stars, groping for my stirrups, swinging half under his belly before I clutched and scrambled and got back. Then he bolted.

'That's done it,' I thought; rage now, blind, bloody fury. "You can't scare me, you swine. You're going to get it, d'you hear, get it? Pull all you bloody like. Pull my arms off. I'll teach you." Crouched low and swearing, with the sky and the turf pouring past, holding him, sitting him, getting control, wheeling him over towards the high jump, yelling at Mallock for the whip. Rougemont was my black and plunging enemy; I hated his guts. We hurtled close to them; I didn't see Mallock come; there was just the flash of a hand there and the whip to grab and a zigzag glimpse of Mallock flinging himself back out of danger and the ecstasy of cutting Rougemont as hard as I could. It was a wicked whip; it felt like slashing with a sword.

But it was all temper now; it had to be; nothing but my flogging hand between him and his doom. "You or me," I panted at him. "And damn you, it's going to be me." It was all hate as we raced at the hurdle, the hate was the bond between us and the whip was the hate made alive, raining down blows that hurt me too. Black rage couldn't stop the lines from coming.

> '*Still on past the gateway she strains in the*
> *straight way,*
> *Still struggles. "The Clown! By a short head*
> *at most"*
> *—and swerves, the green scourges, the stand*
> *rocks and surges—*'

This was it—my knees gripped him, I cut him again and he rose; it was being carried high on a comet's tail.

> '*And flashes and verges and flits the white*
> *post.*'

I heard them shout as we landed; then I flung away the whip and rode him on down the field, saying, "I love you, Rougemont, I love you, I love you," over and over again.

III

As usual I had miscalculated Crusoe's reactions. He frequently fooled me by being larger in mental stature than I expected. This, because I was still accustomed to the littleness of people my own age, whose victory was 'Sucks to you!', whose retreat was sullenness. I thought that he would be cross because I had proved him wrong. He was grinning all over his face.

("You'll get yourself killed one day, you courageous little bastard.")

"All the same, don't get too cocky about it. He may revert tomorrow."

"Not he. I'll swear he winked at me. Christ, I hated hitting him."

"If you are in fact addressing the Son of God," Crusoe interrupted coldly.

"I'm sorry. I'm awfully sorry. I haven't for ages."

"Well, don't. It's shocking bad manners."

"I know it is." We were sitting on the terrace. I had to approach my goblet of cider at an angle; my mouth was all plummy from collision with Rougemont's head. Crusoe drank brandy and water; his dogs lay at his feet, the giant Alsatian bitch, melancholy with her love for him and the stout, bristling toffee-coloured terrier.

"This essay, now?" said Crusoe.

I couldn't switch my mind so quickly. I was still thundering down the field in the loving gallop. And this was peace, sprawled out on a long chair between the magnolia-covered wall and the grey, pedimented urns that formed the balustrade. Beyond the tops of the urns the lake shone greyish-gold. The trees and the parkland sloping up away from it had the veil of evening upon them—their Corot look. A wild duck skimmed down on the water and glided into the reeds. Afterwards there came the 'plick' sound of a fish as it pierced the surface. I wanted to be quiet with all this, and to be riding Rougemont in my head.

"Can you read, with that mouth of yours?" Crusoe persisted.

Certainly somebody would have to read it to him. ("*I save what there is of my eyes for the horses.*") He banned Miss Wood "*because, if there were such a thing as a breathy harp, it would be Miss Wood reading.*" A priest from the seminary at Chalford came once a week to read to him and there was another regular, a retired doctor who was an authority on Dickens. He had the talking book, with records from its library. Not the wireless (which he disliked as much as he despised the telephone) unless there were classical music playing. Seldom did he ask for the newspapers. It was his boast that he had not read a newspaper since the end of the war. He had shown cool astonishment when I told him about our family-drilling in current affairs.

"Current affairs? Do they interest you?"

"Sometimes."

"Shouldn't bother to learn them, if I were you. You'll be living them soon enough. Or, more likely, being killed by them." And he went on to say that the wisest men, unfolding their newspapers, turned at once to the sporting-column, or the nature-notes, or the crossword. "These are passions, after all. You couldn't have a passion for current affairs, unless you were out of your mind."

I went to fetch the essay. I knew that, however poor it might be, I should not do it what little justice it deserved. It puzzled me always that I couldn't put on a performance, except in the show-ring, where I had never known nerves. From the age of four onwards I had been master of that situation. Setting a pony up and showing him off, I was happily arrogant. This ease did not come on the cricket-field, where I sweated with fright; nor, God knows, when called upon to read my own work aloud.

I read it slowly, expressionlessly, trying to pretend that it had been written by somebody else. When I got to the end, he said, "Read the poem again, would you? What's the title?"

" 'Lucifer Sings in Secret'."

"You should mention that. Otherwise your meaning isn't clear. I know what you're driving at, I think, but the judges won't."

I began again. It was much more difficult than 'How We Beat the Favourite' and I gave it a throaty mumble because I liked it so much:

> " '*I am the broken arrow*
> *from Jehovah's quiver . . .*' "

I broke off. "Look, Crusoe, I don't like 'Jehovah'. I wish it was 'Jesus' quiver'. Wouldn't that scan as well?"

"Perfectly. Dropped syllable. Yes," he said, "it is better. But I'm afraid you can't tamper. Go ahead."

> " '*I am the broken arrow*
> *from Jehovah's quiver.*
> *He will not let me sorrow*
> *for ever and ever.*

> *'He will give me a new feather*
> *that is white and not red;*
> *He will bind me together*
> *with the hairs of His head.*
>
> *'My shaft will be jointed*
> *like the young, springing corn.*
> *My tip will be pointed*
> *with a painted thorn . . .' "*

As usual, my voice shook ridiculously on the last two verses:

> *" 'I shall choose the target*
> *His arrow deserves,*
> *I shall trace it and mark it*
> *in scarlet curves.*
>
> *'Small and bloody*
> *as a fallen sparrow,*
> *my own dead body*
> *shall receive His arrow.' "*

Crusoe was silent for a while. Then he said, "That being your last word on penitence? The Devil's penitence, eh?"

"That was the idea."

"It's a good idea."

"Thank you." I gulped some more cider.

"Leave it with me, there's a good fellow. You don't mind somebody else reading it? Lawrence'll be over tomorrow afternoon. I have to hear it more than once."

"And preferably not from me," I said with a grin. "No: of course that's all right. It's damn' good of you to bother with it."

"It interests me." I could hear him thinking now, but I didn't know what he was thinking.

"As you're up" (I wasn't) "you may give me some more brandy."

When I brought it to him he said, "Would your father be impressed if you won the McColl—or discomfited?" This was wave-length again; I had had my father in mind because the essay was, I thought, in keeping with some objects of distrust at home.

I said defensively, "I imagine he'd be quite pleased. In his view, any prize is worth competing for."

"Not really?"

"Yes, truly. Of course he wouldn't be as pleased as if I made a century against the Rovers. He's promised me anything I like if I do that . . . within reason, of course."

"Dear God . . ." said Crusoe. Then with one of his rapid swoops toward consideration, he added, "Not meaning a word against your father. Thinking of you sweating at the Grand Guignol."

IV

ON the morning of the Rovers' match, I knelt in chapel, trying to pray. I stared at the dark choir-stalls, the stained glass and the shapes of the Gothic arches.

> 'We praise Thee, O God,
> We acknowledge Thee to be the Lord.
> All the earth doth worship Thee.'

This was changing. Before Crusoe I had found God placidly remote. I knew the feeling of being one with the crowd who worshipped and praised, but that was all. When it came to the object of our worship, my thoughts wavered and retired. Ages ago there had been God the cross old gentleman who didn't like me to bite my nails; less frequently God the jolly old Santa Claus who responded to my prayers for an electric railway-train. After I grew out of that, he became merely a conviction, a belief without form.

The figure of Jesus Christ endured, friendly and sad. I had long been convinced that I wouldn't have gone to sleep in the Garden, nor betrayed him as the disciples did. In fact the disciples still seemed to me an unworthy lot. But I was accustomed to no further identification of my religious feelings. There was just the conviction, an instinctive hush of politeness in my mind and compassion for Christ when I thought about him. My confirmation-classes had done little to sharpen the view.

A pretty comfortable view, it looked from here. Crusoe, the destroyer, had swept it away. I was confronted with the Blessèd Trinity, the Four Last Things, the Mystical Body and many other new complications. That religion could be adult, philosophical and intellectual was disturbing. Much as it fascinated me, I was sure that my parents would disapprove profoundly.

Perhaps that was why I found it so hard now to shape the prayer that must include them. Their surprised faces kept coming before my eyes. It would have been easy in the old days, when I simply buried my head and bargained: I would have said:

"Please let them say yes without a fuss, when I give them Crusoe's invitation for the holidays. Please let me make a hundred in the match today, because that'll help."

(*"Treating him like a mail-order service is all right as far as it goes, but once you're out of the kindergarten stage, you naturally want to do more than just say please and thank you."*)

I tried again. "I offer you all that I am, and it is yours already, but it is all that I have to offer. Teach me. Show me. Help me to do the right thing. And help them." Their faces looked incredulous and worried.

"I leave it to you," I added faithfully and then wondered if that were a lie. If I could really leave it to Him, I shouldn't still be worried.

"Simply put your prayer on the altar and walk away from it."

Too difficult. I changed my approach and said "Thank you for earlier benefits. Thank you for having got Rougemont over the hurdle and given Eva mumps." Then this, too, showed a sly side; as though I were deliberately decoying Him by a profession of thanks because I wanted something more.

I made a savage effort to look out and not in, to see God as 'the ultimate end of my being, the supreme perfection of my nature'. If I held my breath I could sometimes perform the trick of thinking of nothing at all.

I found that I was doing just that, holding my breath and thinking of nothing at all. Oh, blast Crusoe, I thought. Simplicity was gone.

"The Grace of our Lord Jesus Christ and the love of God and the fellowship of the Holy Ghost be with you always, even unto the end of the world."

Greatly daring, I crossed myself. And as we all poured out of chapel, my prayer, such as it was, received the hint of an answer. I suddenly saw what might be done. But it was up to God to give me the chance to do it.

V

FROM the wicket I could see the green edge of the field, bordered unfamiliarly with the watchers in their chairs; a frieze of colours and shapes that were not there as a rule; usually just the plain edge of the grass with a few empty benches, a space of asphalt and the pavilion behind; then the tall College buildings of yellowish-grey stone, widely scattered and spaced, a casual forum standing back from the field. It was hot now; with the later afternoon the sun had come out, and there were no grey clouds left, only heavy white clouds on blue sky.

I sweated. I was in a daze of concentration that must not let up, and it was like being under an anæsthetic. Part sleep, part superstition, this inability to let my thoughts run out of the grooves that they had worn for themselves in the last three hours; they were hardly thoughts at all, really.

There was a hymn-tune, 'Love divine, all loves excelling',

whose brisk jog-trot lines lasted the pace of the slow bowler's delivery, so that I hit him (when I hit him) on 'Joy of heaven, to earth come *down*'.

That was one safe groove. Then there was a flashing calculation that my eyes and my mind could make, from here to the oak tree at the south corner, beyond the boundary. The words that kept it company were, for no reason, 'How many miles to Babylon?'

I could also, now that I'd done it over and over again, safely glance across my shoulder at the menacing line of the fieldsmen in the slips and think 'There they stood ranged about the hill-side, met . . .'

It was all beginning to be a little blurred. The white figures on the green turf showed a tendency to jiggle up and down; they framed themselves now and again in a coloured prism. Here he came, the fast bowler this time, shooting into sight. He was just a knotting catapult of limbs at the far end, the weapon that fired the ball. It came straight and I timed it and lifted it; the blow on the bat jarred electric needles down my arms. It travelled, high and away, over deep-field's head, to the boundary. (*Away, away, for I will fly with thee;* the little clapping at the side was ceasing to be a noise; it was a thing that I thought I could see, a line of solid smoke coming up.)

Now, though I was out of sight of the scoreboard at this end, I knew I was on the edge of the hundred. Ninety-one (was it?) and four for the boundary; ninety-five. Near enough, anyway. Two more balls in this over. I had time to make the 'How-many-miles-to-Babylon?' flash before the twinkling catapult fired again.

The ball broke to the off and as I hit the air I could already hear the dismal crack of my off-stump falling. But it didn't come. Nothing came. Slowly I dared to straighten up out of my crouch over the grounded bat. From the sigh all around, I knew how close it had been.

"He'll get me with the next one," I said, and at once I was in a panic, finding myself left suddenly naked, the thoughts run out of the safe grooves and writing stolidly on the surface of my mind, 'Bradley (D.), bowled Eldridge, 95'. I couldn't get back. I could only wait, hopeless, and see my thoughts writing that.

Here he was. He was a starfish of white and then he wasn't there. I don't remember seeing the ball. I stepped out to it, which was insane, and there was no electric jarring at my wrists, just a smooth flick and it went where I turned it, to leg. It was the kind of freakish, pretty stroke that left you blinded in a second of power, blinded and running like hell.

I could hear Jarvis, the other batsman, pant as he passed me. We ran two and I wavered, but he was shouting, "Come on!" and he was right. As we raced the third, the solid smoke of applause lifted and stayed. It was still there as I slid the bat over the crease.

Through the sweat that was trickling out of my hair into my eyes, I saw the hands of the man fielding at cover-point come up and start clapping too. It took me several seconds to understand why the field was clapping a lucky stroke to leg. Then I saw that I must have counted my score too low. This was it. I had made the century.

I waved the bat in what felt like a feeble gesture, acknowledging the noise. I felt no sense of achievement; only a sudden, awed belief in miracles.

VI

I HAD made a hundred and twelve not out when the last wicket fell. The school had lost the match; we usually lost to the Rovers; nobody cared. Walking into the line of applause was difficult. I found that my legs still shook; they had shaken on my way to the wicket, a lifetime ago. I had to wave my bat again as I came in.

There was the back-slapping, the glass of lemonade drunk at a gulp, then I was hunting along the line of chairs towards

my father and my mother. They always came down for the
Rovers match.

I could see them now, and even in this moment of placid
relief I could feel the same little shock that they had given me
this morning; as though I had not seen them for a long time.
My father was standing up, waiting for me. Had he always
seemed thus tall and fair and rigid? He was a remote, handsome stranger in grey flannels and Old Laxtonian tie. And my
mother . . . was she still the mother whom I had always known?
Why should I get this detached view of them? I was puzzling
at them, spying on them, thinking that, had they been portraits
instead of people, you would recognise that the same artist had
painted both. There was a likeness in design. What had
happened? I did not know. But it felt as though, without
realising it, I had taken a long step away from them.

"Don dear—congratulations—you did wonders." My
mother shook my hand. It was the carefully 'good-form'
greeting. She was wearing the kind of hat that I used to insist
upon. Now I had no longer any theories about hats. In
younger days I had thought it important for clothes to be incon-
spicuous; the hat had gone on being plain straw with a narrow
ribbon, or, in winter, a small felt cap that hardly showed.
Some day, perhaps, I should find the heart to tell her that I'd
like her to go wild with a hat, as my friend Levy's mother did.

"Good boy, oh, *good* boy," my father was saying. His
pleasure had become mysterious to me. Whether this were
due to Crusoe's verdict on competition, I could not be sure.
But the effect was uncomfortable, making me tongue-tied and
lumpish. I was glad when the Penleiths joined us and there
was more lemonade.

"And now, you know, you can have anything you want,
'within reason' "—my mother whispered to me. "What's it to
be? Have you decided?"

I smiled and shook my head. I stretched out on the grass
at their feet. I could smell the clover in the grass; they did not
cut it at the edge of the field. And the empty field itself looked
different, harmless, longer-shadowed beneath the evening sun.

The oak tree didn't signal 'How many miles to Babylon?' any more. It was just a leafy tree, far off.

It was good to know that the match was done, the hundred scored. But when I shut my eyes the images came back; the catapult-twist of the fast bowler's body, the little line of men waiting in the slips; the white shapes that jiggled and the green gaps between the fieldsmen where the ball must go. I felt as though I had it still to do. I knew that I should dream I was still doing it tonight.

"Don, oughtn't you to change, dear? You'll catch cold."

I sat up on my elbows.

"Your friend Raines didn't come. We were looking forward to meeting him."

"He can't go out on sunny days; his eyes hurt him." I realised now for the first time that I didn't want Crusoe to meet them and this shocked me.

"Too bad. He'd have enjoyed seeing you make your century."

"I don't know. He ain't much of a one for competition." There was no need to have said that; they looked bewildered. Then my father said briskly, "Well, if you'll change your togs we'll go up to the Castle and have a bite of dinner before the train leaves."

Worse and worse. Why should I mind his saying 'togs' instead of clothes and 'a bite of dinner' instead of just dinner? The words had a kind of out-of-date jauntiness. But he had always talked like this and it had not irked me before.

The Castle Inn stood in the market-place; it boasted of being built in 1600. It presented a black-and-white timbered façade; there were hanging baskets of flowers above the ground-floor windows; an old, darkly-painted signboard. The building was divided in the middle by the yard where the coaches used to come.

"Cider for the conquering hero," my father said.

It was an easier dinner than I expected, because of the match. Talk stayed on cricket, then on the horses, on Eva's being out of quarantine and my baby sister's progress with her pony.

But there was, I felt, a second me who watched and listened over my own shoulder. He was coolly out of it; he had nothing to do with this.

After dinner my mother contrived as usual to separate herself from us. "I know you and Don would like a little walk. I'll just rest here in the lounge with a magazine."

We strolled through the market-place and into the public gardens. It was twilight, not yet dark. The public gardens were too formal for my taste, with their planned flower-beds, benches and tidy paths, but we always came here. In the last of the summer evening they were a little softened; a copper-beech tree glowed—I saw—with the glow of the brasses in Whiteford Church. I could hear a thrush calling.

Our feet crunched on the gravel and his stick tapped rhythmically. He was still a little strange to me; I glanced at the profile, the hat-brim and the clipped moustache.

"A great innings, old chap. It really was. You only gave one chance all through—that catch in the gully when your score was at fifteen."

"Eldridge damn near got me with the last ball but one of the over when I was at ninety-seven."

"Hm—I think I'd have cut his throat for him if he had."

"Anyway," I said, comfortably tired, no longer watchful, "it's over. I don't need to do it again."

There was a pause, then a note of anxiety in his voice: "What exactly d'you mean, old boy?"

"Just . . . Well, don't you feel like that when something's over? Something you've tried for?"

He said only, "Good Lord, I hope you'll make a lot more centuries before you leave Laxton," and sounded hurt about it. After a moment, confronting some calceolarias, he cleared his throat, "Well, what's it going to be?"

"Anything I like, within reason?"

"Yes." He chuckled. "Think we ought to have agreed on what we meant by reason! I mean, you don't expect a car, or an aeroplane, do you?"

"No, don't worry."

"I've had an idea, mind you . . . just an idea. But suppose you tell me yours first."

I dug my hands into my pockets. God, I thought, had left me no alternative but to speak now. And I was strengthened by a maxim of Crusoe's: '*Once you begin thinking out what you'll say in advance, you're bound to end up with a singular poverty of display when the time comes.*'

I plugged at it. "What I'd like best is to spend one week of the holidays at Whiteford. Crusoe has invited me."

My father greeted it with dead silence.

"I'd like to go for the Merrowdown Race Meeting, that's the last week in August."

Still silence.

"There are new colts coming along," I said. "And there's Rougemont; I told you about him in my letter, the two-year-old who looked like being a refuser. He's nearly cured, but he's still better with me than with anybody."

My father said, "*That's* what you want? More than anything else?"

"Yes."

He took a few more steps.

"It seems very extraordinary."

"Why does it?"

"Well . . . I mean . . . it does."

I wondered whether, after all, God were letting me down.

"Doesn't it?" he repeated. "I meant to give you a really decent present. Run to anything reasonable, I told you so."

"I'm sorry. What was the thing you were thinking of?"

He said in his hurt voice, "Oh, that doesn't matter now." Then he gestured with his stick towards an empty bench. We sat down. He punched little holes in the gravel with the end of his stick.

"Really thought about it seriously, have you?"

"Yes. Very seriously. I hope you've no objection." Now I sounded as stiff as he sounded.

"I promised you what you wanted, Don, and I keep my promises."

"Thank you."

"But I must say I'm surprised. Surprised and a little disappointed." He went on punching holes. "Just why is it so important to you?"

I said, "You know I like going there."

"Yes, but—I mean you have Raines and his horses all through term-time. I should have thought that in the holidays —well, never mind." He sighed heavily. "According to Penleith he's rather a peculiar chap; some people think he's not quite right in the head."

It made me angry; I had to swallow hard and develop a sarcastic sneer. "Well, his spine's all smashed," I said, "and there's a damage to his eyes—that's why he's half blind. So I dare say his brain's affected too. He happens to be the most brilliant person I ever met, but pay no attention."

"There's no need to get huffy and rude and spoil the day." (It was a familiar accusation. I had, it seemed, been spoiling the day since I was six.) "I'm not attacking your friend. Of course I'm sorry for him—who wouldn't be? But he's been like it for years, you know. Raines must be fifty."

"Fifty-two, in fact."

"What's so fascinating about him?"

"You'd see, if you knew him." This I doubted, but it seemed the safest answer.

"I hope we shall meet. You realise, your mother and I aren't in the habit of letting you accept invitations from people we don't know."

"I think he'll pass muster if you check him in Burke. The family goes back to the fourteenth century."

"That's enough sarcasm for now, old boy."

"Sorry."

"I presume he'll be writing to us?"

"Yes. Rather. Of course he will."

My father rose from the bench. As we walked to the gate he said, "Er—Raines will have other guests while you're there, I suppose?"

"I expect so. He seems to know everybody in the world."

My father put on his facts-of-life voice: "Naturally you're getting to an age when you'll meet all sorts of people—know what I mean by all sorts of people, don't you?"

VII

THEIR train drew out and I walked back alone. I took the short cut from the station, over the level-crossing, down the embankment, towards the Whiteford road. The moon was rising on one side of the sky and the sunset still coloured the other. An owl flapped past me. I crossed the Whiteford road, climbed the fence and ran down the steep bank to the river-field. There was a cow to keep me company. She walked behind me; I could hear her blowing breath and her hooves that squelched.

God, I thought, had tricked me into a trap. Supposing that I had asked for something else? For a gun or a watch or a pair of riding-boots, and let Crusoe's invitation come unannounced? What then? Would they have refused? Perhaps not. Because I hadn't dared to risk that, Crusoe was now an issue between us. I had put him into their full view; and I felt that from tonight he was endangered. I had handed him over to the enemy.

Oh, but it couldn't be true, I thought. They couldn't be the enemy. I couldn't really dislike my father and mother. It was just a feeling, a feeling that would pass. I mustn't go on with the thoughts in my head.

Guilt haunted me. Guilt for that, guilt for 'spoiling the day' and disappointing my father. I remembered the happiness in his face as I came off the field. I fingered the two new pound notes in my blazer-pocket. I prayed—"Oh please. Let me like them again."

But had I ever liked them, really liked them? The thought nibbled on; reminding me that as a small boy I had adored my

mother, until I found that she was not to be trusted. It had
happened gradually. A sudden show of guile would take my
breath away; then I would forget it until the next time it
happened. A 'secret' that we were supposed to share turned
out to be a diplomatic way of curbing some project of Eva's.
A plan that sounded spontaneous ("I've just thought . . .
wouldn't this be a good idea?") had been hatched between
her and my father; she, the cleverer of the two, was deputed
to sound me. She would break my confidence and give me
the best of reasons. Smiling and smooth, she 'managed' us
all. My love had died of this smoothness.

Now I turned to him in my mind. Except when we were
with the horses, I could not recall a moment of being honestly
happy in his company.

I thought of other people's parents. Of Levy's father and
mother, small and Jewish and comical. Of Richardson's
parents who came down in the most awful old car and took
three of us to see a Marx Brothers movie in Gloucester. Of
Peyton who had no father, but a mother who looked little
older than he did. The two of them never stopped talking for
a minute and I had seen them weak with giggles over some
private joke in the lounge at the Castle Inn.

I recalled the remark made by the highbrow Hemingway.
They had hated Hemingway. He was a Socialist and when he
engaged my father in political argument I thought that my
father got the worst of it. A disastrous lunch. But, walking
back afterwards, Hemingway said, "*Adore* your family. Pure
Edwardian. Awfully rare."

I climbed the wall and jumped down into the playing-field.
It was almost night now. I saw the dark shell of the school
buildings, the long lit rows of dormitory windows, the taller
lights that were the windows of study, library and hall.

"*A parent, if it lives long enough, can always repay its child in
kind for the anxieties that the child has once given. It turns back
into a child itself, with all a child's egoism, dependence and
demands; all the selfish unreason that makes communication
impossible.*"

"Oh, God, Crusoe, if you're right, I can only look forward to its getting worse."

I was resenting him as I walked across the ground. "It's your fault, you know. You've shaken everything up. You're the only sort of father I want; the only teacher I want. You've become my yardstick. Nothing'll ever be the same again."

I went up the stairs.

"*One of the signs of true unhappiness is a regular, placid relief at the sight of one's own bed; to be at peace with the knowledge that the day is over.*"

I had never felt it before.

VIII

I WOULD have thought that I knew all there was to know of Crusoe before I stayed in his house. But there was, I discovered, a marked difference between the perspectives of an afternoon visitor and a guest under the roof. At first I was shy and jittery. I had mistrusted fate for nine weeks, believing that some last-minute stroke would stop my coming here. Setting down my new suitcase on the floor, looking about the room that was to be mine, with its bookshelves, its bronzes, its tapestry curtains, I felt inadequate; inadequate alike to the adult frame and to the task of enjoyment.

Almost I wished that I were still at home and straining towards this.

I opened the window and leaned out beside the dark magnolia leaves. I saw the terrace below, the tops of the grey urns and the lake; a new picture of an old landscape in the August evening.

My further discoveries of him began. I learned the shape of his day. Even when it was a good day, it was a day of battle. I could not, for him, reconcile myself to its physical slowness;

the journey from bed to bath, from bath to chair; from the chair to the irons or the black torpedo; the continued dependence on a hand or a shoulder or a voice reading aloud. He seemed more emphatically a prisoner than ever. A prisoner whose gaolers paid kindly and regular attentions. The man-servant dressing him and undressing him; the doctor and the masseur; myself and Miss Wood; our functions underlined his captivity.

I breakfasted with him on the terrace; the details are still sharp: the table laid between the magnolia-covered wall and the grey urns; the Italian china; the smoky taste of the bacon, and the eggs that were fried on both sides; the fat silver coffee-pot; his dressing-gown's peacock pattern and the smell of his first cigar.

I came to that breakfast hungrily because I used to go up to the stables at seven, riding in the lorry that collected the milk-cans. The early-morning gallop was the best of the day. Afterwards the lorry brought me back. I walked through the garden and round the house to the terrace. If the fat terrier came to meet me, I knew that Crusoe was there already.

He was as fluent at breakfast as at dinner. After it, he went to tyrannise first over Miss Wood, next over the gardener, and I did not see him until lunch-time. The stables were for the afternoon. Then he rested. Our longest meetings were at evening.

Crusoe drank slowly but steadily from six o'clock until the early morning; brandy before dinner, champagne with dinner, brandy after dinner. It did not change him at all. I could never sit up as late as he did; he was a poor sleeper and he made no effort to sleep. I would hear the music coming up long after I was in bed. His appetite for music was immense; he could take three symphonies in succession, reminding me always that I need not listen if they bored me. He liked the evenings. He greeted them with a velvet dinner-jacket. (It was my shame that as yet I had no dinner-jacket.) We played chess; he never looked at the men; his blind hand moved with assurance, any strategy of mine seemed to be known in his head before I made it. When I got my nerve back I beat him twice and he was delighted.

While he endured as a prisoner, I was knowing more freedom than I had thought could exist. It wasn't only because I could do as I liked; though he gave me the run of Whiteford, from the stables to the bookshelves; though he let me drive the car and swim in the lake and fish the stream. Freedom was more than that. It was in the knowledge that, all day, nobody would be hurt, perplexed or questioning, if I didn't fit to a required pattern. It was in the removal of the guilt that haunted me at home.

'Perhaps,' I said to myself, 'I'll be killed at a jump and not have to go back.'

He insisted that I finish off the essay before the Merrowdown race-meeting opened. "We shan't know a moment of peace after Thursday. Why don't you go to the study and do it now?"

"Now?" It was near midnight. We had just finished our chess-game.

"Why not? There's no time like the night for working. I forgot, though, you are young and healthy and sleepy."

I said, "I don't need to really *finish* it before next term, you know."

"That," said Crusoe, "is a splitting of straws, not to mention infinitives."

He was restless tonight; since he seemed to want me to go, I retired to the study to sit blinking like a cat over the essay. It surprised me when I went back to say good night to him, that he should have gone to bed.

That was the prelude to the interminable day; the only bad day while I was there. Joel served me my breakfast on the terrace. Joel said, "He'd like you to go to him when you've finished."

The curtains were drawn; there were screens between the canopied bed and the window. All was shadowy. He lay hunched on high pillows in a position that looked desperately uncomfortable. I could see that he was braced and watchful with pain. The Alsatian bitch lay on the floor beside the bed, still as a rug.

"It happens," he said drowsily, "from time to time. I just wanted to say good morning to you and tell you not to think you need hang around. Have a nice day. Come back and see me this afternoon."

"Isn't there anything I can do? Would you like me to read to you?"

"Later on, perhaps." He turned his head and I saw the gleam of sweat on his face. I sponged him and dried him. Then he sent me away.

Though I was used to spending the morning alone, time now hung heavy. I finished the fair copy of the essay, but the thought of him went on nagging me all the time. When Miss Wood came into the study, I was glad to see her. I badgered her. "How often does this happen? Can't they stop it? Why doesn't the doctor come?"

"He'll be here later. There isn't very much that anybody can do. It passes off. He's terribly brave; he doesn't complain." She was no comfort.

I took a swim in the lake; as I came up the garden in my trunks I met Mrs. Irvine.

She said, "I wondered if you'd like to come and have lunch with me?"

"It's awfully kind of you. I think I'd better stay here, in case he wants something." I couldn't explain to her about not deserting in time of trouble; I expected her to argue kindly and firmly. But she didn't. She said, "Of course—do what makes you happier. And come another time."

It was, I supposed, a useless vigil. He did not send for me. When I had eaten my lunch, Joel brought me his instructions about the colt and I went up to the stables. Here I missed him astonishingly. Over the horses, he could be exasperating, demanding and unreasonable. But it was only half the fun without him.

I saw the doctor's car drive away as I came into the garden. Joel was in the hall.

"Is he any better? What did the doctor say?"

"He's a little easier, I think. Doctor O'Neill isn't worried. The lamps help him; the violet rays. They'll be giving those later." Their attitudes were all accustomed, Olympian. I felt shut out.

When I had changed out of my riding-clothes I hung around in the panelled room until I could bear it no longer. I crossed the hall and knocked on the door and went in. His voice came out of the cave of shadows.

"Who's that?"

"Don."

"Very opportune. You can give me some more brandy."

He was still in the hunched mould of discomfort. "Only position that helps," he said. He raised his tortured head a little way and drank.

"Does the brandy help?"

"Oh yes. Pushes it further away . . . Give me another."

"Ought you to?"

He chuckled. "Long ago, my son, I had to decide between a bullet and the bottle and I chose the bottle."

"You don't rely on it all that much," I said. I came to the bedside with the glass. He drained it, winced and lay back.

"Know what my situation is? 'I am defeated, but I refuse to capitulate.' Obstinate type; always was. Now there's a point. You'll very rarely hear anyone admit to obstinacy. Most people, speaking of themselves, call it 'firmness' or 'conviction'. It's only when they meet the same quality in somebody else that they call it obstinacy. Always interesting, those little things."

They came with the lamps, laying a black cloth over his face to shield his eyes. I sat beyond the harsh violet circle of light, reading aloud. I felt tired. I had discovered this day that it was harder to bear another person's pain than to bear my own.

"You make the perfect audience, Don. Realise how easy it is to behave well when somebody's watching?"

"I'd have thought it was easier alone."

"Bah! That's real merit—good behaviour when there's

nobody there to appreciate the performance. I wonder how many men have died bravely alone on a raft at sea."

IX

THE next day it was over. Having seen him in such agony, it seemed impossible that he could ever come out of it. But he was at the breakfast-table when I returned from the morning ride. I hadn't dared to believe the signal made by the fat terrier coming to meet me. "Doesn't last more than a day, as a rule. If it did, I'd be dead," said Crusoe. "Help yourself to sausages."

There was a letter beside my plate.

'MY DEAR DON,

'I hope that you are enjoying yourself as much as you expected to. All well here and no alarms or excursions.

'As it turns out, I have to be in Gloucester on business this week. Your mother and I have decided that it would be nice to make a little jaunt of it. We will drive up in the car, come over to Whiteford on Sunday and fetch you, then all drive home together.

'Eva has a friend coming to stay with her, or she would join the party.

'Please give my kind regards to your host and ask him if it would be convenient for us to call for you at about five o'clock on Sunday.

'Mum sends much love and so do I.'

"God's truth," I said.

"Only a small manifestation of it, but painful, I agree," said Crusoe. "Never nice when young, to be fetched home. Even from parties. I don't know why."

"It isn't only that." I hesitated. He made the hawk-movement with his head, picking up my thoughts.

"Only two attitudes about one's family—have you noticed? One can feel that they're sacred, that it's a privilege for the outsider to be admitted to their hallowed circle and a thundering impertinence for him to expect the privilege . . . in which case one is a bore. Alternatively——"

"Alternatively?"

The black mask seemed to be watching me with amusement. "Alternatively, one sees them as one's private burden of mediocrity; to be kept in the background; for whose appearance in the foreground no apologies are enough. In which case one is a hyper-sensitive ass."

The hyper-sensitive ass whom he addressed was reviewing the letter. 'As it turns out, I have business in Gloucester' wore a look of laboured transparency. They had thought this up for the purpose of inspecting Crusoe; an instance, no doubt, of my mother's smooth planning. ("Well, and why shouldn't they, after all?" I groaned to myself in a weary effort at justice.)

"I suppose you couldn't say it *wasn't* convenient? Then I could meet them in the village."

"That would be bloody rude on my part," said Crusoe. "What's the matter with you? Have they got three legs each?"

X

By Sunday afternoon, when they arrived, I was looking back on three days that were glitteringly, noisily different from the first half of the week. It seemed as though the bulk of Crusoe's enormous circle of acquaintances had come within range for the Merrowdown meeting. We met them on the course; we brought them back for drinks and they stayed for dinner. Now I met for the first time the remnant of the aristocracy and found the remnant good fun. They were easy talkers and devoted drinkers. I discovered also for the first time that champagne-corks really popped and went on popping; the accompaniment to gaiety as I had read of it in old-fashioned novels.

It was perhaps an old-fashioned assembly. Crusoe at the centre made the most noise, bellowing and roaring, never attempting to introduce anybody by the right name. Even half a glass of champagne made me fuzzy-headed, and I would go through the evening talking to Bucky and Bimbo and a woman whose nickname was Poodle, with little hope of identifying them afterwards. ("Good God, *I* don't know. 'Flanders' Barrington, was it? Red moustache? No moustache. Well, point him out to me tomorrow.")

For once he seemed to have cause for vagueness. There was a stamp of uniformity upon them; the women's voices all had the same timbre; the men all had the same immense affability. Here at last were adults who looked and sounded as though they were having a good time. No matter if it owed itself to champagne or to a ten-pound bet on an outsider. I could see them kicking up their heels.

With them there would come an oddity like a portrait-painter or a Monsignor, and an expert dietician knighted for services to the Ministry of Food; these fitted into the group without effort. Effort indeed was missing from all of it. I had, I thought, struck a world of non-worriers.

Sunday morning had flooded the house with them from twelve until half-past four, when we sat down to tea. Only the Monsignor stayed for tea. He fascinated me with his robes and the triangle of purple silk below his collar, his narrow silver head and goat-like profile. Crusoe called him Johnny. They had been at school together.

But it was getting too near the end to be fun. Crusoe had tried to teach me the mental process that he described as 'sitting on Now' until the last minute. It should be perfectly possible, he said, to sit on Now, without any sort of painful anticipation, until the firing-squad had pressed their triggers.

I couldn't do it, nor anything like it. Their voices thinned out on the air. I wasn't sitting on Now, but playing the reverse trick, turning Now into Then, walking back through all of it.

I sat there tugging at the terrier's ears, but I was riding uphill
with the milk-cans at morning; I was saddling Rougemont; I
was running the colt around the field on the exercising-rein;
I was cleaning the stables. Now I sat opposite Crusoe at the
chess-board; now I heard the chorus from the Ninth Symphony;
now I crouched in my chair at his bedside, with the book on my
knees and the violet lamps crackling.

I grew ashamed of it. I struggled back to their talk. Which
seemed to be about talking.

"I mistrust and despise the inarticulate," Crusoe was saying.
"Along with 'Nature's Gentlemen' and people said to have
quiet charm. There's no such thing as quiet charm. Except in
cats."

"Don't you like silence?" I teased him.

He gave me a withering look, "Not when I want conversation, oddly enough."

"What about the people who honestly haven't got anything
to say?"

"Well—what's the matter with them? Why haven't they got
anything to say?"

"They might be ignorant of the subject under discussion."

"Bah!" said Crusoe. The Monsignor said, "Come, come.
Ignorance never kept anybody quiet yet."

I held to the attack; it was at least a diversion. "Crusoe—
listen. Suppose that two people were discussing the inside of a
motor-bicycle."

"I don't know how your imagination runs to these horrors.
Why should they be? And if they were, such a discussion
would not rank as conversation."

"Well, but they might think it did. Suppose they were
fascinated with the rival merits of two motor-bicycle engines,
comparing dynamos and magnetos—and going on and on
about it—and you had absolutely no views."

"In the unlikely event of my finding myself in such company," Crusoe said, "I should leave at once."

"There's nothing I used to like better than riding a motor-
bike," said the Monsignor.

I surrendered.

"To sum up"—Crusoe's sideways thrust of jaw and beard preceded it—"a speechless person is a curse on the company. If you're in company it's because you want to talk."

"Or listen."

"Talking implies listening. Otherwise I should use the word Pontificate or Declaim. If it's silence you want, you stay in your room."

The Monsignor said, "How I admire your passion for attack. Inspired by the simplest human institutions. I believe you could whip up a polemic against washing."

"By Heaven, I could . . . Beginning with a denunciation of Transatlantic bathroom-worship and ending with the abysmal misconception, 'Cleanliness is next to Godliness'."

The glass doors opened from the hall on to the terrace.

"Crusoe, darling—oh, my darling, how are you? I did mean to come to lunch . . . I did try to come to lunch . . . I was deflected." She embraced his head. She was as lovely as a Madonna and she wore trousers. Crusoe said, "Bless you. But it's quite all right. I didn't ask you to lunch."

"You didn't?"

"No, darling."

"Then I have wasted hours of guilt. Hullo, Johnny dear." I had risen to give her my chair. "Oh, but *how* kind of you," she said, as though I had rescued her from drowning.

"Do you know Don Bradley?" Crusoe asked, adding, "This woman's name escapes me for the moment." It was obviously a name that I should know, because the Monsignor chuckled.

"Crusoe, you are too horrid. There's nothing to touch the embarrassment of having to say one's own name aloud."

"Americans do it naturally," said the Monsignor.

"Well, but I can't."

"You must try," said Crusoe.

She did not. She said, "Do you think that as I wasn't invited for lunch, I qualify for tea? I really have had the most cruel day . . . beset, beleaguered. Tell me, do you simply hate your school?

My son accuses me of having sent him to a concentration camp."

"Really it isn't so bad," I began.

"You won't have been out of it ten minutes before you understand just how bad it was," snapped Crusoe.

"Of course, I had no education, merely governesses," sighed the Madonna. "But Billy appears to learn nothing. And to *read* nothing—since last term when his collection of comics was confiscated. Do you read comics, Mr. Bradley?"

"Well, no, I don't any more. I used to."

Her enormous eyes pleaded with me. "But could you understand them? Could you *really*? To me they are more difficult than Aristotle in the original or Karl Marx."

"Only trouble with Marx is the poor quality of his translators," said the Monsignor.

"*Only* trouble, ha? Page the Pope," said Crusoe.

"Mr. and Mrs. Bradley," Joel announced.

They were as much out of context as two giraffes would have been. No; two giraffes would have been all right. Crusoe would merely have summoned Mallock to see that they were accommodated at the stables: and the Madonna would have fed them with cucumber sandwiches.

No such dispensation awaited my parents, caught between three fires of embarrassment; the Monsignor in his robes, Crusoe in his chair, the Madonna in her trousers. I noticed that when my father shook hands with the priest, his attitude was one of subdued sympathy as though the Monsignor were an invalid; while with Crusoe he adopted the opposite technique, looking him straight in the face, shaking his hand heartily, breathing out strength-through-joy; trumpeting compliments on the weather and the house and the horses.

At first it seemed as though I need not speak at all. The Madonna was saying to my mother, "You've come to take him away? Oh, how sad. I was hoping to hear an unbiased sketch of Laxton's horrors."

"Horrors?" My mother made a bright effort at adjustment. "Well, now, Don, what *are* the horrors?"

"Idle to ask. As a gentleman, he is obliged to spare our feelings," said the Monsignor.

Out of my left ear I could get snatches of my father's speech to Crusoe. ". . . Awfully kind of you . . . hope he hasn't been any trouble . . . good seat and good hands . . ." and Crusoe replying, "Only too delighted to see the last of the little rat. Keeps me up till all hours and beats me at chess."

Joel came to ask whether drinks should be served here or indoors.

"Out here. Nobody could be cold."

"Crusoe, I'm *freezing*."

"Bring an asbestos suit for her ladyship and an ice-cap for everyone else. Spare us the feverish footman, Don. You know his feverish-footman moods, Mr. Bradley?"

"But you could, if you were as saintly as your appearance suggests," the Madonna murmured, "bring me a coat. Any coat. Crusoe has hundreds of horrible coats in the hall-cupboard. Not one of the loud tweeds. There's a muted green ulster in which I shall look like Sherlock Holmes."

As I hurried indoors, my right ear established that my mother was caught with the priest. She was saying something about Harvest Festival.

I shut the glass doors. I found the muted green coat for the Madonna. But the sight of my new suitcase standing in the hall desolated me and I had to make a rapid tour of the down-stairs rooms; I hoarded things that I liked and must remember; the leather backs of the books; the giant globe beside the study table; the little clock set in a silver skull; the cloudy painting of the galleon above the library mantelpiece. I would take them home in my head. ("*Safest place for keeping what you treasure.*")

I returned. My mother was saying, "Our curate, who is as a matter of fact *very* High Church," but her eyes were fixed on the Monsignor's glass of gin-and-bitters. The Madonna was moaning, "Poor, *dear* little boys. It is a barbarous custom . . . but if they weren't at school, they'd only be with *us* all the time, wouldn't they, and that would be so much worse."

"You'd match your own barbarous customs against those of

the English public-school system?" Crusoe inquired. I saw that my father wore a determined smile; reminding me of Mr. Stephens on the afternoon when Crusoe first became real for me. I had just helped myself to ginger-beer when a confused bellow sounded from the hall. An enormous figure in a black and white check suit rushed through the glass doors, and embraced Crusoe. He was Bobby Durand, V.C., golden and ruddy and—at the moment—rather tight.

"*Ah, mon vieux!*" He hugged Crusoe, kissing him on both cheeks, Crusoe bellowing back, "*Salut, mon brave*, and about time too."

"I bury my head in your chestnut beard. Forgive me," said Durand, taking in the assembly with a wild and merry eye. "Been in love with Crusoe for years; of course we don't talk about it. Hullo, Don; Ganymede with the ginger-beer. Madly jealous of you, I am." He surveyed the bottles. "It's a Bacchanal. So it should be. Do you realise that my miserable horse, my runt, the stable stinker . . ."

"Yes, Robert, we know," said Crusoe smoothly. "It won. And you warned us all not to back it. A chiseller's way with the price, if I may say so."

"How much did you put on, yourself?" asked the Monsignor.

"Johnny, your calling gives you a suspicious nature. Not a penny. It's the thought that counts. . . . Oh, all right; a hundred pounds." He straddled beside the bar. "*Crusoe, mon preux chevalier, mon fond-du-bain*, have you no white mint? How the hell can I make a brandy-float?"

"Ring the bell. And pipe down," said Crusoe—"May I introduce——"

"Of course you mayn't, you monster. You can't. Last time you tried, I was somebody who'd been dead for years. Besides, I know everybody, don't I? How *are* you, sir?" he said to my father: "Hullo, darling" to my mother; ending up with the Madonna, whom he enfolded, "Haven't kissed you since breakfast. Oh, my God, that reminds me. I've left my mistress sitting in the car." He rushed at the glass doors, turning back to say, "Not a *word* of truth in it—she isn't my mistress. Up till today I rather hoped. Then she broke it to me that she was in love with a Chartered Accountant. But alas, my poor doxy, how could I treat her so?"

"We must," Crusoe said, "excuse him. A man of good-will, but his winnings have gone to his head. With the brandy-floats. I apologise for him, Mrs. Bradley."

My parents said little afterwards. There was the tempered adjective 'amusing' applied to Crusoe; my mother remarked on the Madonna's beauty; later, my father wondered why Roman Catholic clergymen always had to dress up; the vicar, who was as good a Christian as he knew, frequently appeared in flannels. And that was all. In my innocence, feeding on memories, I did not realise that there would be any more.

XI

AT times I still think that there might have been no more, that the decision was only pending in their minds until I made some move that would clinch it. I don't know. The keeping of it in cold storage for three weeks may have been strategy.

Meanwhile, sunnily, I thought that the last part of the holidays went rather well. I was helped by some lines from a book read at Whiteford, '*We should wish one another, not so much surroundings more congenial to our temper, as a temper more congenial to our surroundings*.' I used it when my patience showed signs of growing short. And breaking my rib was another help. This happened when I was thrown at a jump. It reminded me of what Crusoe said about the world's appetite for drama. Strapped in plaster and taut with pain, I was dramatised; a comfortable situation that removed many occasions of sin.

And perhaps, if we hadn't fought over Benjamin, nothing would have been said. This happened two days before the holidays ended.

It was the first day that I had ridden since my accident. Between my father and myself I could feel the near-understanding that came when we rode. We met Benjamin cantering home; with his grey curling hair and his little red face, he looked like an ostler. He was the father of a large family; they lived only a few miles away, in an Elizabethan farmhouse that I coveted; I liked Benjy and I liked his children, but we only met them out hunting.

He called Hullo to us and rode on. The fight did not begin until my father and I were walking back up the short avenue of chestnut trees that led from the stables to the house. As a moment just before a war, it was full of peace. Autumn was in the air. You saw it in the mist on the moors, the blue of the smoke at the chimney-tops, in the bright, formal dahlias growing beside the house. Overhead the chestnut-shells were swollen and split, showing glossy brown streaks set in a lining of white kid. There was an adventure to autumn. I saluted it. My mind went ahead of today and tomorrow, travelling down the Whiteford road.

"Most extraordinary about Benjamin; I really don't understand it," my father said.

"What's extraordinary?"

"They're talking of making him Master next year. This may be Randolph's last season, you know."

"Yes. I know. Well, why not? Benjy'll make a good M.F.H., won't he?"

My father made a blowing hrrumph like a horse. "Funny choice, isn't it, a Jew?"

We had had it out about Jews before. It always made me angry and this time I did not pause to wish myself a temper congenial to my surroundings. I said, "Oh, for Heaven's sake —*that* old nonsense." He reddened perceptibly before he said, "Well, there are a good many people round here who feel as I do, I assure you."

"More fools they. Benjy's a magnificent horseman; he knows the country backwards and I should think in fact he'd done more for the hunt than anybody."

"Well, of course he has. One way of getting in, isn't it? Hmm?"

"What precisely d'you mean by 'getting in'?"

"In with the county. A nice rich Jew can always do that, you know."

I made a belated effort to keep calm. I tried to think what Crusoe would have said. It came out authentically, but, I imagine, surprisingly from my lips, "The racialist would do well to remind himself once a day that Our Lord was a Jew."

On my father's face now blended the looks of a basilisk and a bullfrog. "I *beg* your pardon?"

I repeated it; standing at the front door, switching my gaiters in imitation of Mallock.

"Where did you get *that* from, may I ask?"

"It's true, isn't it?"

He said, "Are you trying to be impertinent?"

"No."

"It's not the sort of talk I care for, Don."

"I'm sure it isn't. But if you ever could explain to me the difference between Jews and gentlemen, I'd be awfully grateful."

He was silent. We went into the hall. We put our riding-crops on the rack. I turned towards the stairs and he said, "Just a minute. Come into the study, will you? I want to talk to you."

I followed him in. He motioned me to the big chair and stood before the mantelpiece, his hands in the pockets of his breeches.

"I've been worried about you for quite a while now. So has your mother."

I was expecting a follow-up on the Jews and this put me off-balance. "Mm?" I grunted cautiously.

"That kind of remark confirms what we've been thinking. Not only your mother and myself. To show you that we're not entirely alone in our opinion, I'd like you to know that Penleith—er—backs us up to a certain extent."

What on earth was coming next? Jews . . . Penleith . . . something to do with my friend Levy, the school satirist?

"I'm talking about your habit of making unsuitable friends."

"Who? Levy?" I hazarded, still blind to it. "Really, Dad——"

"Nothing to do with Leevy."

"He pronounces it Levvy."

"Never mind. That's not what I'm discussing."

"What *are* you discussing?"

He shifted his feet. "The person I have in mind is your friend Raines. I want you to know that I'd prefer you not to go to his house again."

I sat still, feeling an odd, cold sickness. I said nothing at all.

"Is that understood? Then we needn't have any argument, need we?"

Still I said nothing. It seemed safer for the moment just to sit there, looking at him.

"Quite easy to do it tactfully . . . simply tell him you've too much extra work this term to go on exercising his horses. Perfectly true, with the exam coming along. Penleith tells me that he'll write Raines such a letter if necessary."

The cold had passed. Slow red fires seemed to be burning inside me, mounting towards my head.

"Would you mind telling me why?" I said at last.

"I shouldn't have thought I need. You have only to cast your mind back. The things your mother and I heard and saw at Whiteford——"

"What were they?" My voice sounded ugly and strange.

He said, "I don't want to discuss it in detail. Just take it from me that those people are very unsuitable company for somebody your age."

Still I could keep the fires banked down. But the effort made my hands shake and my rib had begun to hurt viciously.

"Well, well," I said, looking past him. "Was it the priest? Or Lady Felicia's trousers? Or Durand with his doxy?"

My father said only, "I've never been more disgusted in my life."

"With Durand?" The cold, ugly voice had changed to a

lighter certainty. "He's a crazy man. All ex-Commandos are a bit crazy. Nicely crazy."

"You call that a *nice* exhibition?"

"What exhibition? Oh, my God," I said. "You don't mean his hugging Crusoe?"

My father was now all bullfrog. "That wasn't the whole of it, revolting as it was. Perhaps you didn't hear what he said."

I got up out of my chair. "For the love of Heaven, don't tell me you took any of *that* seriously? You couldn't——"

I was near laughter; and he saw it and stamped his foot. "All I mean is you're to keep away from such people in future. D'you understand? It's a great pity that some of the British aristocracy should have these extraordinarily loose manners and morals, but there it is. I don't like it for you and I'm not going to have it. I'm sorry——"

"I'm sorry too." My breath was running short and he jumped in:

"Naturally one makes mistakes about people—when one's young. And of course you like going there for the horses. But when that sort of things bring you together with people who live outside all decent codes, it's got to stop."

"It's not going to stop." I managed to croak it out at him before my breath went again.

"I *beg* your pardon!"

"God," I panted, "you make me bloody angry."

"That's enough bad language. Pull yourself together, please."

"How can you be so utterly small-minded, and smutty—and stupid"—I must breathe deeply, I thought, or never finish a sentence again. And to breathe deeply hurt my side.

My father was turning purple. "You'll apologise at once or you'll leave this room."

I had got some breath. I made a final, reeling effort. "All right. I apologise for swearing at you and for being rude. Will that do?"

He snorted.

"I can't apologise for losing my temper. And I can't accept your ban on Crusoe. And that's that."

The purple flush subsided a little, but he did not speak.

"I couldn't, possibly. Because it's idiotic. He's a great man, he's the best friend I've got. Damn it—sorry—I could see you were a bit out of your depth with those people. They are funny, the first time you meet them. But to jump to conclusions about their morals is just fatuous."

"You will leave the room, please."

"All right. But I'm dead serious. If you insist on banning him, I'm afraid I'll have to fight. I shan't leave it with Penleith. I shall take it to the Head and get his ruling." As I reached the door I fired my shot: "He happens to be a friend of Crusoe's."

I shut the door quietly, longing to slam it. I felt sick and shaky. I went up to my room and met Eva coming out of hers.

"Don, you look *green*. Rib hurting you?"

"Not rib. Row," I said.

She followed me in. "If you don't want me, I'll go away."

"Please don't go away. Let's talk. How do *you* do it?" I muttered. I envied her; she was so smoothly able to slip out of trouble where I always met it head-on. She was pretty, with my mother's prettiness. She was tidy and cool. Her hand on my forehead felt cool.

"Poor old Don . . . perhaps I don't try to do the things that you do."

"Well, to hell with it anyway."

"It's because you will make sort of crusades. I just keep quiet about all my stuff." She sat on the bed beside me. I didn't really know what her 'stuff' was. "That makes for less fuss, you see," she said.

"It obviously does."

"Do you feel sick? Would you like a glass of water?"

"No. I'm all right. I just got too angry."

"What's it about this time?"

"Crusoe Raines."

"I thought they'd be putting a foot down."

"Did you? Why?"

"Heard them talking." She always heard them talking. "Want me to tell you what they said?"

"No, thanks. I can guess. And I don't want to get angry all over again. Look, Eva, how bloody are they, really?"

"Pretty bloody, poor darlings," she said lightly. "Comes of being afraid."

"Afraid of *what*, for Heaven's sake?"

Eva wrinkled her nose and stared ahead of her. "I'm not quite sure. 'What People Will Say' is one bit of it. Sometimes I feel as though they were waiting for an inspector to call, don't you?"

"Inspector?"

"Somebody to make sure that we're all doing the things that 'Nice People' are supposed to do." She cocked her head on one side. "And another bit is the fear of *seeing* that anything's wrong. Putting a bright face on it all—you know. 'Let's change the subject, shall we?' Refusal to face facts. Particularly *queer* facts. Anything that isn't 'normal' is a terror. If you ask me, I think their trouble is that they just have no imagination at all. They can't see further than their poor noses. So they've never really grown-up, and they're out of date."

She sounded compassionate. I said, "Can you be sorry for them? I can't today."

"Yes, I can. Quite often. I don't blame you for not, though. Did he say Crusoe Raines was a pansy?"

"Hinted it."

"Is he?" The lightness of the question shocked me a little, coming from Eva, but it wasn't offensive.

"No," I said. "Not only because he's quite impotent but because he just isn't that sort. Why should he be? What makes me so livid is their poisonous pettiness and smugness and smuttiness."

"They're hipped on sex. All parents are, I think." She looked at me. "Does Crusoe talk to you about sex?"

I recalled his words, the oblique phrases, as though he were talking to himself, "*I remember being worried by the fierceness of that private impulse. It seemed so lonely and misdirected. Silly of me; because so eager a loneliness can only argue the logical sequel of companionship ahead.*" This I had found reassuring.

I said, "Only once that I can remember. In the abstract. He can talk abstracts by the hour."

"What are you going to do, Don?"

"Fight them."

"How can you?"

"I must. Even if it means never coming home again."

She was silent; and I looked about my room; at its familiar chintz and carpet, at the photographs of the horses, the silver cups on the mantelpiece and all my things. What I had just said awed me. It left an echo like that of a bell striking.

XII

I MEASURED it up and tried to see what my father would do. Silence clamped down. The last day was made hideous by our pretences, particularly by the brightness of my mother. I guessed at his strategy. A letter to Crusoe himself? A last-minute ultimatum to me, that I must submit or be removed from school? Nothing to do but wait for it.

It did not come until they stood on the platform, waiting for my train to pull out. Then my mother kissed me and drew Eva back beside her. My father said abruptly, "Well, good-bye, Don. Have a good term. By the way, I don't like keeping things from you—better for you to know I've written to the Headmaster myself."

The whistle blew. "All right," I said aloud to the empty carriage, "now we know where we are." I tried to feel tough and confident.

I pictured the letter. I saw phrases like these: 'Not wishing to say a word against your friend . . .' 'An impressionable boy of Don's age' and 'Ask for your kind co-operation'. My mother had, no doubt, helped him in the writing of it.

I pictured the Head's reaction. I knew more of him from Crusoe than from my own first-hand view. He was easy-mannered, unorthodox, something of a thorn in the flesh of the Governing Body. "His aim being to open a few windows upon the obsolete stuffiness of the private-school system," Crusoe had said, "he will—inevitably—be replaced."

Would he, conceivably, take my side? No. No good fooling myself. He couldn't go against even the silliest of parental wishes unless it interfered with his rule. And this did not. He might show me a gleam of sympathy, but he would enforce the ban. He would have to.

"So," I said, "two choices. Pipe down or fight."

How to fight? I didn't know. But when I considered the other way, I saw that it would have to be fighting. My relationship with my father and mother had changed with alarming speed; I'd seen the beginning of this moment, I thought, on the day that they came to the Rovers match. Not by the most strenuous effort at detachment could I put myself on their side. I could think it out impartially, see what their side was, explain it to an audience. But I couldn't take it. They had become the advocates of a cause that had long bewildered me, but that now made me sick.

It was frightening to weigh them in the balance against Crusoe. There wasn't enough loyalty left to budge the scale. He who had opened the doors, lighted the candles, pushed back the horizons—I would not lose him. Yet there was in my mind an awful hint that, even without his existence, I could bear them no longer.

I would not lose him, I said. But how to win? Surely I couldn't win.

"He'll help me. As soon as I've talked to him, I'll know what to do." Then I was pulled up in horror by the thought of telling him. I could hear his voice already, 'Not, in their view, a fit companion?' And I would squirm and keep my father's obscenely ridiculous words inside my head.

"Leaving you right out of it," I argued with his image. "It's still all wrong. I can't make peace with them because it would be making peace with ideas and views that I loathe. I've grown out of them and that's that. I didn't want to. It just happened."

"And the alternative to making peace?"

"Well, surely—making war."

I could hear his 'No' echoing; and I shut my ears to it. But I could still see the size of my boast. Could I only be brave in boasts? That was the test ahead.

Certainly he'd know the answer. But would I get the chance of him again?

I had written telling him that I would be at Whiteford tomorrow afternoon. Tomorrow was Saturday. We always reassembled on Friday; the week-end was convenient for what Penleith called the Shaking-Down. I measured it. Just so long as authority did not utter between now and two o'clock tomorrow, I was safe.

XIII

AUTHORITY did not utter. In a less clamorous state of mind I might have foreseen that. A headmaster on the first day of term was a busy man. My father's letter would, in a little while, silt down to his attention through the mass of more urgent things. Penleith might have uttered, but I suspected that a stiff little note had already informed him of the new stage. Even so I got no peace. It was only when two o'clock came without incident that I could relax and see how safe I had been. I went up to my dormitory and collected the snapshots of the hunters, for Crusoe. (I never knew how much he could see, but he always asked for them.)

It wasn't the same escape today, across the playground, over the wall and down to the river-field. I had no impulse to turn a cartwheel. They had taken that from me, the old gay run into freedom. I felt too desperate a need of his reassurance. It made me superstitious, as though when I got there I should not find him.

'Don't be an ass,' I told myself. 'He's there. He's waiting for you.'

It was a hot afternoon. The pain of the cracked rib came up as I walked, like a stitch; the strapping pulled a little.

I couldn't, I thought, jump the stream today, even at the narrow part, without hurting myself. I would have to skirt the marsh and cross by the stepping-stones.

Before I reached the stones I saw the thing. At first it was just a cloud of flies and mosquitoes buzzing over the wettest patch of ground, on the far side below the steep bank that ran up to the road. Then I saw that there was a pinkish-brown bar under the flies. As I came level with it, the end of the bar moved and bubbled. It was a calf, stuck in the mud, almost submerged; just his back and part of his head showing. His nose was down in it and I could see the white rolling of his eye.

He looked almost dead.

Perhaps he had slipped in off the steep bank. I noticed a piece of wood sticking up at one side of him. Had somebody laid planks across the mud and deceived him into thinking that they would bear his weight? It couldn't be deep; there was no depth in the marsh at any point. He had just wallowed in it and dug himself down until he was too tired to scramble out.

Blast him; why did I have to find him? Well, there it was. I tried to gauge the depth of the mud. At worst it would be over my knees. It was really only the smallest struggle in my mind, because if I missed the bus I could always thumb a lift into Whiteford. I was free till five-thirty. It couldn't take me long to haul him out. But I didn't want to arrive at Crusoe's with mud all over me. I took off my blazer and trousers, my socks and shoes. In my shirt and my undershorts, feeling improperly silly, I stepped down on to the greenish mud; it came up around my ankles with a sucking noise, then higher until it felt warm and horrible.

There were flies about my own head now. I slapped them away. At the place where he was, I went down a little deeper. He had buried his nose and he was bleating and snuffling, bubbling the mud. I got my hand down, groped and found his chin. It was quite easy to lift his head, but as soon as I took my hand away, he dropped it again. So I held him and used my other hand to scoop some of the mud from his mouth and nostrils.

Already it was much nastier than I expected. He had surrounded himself with his own dung. The flies and the mosquitoes were thick.

In a sudden spurt of new energy, he threshed a foreleg free, pawed at the surface, then let the leg sink in again. He sagged down. My feet were on solid ground; I got a purchase on his neck and shoulder, but he was heavy beyond my reckoning and the effort sent stabs through the cracked bone.

There was a second plank on the other side of him. It looked now as if somebody had tried to help him by putting the two planks under his belly, and then had given up and gone away. I got one plank free of the mud and tried to use it as a spade. I had to keep stopping to beat the flies away. The mosquito-bites began to tickle, but my hands were too filthy to let me scratch my face.

I rolled him to this side and that. Surely the fool could stand if he wanted to. I couldn't feel really cross with him; he was too beaten and his eyes were too frantic.

"Get on, old boy, make an effort, can't you?" I pulled at his head. He groaned. The plank was no good; I couldn't push it down far enough.

Now I heard the Whiteford bus on the road above; I heard its brakes and the slowing of the engine, then the engine starting up again and the sound going away.

Perhaps because of that, I began to see what I had let myself in for. I couldn't get him out like this. 'It'll take a rope,' I decided. 'And we'll have to pull him up on this side, the steep side; we could never haul him through the marsh on to the flat bank.' We? Who were we? There was only I. Oh, but surely somebody must come. I looked up and down the river-field. People came here for walks, didn't they? Often; I had met them.

Nobody came now. There was just the hot silence broken by the humming of the flies; occasionally a rippling, sucking noise as the calf threshed a leg.

The thing to do was to get out of here, find somebody, find a rope. I was doing him no good.

"You wait a bit, will you, like a good chap?" I said to him. "I'll be back." I patted his saddle; I waded away, trying not to hear his despairing bleats. Presently they stopped. When I was almost at the bank I looked round and saw that he'd buried his nose. "Oh, hell," I said and waded back to him.

"*Can't* you keep your head up?" I besought him as I cleaned his nose again. His eyes looked glazed now and his tongue lolled. "Blast you," I said. "I've got to get to Crusoe. Crusoe's waiting for me."

I saw that he was one more in the line of helpless, horrible things; he joined with the yearling that broke a leg, with the drunken old woman in the lane, with the dog that the car had smashed. And I had to stay by them. I had 'vowed my vows in another place'. But this was surely the lowest bid yet made for the worth of the vow. It was ridiculous; it was hot and smelly; it hurt and it tickled; there were no heroics here, no drama to satisfy the appetite identified by Crusoe. It was just a mess. And suddenly I wanted to cry.

I began to swear aloud; all the words that I could muster; short, ugly lumps of words. The sound of them checked me. And I remembered, '*Merit in good behaviour when there is nobody there to see.*' I stopped swearing. I said, "Sorry" and felt better.

For another long period I struggled at him, getting a foreleg free again, raising his shoulder, trying to turn him towards the bank. Then, to my enormous relief, I heard voices above my head. Two men were coming down the steep path under the trees; large townsmen in blue suits, on a Saturday afternoon walk. They began to laugh when they saw me. "Hullo—hullo! What have you got there?"

"A calf. He's stuck. Will you come down and give me a hand?"

They came on. They stood on the edge, looking down at me. "You'll never get him out like that," one said after a time.

I was short of temper. I said, "I probably could, if I hadn't got a broken rib."

They exchanged glances. "How'd you break your rib?"

"Riding." I thought I'd better be polite to them, because I needed their help and from their grins I judged that I might not get it. I said, "But two of us could get him out. With a rope."

"'With a rope', he says. What d'you think of that, Arthur?" This question appeared to be a slogan of a sort, for they both repeated, "What d'you think of that, Arthur?" and laughed heartily. "Look, you'd better get out of that muck, hadn't you? Getting plenty bitten, aren't you?"

"I can't leave him. Do come down and help me. Perhaps the three of us could do it without a rope."

"Honestly, son, it's no good. He'll be all right. They'll haul him out fast enough when it's milking-time."

"He'll suffocate long before then. Don't you see? He drops his head; he's so bloody tired. Besides," I said, "the field goes for miles; they may not find him." I struck at the mosquitoes. The imperturbable faces watched me. I began to feel like crying again.

"Please . . . if you won't help me—would you go and fetch somebody who will? Ask the people at the cottage by the bus stop if they've got a rope."

Again the exasperating silence.

"Know the time, Arthur?"

"Getting on for half-past three."

What on earth had the time got to do with the calf? It had something to do with me, or perhaps it was ceasing to have. My head felt light and queer. I began to dig at the calf again; his eyes were almost shut; there seemed very little life in him. Far away on the bank, dry and clean and free of the cloud of insects, they stood, my enemies.

One said, "Perhaps Robinson's got a rope."

"All right, son. We'll see what we can do. But I'd get out

of that, I really would. It's not healthy." They moved slowly
up the hill.

'Now,' I thought, 'this has been going on all my life; I have
been here all my life; and there never was a time when I didn't
tickle and my hands weren't too filthy to scratch; and my side
has been hurting all my life; and I've never had anything to do
but hold up this damn calf and try to dig him out. Why doesn't
he die?' But I didn't want him to die.

I had to scratch my face. I wiped one hand on my shirt until
it was almost clean, and scratched. It was as good as a cold
drink when one was thirsty. I went on tearing at my skin with
my nails until it hurt.

The calf opened his eyes a little way and threshed again.

God knew how long it had been going on; I didn't. The
light feeling in my head had turned to dizziness, and I thought
that the men had been gone for hours, but I could still hear
their voices above me on the slope. I looked up. Yes, they
were there. No, it was not they. A procession that in any
other moment I should have thought ludicrous was coming
down through the trees; a very large policeman and two very
small Boy Scouts. The policeman was carrying a coil of
rope. The scouts began to yell at me, their voices shrill as
whistles:

"Is he all right?"

"We put those planks there."

"We biked into town."

"We'll help you."

"The Bobby'll get him out."

It was the nearest that I ever got to hysteria. I saw the
solemn policeman making the slip-knot; I saw the two eager
little boys in khaki. I saw me in the mud without my trousers.
'As drama, Crusoe,' I said to him in my mind, 'you must admit
that it lacks something.'

"Can you get it round his neck, sir, if you can't get it round
his middle?"

"Won't he strangle that way?"

"Well, just have a shot," said the policeman. "I'll come in if you can't manage it. But these boys aren't big enough to pull him."

They threw me the rope and I got the loop around his neck. Plunging and weaving in the mud, I braced him up from below.

I said, "Haul away."

The scouts tugged on the rope with the policeman. The calf's head and neck came out; his chest came clear. Then he began to throttle and scream. I put my shoulder under his chest. I worked the knot loose from his throat and down as far as I could. I couldn't get it around his belly, but the strain would come on his chest if I held the rope so that it did not ride up too fast.

"Haul away."

I flung myself against him as they hauled. This time it worked; somehow he came out of the mud, a screaming, filthy bundle, with my hand caught in the rope and the rest of me under him, shoving him up to the edge of the bank. I freed my hand from the rope. For a moment I thought he would topple back on my head, but the little boys were there, grabbing him, clutching him, sliding the slip-knot over his weak legs to his belly. Then I saw him drawn up, kicking and screaming, to the path. The scouts yelled, "Hooray!" and, for all the absurdity, there was an odd moment of triumph when he rolled over and stood upright. It was strange to see him stand; his legs shivered. As the policeman untied him, he kicked out suddenly, tossed his head and trotted away under the trees.

I climbed out and sat on the edge, dead-beat. I thought that the scouts would laugh because I had no trousers on, but they said, "We'll get your clothes!" and dashed across the stepping-stones. The policeman wound the rope. He said, "I expect he'd have croaked if you hadn't held him up." He grinned, watching the scouts race back with my clothes. "Good kids," he said reflectively.

I always found Boy Scouts embarrassing; my father had been a scoutmaster at one time. The policeman was right, though; they were good little boys.

"We've got some water in our tent, sir. Wouldn't you like to wash a bit?"

"Got some smashing stuff for mosquito-bites, too."

I walked between the two virtuous pygmies. I was so tired that I couldn't thank them properly. I washed off the worst of the mud in the tent. My undershorts were so dirty that I had to roll them up in a bundle. I thought that I would throw them away as I walked back. To do it here might shock the scouts. I dabbed my swollen face with the liquid from their bottle.

"Piece of lint, sir?"

"Thanks very much. Do you fellows know the time?"

"Quarter to five," they said in chorus, looking at their enormous wrist-watches.

That was that. For the moment I did not feel it very much. My rib was hurting like hell. I walked back to the college, to telephone Crusoe.

The nearest telephone was in a box outside the Bursar's office. I lurched up the steps, found three pennies and put them in. As I waited, looking at the scribbles on the wall above my head, I forecast Crusoe's comments. Certainly he would laugh. Probably he would compare it with the time that I'd had to pull him and his chair out of the mud.

I heard Joel's voice and I asked if I might speak to him.

There was a pause. Then he said, "Oh, Mr. Bradley . . . you haven't heard?"

"Heard about what?"

He said, "About the accident this morning."

XIV

I CAME to Whiteford on Sunday, after chapel. There was no hurry, nor ever would be again, but I took a taxi instead of the bus. As we drove up the village street, past the almshouses and the curved shop-windows, I looked out at the pavement gutters; they were running dry. We came past the church, down the other hill and over the bridge.

I sent the taxi away. I went in, through the gates, down the green ride to the water.

The garden was changed with autumn; there was a hot, dead stillness upon the lake. The blinds were drawn at the windows of the stone pavilion; dark red blinds; I did not remember noticing them before. I saw the cat in its favourite flower-bed. I looked at the board across the middle of the steps and thought, 'They can take it away now.'

I didn't ring the bell. I walked round the house, as though I expected to meet the terrier half-way and to find Crusoe at breakfast under the magnolia. Nobody there. I mounted the steps to the terrace and went through the glass doors into the hall.

Down at the front of the hall Mrs. Irvine stood; talking to a man who had his back to me, a man with fair, reddish hair. I could see her face looking up at him, the pointed face on the neck of the prim swan. Then she saw me and made a gesture with her left hand; a sympathetic hand stretched out to draw me into their company.

"Livesey, you haven't met Don."

I looked into the face of 'my brother Livesey'. The only resemblances to Crusoe were in the colouring and the straight nose. Otherwise it was just a fair face with blue eyes, and queerly hard lines on the forehead that gave him a look of perplexity.

His voice was like Crusoe's, though: "You know it's over, don't you? At two o'clock this morning."

"Yes. Joel told me. I telephoned before breakfast."

"Livesey, I'll leave you now," Anne Irvine said. "Do you mind if Don walks with me to the gate? There's something I want to say to him."

"Please do. But you'll come back, won't you?" he said to me. "I'll be waiting here." I was aware of him as we went, standing, large and still and beaten, in the middle of the hall.

Mrs. Irvine put her arm through mine, leaning upon it a little.

She said, "He never recovered consciousness. I thought you'd like to know that." Her nose and her eyes were quite pink.

"Not at all?"

"No; not from the first minute."

So I never could have seen him alive again. He was virtually dead while I thought that he was waiting for me. She was right. There was a huge and practical consolation in this, though it didn't last.

"That's the first thing," she said, stopping and biting her lips, staring at the wall above the herbaceous border. "Pretty —those red leaves. Then I remembered something that he said—after he read your essay, I think it was. He said he'd never realised that he wanted a son until you came along." She patted my hand briskly. "And there's this. I know that when somebody dies, the worst of it is remorse; remembering the times when one has failed or been unkind. I know, because I've had that. And that's the one thing you can't have; what you have is just the opposite; the knowledge of having given him nothing but pleasure. And you've known a great man. That's all, my dear. Go back to Livesey." She raised her hand in farewell; the tears were running down her face, but they didn't seem to embarrass her at all. I saw her thin, dark shape walking away up the green ride.

Livesey was standing exactly where I left him, contemplating his shoes; they were chunky, well-cut shoes, rather too bright a brown.

"Hullo. Sit on the terrace, shall we?" I followed him out. He said, "You know how it happened?"

I said violently, "What possessed him to do it? Take the colt out on the rein? In the *chair;* it was crazy. Why did they let him?"

"Oh, look here. Knowing Crusoe as well as you did—how could anybody have stopped him?"

I asked, "Was he angry about something?" It seemed the

sort of impatient gesture that he might have made if he were in a temper with Mallock or Gill.

"No, I don't think so. Just amused by the colt. Mallock'll tell you."

"Was he kicked, or was it the chair going over that killed him?"

"Kicked on the head. Fractured his skull." Livesey took a pipe out of his pocket and filled the pipe meticulously. His hands were like Crusoe's hands.

I said, "You weren't here? They sent for you?" Somehow I had thought of Livesey as being on the other side of the world for ever, but he said, "I was on my way. Just got back from America."

I thought about the homecoming. I said, "How bloody for you." Now he lit the pipe and raised one eyebrow, his face becoming more cryptic.

"You do realise that Crusoe wouldn't have lived much longer, anyway?"

"No, I didn't."

"He didn't tell you?"

"No."

Livesey said, "There was a progressive disease of the kidneys. It's been gaining for the last few years."

"He never talked about it. About any of it. I don't even know if he got it playing polo or hunting."

"Neither," said Livesey, "he was hacking home; a lorry driven by a drunk hit them."

"When was it?"

"Oh, he was about your age. Seventeen."

I stared. "You mean—but then he never had any life at all——"

"He had plenty," Livesey said. "He made it. You know, I think he was a genius. Only a genius could have lived it his way."

I couldn't take it in. Always I had thought of the thing as happening long after he grew up. No manhood, I thought; no true love; no more riding. For nearly forty years. It made him twice the hero.

I was silent. I saw the calm blue eyes looking at me. "Would you like to see him? Before you go up to the stables?"

It was nice of him to know that I wanted to go up to the stables.

As we went into the hall, he said, "Don't do this if you'd rather not."

"I'd like to, please." I braced myself and followed him in.

The effect of the room was to make me think that he wasn't dead at all; he still seemed to be alive and all over it. It was no more shadowy now with the blinds drawn than it had been on the days when his eyes hurt him. We went up to the canopied bed.

I looked down on a face that I did not know; the face without the black bar across the eyes. This face looked smooth and pale, somehow Biblical. Perhaps that was the effect of the white sheet and the pointed beard. Anyway he did not look like Crusoe. His stillness made a demand; the silence of him went on and on.

He was only the second person whom I had seen lying dead. And the first time I had not known what I saw. The first was the old lady in the French hotel, the Duchess; she was the first eccentric, the first clown and tragedian of my life. And Crusoe was the second.

I hadn't thought of the Duchess for a long time; she had receded far behind the vow that I had made because of leaving her. She bobbed up in my memory now with the dance of a mechanical toy; the funny, wise, highly-coloured old creature who had been more enchanting to the mind of a thirteen-year-old than she could ever guess.

(She, too, had been banned for me.)

Perhaps they sent you that sort of person once in a while, as a signal. Sent them and took them away again, leaving you to draw your own conclusions.

I couldn't think of anything to say to Crusoe except—"Thank you for everything", and then I wanted to appeal to him—"This doesn't mean they've won, does it?", but the peaceful, remote head denied me. He couldn't be bothered with such questions now. I left him.

I found Livesey waiting outside the door. He said, "Want to take my car and drive up?" Never was anybody so un-obtrusive on his own ground: he made no claim.

"I can drive, but I haven't got my licence yet. Is that all right with you?"

"I'll trust you. See me when you come back. Bloody solicitor'll be here soon. Spoiled his Sunday," Livesey said.

The car was a black Rolls, this year's model. For a few minutes I was shocked that I could be having fun driving it. Then I saw the fun as a present that Crusoe had given me by his death. I parked it gingerly outside the stable-yard.

I found that, despite the shrinking at my heart, I had to have the details from Mallock. His face looked smaller than ever. The stable-boy was cleaning out Rougemont's stall. We talked over mugs of tea.

"He was in top form, Mr. Bradley, he really was. We didn't expect him up here before lunch, you know he'd usually wait till the afternoon. But he was feeling too well, he said. Laughing and bellowing at all of us. Then he said he'd take the colt and I said, 'Well, I wouldn't if I was you,' but—lord!—I got a proper rocket." There were tears in his eyes and he gave a kind of whistle and went on:

"It was just beyond the big jump at the top of the field. They'd gone round once and it was all right; then something scared the colt. I couldn't get to him. The chair went plunging along, half-tipped over, got tied up in the rein, then the colt backed right on top of him. I knew it was all over when we picked him up. He didn't suffer, Mr. Bradley."

After a time he said, "You'll be coming here again, sir? To ride? I think Mr. Livesey'll stay now. If you ask me, he always kept out of the way because he knew Mr. Crusoe liked to have the running of the place. He's—sort of shy, Mr. Livesey is. But he won't let the stables go. And perhaps Mrs. Livesey'll come back. Anyway, we've got lots of work to do . . ." and he gave the whistle again and led Rougemont into his stall.

I said, "Yes, I'll try and come." But I didn't know if I would want to. I went the rounds of the horses. At first I did not pet the colt who had killed him; but I saw its bright eyes and innocent head looking after me and I went back because I knew that Crusoe wouldn't blame it nor wish me to pass it by. I left Rougemont to the last. After I'd hugged him, my mouth began to shake and twitch and I couldn't say good-bye to Mallock.

I made an awful mess with the gears, driving down. Livesey was in the garden.

"Would you like to stay for lunch? Not much fun for you, I'm afraid, but perhaps better than nothing."

I shook my head, tried to thank him and gave up. The effort not to cry made me shiver.

"Well, now," Livesey said, looking past me with tact, "can't we give you a lift home?"

"Thanks. I'll walk. Get a bus in the village. I'd rather, really. Sorry." The bristly terrier had suddenly appeared on the gravel. If I could start walking I should be all right. Livesey's large hand hit my shoulder. "I'm here, if you want me. Get going now." It was the best advice.

As I came out of the green ride, to the gates, I said aloud, "You've got to cut this out. Can't walk along crying, damn you—— Damn you, stop. But it isn't fair. Oh God, it isn't fair. I can't *not* see him any more. Everything's stopped . . . everything . . . all the things. Nothing will ever be exciting again." It was all said aloud in a sobbing, blubbering voice. I couldn't quite believe that it was I who talked. I sounded mad. "Why did you have to do it, Crusoe? For Christ's sake, why? Why did God have to do it? I prayed all night for you not to be dead. I could have sat with you, watched with you; even if you didn't know I was there. And instead I had to stay with the stupid calf. But that was all right, wasn't it? You'd have said it was all right. Oh God, come back and tell me it was all right."

It was too easy to go on talking aloud, sobbing aloud. I was at the road. I must stop. I got out my handkerchief and blew my nose hard and wiped my eyes.

My breathing sounded funny. I whistled like Mallock. I came to the bridge. I got up and leaned over, staring at the water. The movement of the water made it all go more quietly.

"But they've won," I said. "I think I mind that most of all. It's their victory."

"*Don, for a man of good will, you are sometimes exceptionally foolish. Do you really believe that they've won? Don't you see that, as a retort to their poor little strategy, death has a certain magnificence?*"

My thought. But I had put his words around it, a conjuring trick to be grateful for.

"Yes. Thank you. I hadn't thought of that. But what do I do now? Tell me . . ."

To think that he could not tell me dropped the black tent again. "All the things that we'll never talk about . . . I'll be so bloody lonely with them inside my head. And you'll not know if I win the McColl medal, so now I don't care if I win or not. I don't care what happens.

"No, that's wrong. I must care. It's rejecting you if I don't. I must remember it all. I must hoard everything you ever said to me."

And live by it . . . But how to live? I saw that I was still put to the test. I had said that I would not make peace with certain things. Were those merely words? Gestures of defiance? I should never know what he would have said to them. He had left me to make my own decision.

And this suddenly made his death logical, as though I couldn't have known my own mind by any other way.

And so I knew it. Those words were still the truth, here on the bridge. There was no defiance in them; they were certain and sad, spoken in a moment of knowledge that cut the links with me as I had been. I was a different person now. I did not know this person yet. I did not know what he would do; except that he must break free from the things that he could not stomach nor believe. It felt as though he were setting out on a very long journey indeed.

III

THE ROAD BY THE RIVER

Told by Three Voices

I

Penelope's Voice

I WAS sitting in the summer-house that perches on a hump of the garden between the hotel and the Corniche Road. My manuscript lay spread out before me on the scarred wooden table. A three-sided shell of whitewashed walls enclosed me; I stared at the view, well known and well loved. The open side of the summer-house framed the light, glistening green plumes of an umbrella-pine, with a red rock path looping below; then the stone parapet that bulges at the point where the road curves out into a buttress above the garden. The rest of the view is the sky. Since this was a clear morning, I could see upon the peacock-blue a crinkle of white mountain—the Alps far off.

Had you asked me who I would like best to be at that moment I should have answered unhesitatingly 'Myself'. Penelope Wells, aged nineteen and writing my novel.

Or, more accurately, thinking about my novel, with the ink long dry on the last words written. I was merely drowning in warmth and peace and the scents of the garden. The lazy mood had come on me while I reflected that this was the last day but one. The summer holiday was almost ended. The day after tomorrow I should travel back to Oxford.

Because of that, I had begun to turn the scribbled pages, first to see how much I had written in these seven weeks, then, fatally, to re-read, and now to dream. In the dream there was my first novel, printed, bound and respectfully reviewed.

It would not be, in truth, my first novel. I had written my first at the age of fifteen, in two marble-boarded exercise-books bought from the *papeterie* at St. Raphael. It did not say much, but it was at least finished. It was severe, formal and gloomy. Half a fantasy, full of Celtic twilight, had come next. Then

133

there was the saga of an English family, planned to run through three generations and at least six hundred pages. For this I had lost my appetite early. The novel in progress, then, was really novel number three and I hoped that it would survive.

Like its predecessors, it would be dedicated to the Duchess. The dedication took a new shape in my mind, a shape made of this peaceful mood:

'To Violetta di Terracini
Out of the freedom that she promised me.'

And perhaps, I thought, I would add the translated epitaph from the Greek Anthology:

'As small this stone, so great my love. And you,
despite all Lethe, friend, remember too!'

Yes, she would like that. I came to know her better as the years went by. Francis had made me keep all her letters, the copious letters written to the child who did not understand nor care. Lately I had mounted them in two fat albums. I returned to them often. Much of my philosophy came from those pages, the exquisite angry script on the azure paper with the crest at the top.

'The freedom that she promised me,' my thoughts repeated, and the magic was there. It was unidentifiable; it was just the whole atmosphere of Now; the waiting hush, the excitement that burned down below, the solitude that must, and must not, be broken. I had written:

'The sun and the shadow walk over the wall,
but nobody comes to the garden at all.
Except, as I wander, the thought in my mind
behaves like a footstep that follows behind.
I listen until it is quiet, and then
I walk to the end of the garden again. . . .'

It was like that, I thought, the freedom that the Duchess had promised me. She had said that I would emerge from the self-imposed sorrows of my childhood into light-heartedness and tranquillity. It was so. My wars were over. And if at nineteen it was not yet possible to make peace with the universe, I had at least signed comfortable truces. Francis, on reading the half-finished saga of England, had commented, a little disturbingly, "Now you know all that there is to know—except facts."

"But facts are important."

"No," said Francis, "there are too many of them."

It was Oxford's business, I had said, to teach me facts. But still I knew that wasn't what he meant. "When you meet one head-on," he said, "and it hurts you, it becomes worth learning; so you learn it."

Which implied, I thought, that I was at present ignorantly serene. And serenity was surely a middle-aged virtue, a foothold attained after difficult climbing. But I suspected that I had come to it early and that Francis, bringing me up, as the Duchess had said, through-the-looking-glass, was responsible. And was this, perhaps, why I could not yet write a novel? I was too happy. I was too tidy in my mind. All the best books, I was sure, were written out of chaos and rebellion, by cross people.

Well, all right; in that case I should never be a novelist. Nor, following in Francis' wake, a poet. The verses that I wrote were derivative, jingly, feminine. I was fond of them, but this was only the maternal instinct. In detachment the most that I could award them was an affectionate shake of the head.

The lazy mood held. I could not take up my pen again, nor open the letter that had lain on my table for more than an hour. The postman, having spied me on his way through the gate and mounted the path to the summer-house expressly for the purpose of giving it to me, would be rightly aggrieved. But the letter was from Marius, my friend, my enemy at Oxford. Marius was unpredictable. I liked best the things—and the people—that went on being what they were. Moods, temperament, sudden changes of face, disturbed me. You could never foresee the mood of Marius, because he was always determined that you should guess it and guess wrong. Preparing for an encounter with him was like dressing for the day when you had no clue to the weather outside.

Even the handwriting on the envelope seemed now to offer the same self-conscious challenge. I let it lie.

The silence broke. A large grey bus came roaring down the road, the side of it almost touching the parapet above the garden. At the windows I could see young faces and uniform black shoulders. These were seminarians from St. Ignace. The bus pulled in, as always, to the buttress-curve and they climbed out and scattered, admiring the view. They crowded the sky-line. I could hear their voices. I could see them pointing variously towards Cannes, the Alps and Corsica. One climbed up on the edge of the parapet; his black skirts blew; he waved his arms and pretended that he would jump.

The one whom I knew was not talking today. I could see him, taller than the rest, walking a little apart, reading his breviary. Sometimes he leaned on the parapet and waved to me. I had known him when he was thirteen, and Father Lasalle brought him here occasionally, but we were shy of each other. I never asked him the questions that I wanted to ask.

They were so very young, the boys in their black robes. They drew my eyes always, and my thoughts, and they made a question-mark in my mind. At Oxford I met the determined atheists, the self-styled free-thinkers who seemed not to be free at all, so bound were they to abstain from speculation, so sworn to observe the limits of their own perceptions. And there I met also the mockers, the purveyors of careful acid, and the strenuously broad-minded and the demolition-units of despair.

Meanwhile there were the shouts and laughter of the black-robed young men up there against the Mediterranean sky. For a moment these echoed to me more freedom than ever sounded from the gnawing Oxford arguments. But now they piled back into the bus, and as they drove away I saw only the narrow uphill road ahead of them. I would rather be me in the summer-house. That road was steep and there was no top to the mountain that I could see.

They left a hint of restlessness behind them, the magic disturbed. So that I rose, without any idea except to stretch myself, moving out into the full sunshine; I heard the whirr of the crickets; I blinked at the black cypress and the dimming purple blaze of bougainvillæa down the white wall. Summer was on the wane. Though here, I thought, the seasons pause every step of the way and trick you, in England the apples will be ripening on the trees.

As though to point the validity of England, my Aunt Anne now came out on to the veranda of the hotel. She was a neat figure in blue linen, topped with a huge, conical, coolie's hat which she had bought yesterday in the street at St. Paul-de-Vence. She carried a picnic-case. Today, I recalled, Francis and Jeanne were driving her to meet some friends in Valescure. Her fortnight with us was punctuated by these small expeditions. She waved to me and came up the path.

"It's hopeless to be on time in this place. Francis is still in the kitchen doing something about lobsters," she said. Her tone was benevolent. "I don't suppose we'll leave before eleven now. Wonderful to be born without a sense of time. Or money," she added, sitting down with a flourish on the step of the summer-house and showing her sensible, closed knickers as she drew up her knees.

She has a misleading look of Francis; the pointed Spanish face on the long neck; our family runs to long necks. She is not in the least like Francis. She is eager rather than gay, at odds with her world, not at peace. In Aunt Anne, all is suppression, as though her life had been devoted to putting down a revolution inside. And indeed I suppose it has. Too late, at fifty, to let the Jacobins out.

Aunt Anne is a lady, an English country lady, a rider to hounds, a gardener; an aristocrat of the village, with every kind of local preoccupation, from Women's Institute to church flowers. And it does not satisfy her to be this person.

Her mind makes pictures of freedom that are a little dated

(just as her life now has an old-fashioned look and Whiteford village itself begins to seem a quaint pocket of survival, with the world active in terms of cold war, nuclear fission and state powers). Aunt Anne's dream of emancipation was formed in her youth, when she wanted to live a Bohemian life. In the dreams she still lies on a studio floor, wearing floppy trousers and drinking absinthe, flouting time, taking lovers, arguing about Art and eating sardines straight from the tin.

But in fact she loved, married and buried a simple man. She bore two dull children who grew up and married and went away. One lives in Leeds and the other in Australia. Aunt Anne stays on in the village. All that is left of the dream is her passion for the odd and the eccentric, and this grows with the years. No demonstration of unorthodoxy is too small for her approval. She applauds the daring of the holiday-maker who goes to Matins without a hat. She has protested with me because I will not walk about Whiteford wearing shorts and sandals.

Here with us she welcomes every proof of the native inconsequence. She loves the atmosphere of moon-madness that charges our four walls; it is far more noticeable to her than it is to me. In childhood I was acutely aware of the oddities. Now I see them seldom; I take them for granted; they are predictable and rhythmic, therefore scarcely oddities at all until Aunt Anne, with rapture, draws my attention to them. "Oh to live like this always," Aunt Anne will cry, because we are dining at ten o'clock.

Still I believe that the thwarted dream makes her happier than it would if it ever came true. According to the Duchess, it is never so enjoyable to escape from a cage and prove the delights beyond the bars as to stay in the cage and picture them.

"What are you going to do with yourself all day? . . . Not just sit and work, surely——" Aunt Anne wailed.

I said that I wanted to get to the end of the next chapter, my target for this holiday. And I added, to console her, that I was happier doing this than doing anything else. Still she looked disappointed. I knew that I often disappointed her in these days. When I was a precocious and peculiar little girl, the yearly guest in her house, I must have been fun for her. (Then my love for law and order was largely concealed, a private shame, a source of guilt. Now I admitted my passion, the diametric opposite of her own. Aunt Anne found it sad warning of a future, self-appointed stuffiness.)

"Oh, take a day off—come with us," she pleaded. "You'd like the Puddie boy, I know you would. He's just out of the Army; he's interesting; he wants to write. Apparently he got in some kind of state and was discharged by the Army psychiatrists—so wonderful that they have them, isn't it? He *looks* interesting, too. Haunted . . . a long lock of hair on his forehead."

"With the name Puddie . . ." I mused.

"What a lot *words* mean to you—just like Francis," said Aunt Anne.

"Penelope Puddie——" I offered her darkly.

The suggestion that anything so conventional as matchmaking had crossed her mind was deeply offensive to my aunt. She said that she thought I might find him 'fun to flirt with' and immediately asked after Marius.

She has shown the liveliest interest ever since in an unguarded moment I told her that Marius wanted me to be his mistress. Aunt Anne was delighted with my reply. I had said that, if he would excuse me, I preferred to wait. To her this attitude was evidence of comical sophistication. It was nothing of the kind. It was, on the other hand, nothing of a kind that I could conceivably explain to Aunt Anne.

"Marius . . . well, I don't know how he is. There's a letter from him, but I haven't opened it."

"Are you quarrelling with him?"

"No, indeed. I never do. It is he who does the quarrelling."

"But why haven't you opened the letter?"

"I wasn't quite in the mood for it, I thought."

"How wonderful you are . . . I couldn't leave a letter unopened. But of course," she added with envious delight, "Francis never opens letters *at all*, does he?"

"Fortunately," I said, "Jeanne opens them for him." At which point Francis came out on to the veranda and stood beside the car with the martyred air of one kept waiting. "Really," said Aunt Anne, "he is very naughty."

I watched them drive away. My solitude gave me a reassuring wink.

> (*'And this is adventure, I tell you, to tread*
> *alone with the thought at the back of your head.'*)

I paced the garden. I worked for a while. At the sound of the midday carillon, I decided to read the letter from Marius and afterwards swim. Disturbances were unlikely; it was the end of the season. Except for Aunt Anne and a minor poet, at present in bed with sunstroke, we had no guests.

Marius was, as usual, on the west coast of Scotland. His enthusiasm for the place was such that he might not merely have owned it but invented it. He made a spiky reference to 'your fashionable Riviera life, which we do not envy'. He knew perfectly well that I lived simply here, that I helped Francis and Jeanne with the work to be done. Towards the end, the letter became affectionate and bawdy; then told me that he would meet the boat-train on Friday evening.

I felt the jangle of his personality from miles away. I liked him less in absence than in presence and I did not know what this proved.

Some of the later phrases, with an echo of Aunt Anne's invitation to 'flirt', set me brooding again upon the flesh; upon the whole unexplored adventure of the body. It was an adventure that I did not want. My knowledge of it was theoretically complete. I could talk of it with detachment. I had read of it extensively, in the classics, in set books of psychology, in contemporary fiction. Indeed, it belonged to literature, where, mysteriously, the characters enjoyed it.

Perhaps I was abnormally made. The preludes, which were all that I knew, had convinced me that it was both horrible and absurd. I could not let anybody kiss me on the mouth again.

I had allowed it to happen because I felt that there would be some prestige, some sense of achievement, in the act. And there was not. There was only embarrassment, repulsion, a struggle to end it. It had happened to me three times in all and the last time was with Marius.

Had it shocked me? Perhaps. According to the Duchess, the adult mind could be shocked by no aspect of human behaviour except cruelty. Though I dared not pride myself yet upon the possession of an adult mind, I was always aiming towards one. And here it was surely my body that had been shocked and not my mind.

Marius, being, he said, an unusually sensitive person, had pronounced himself hurt. People were always, it seemed, hurting Marius, and now I was one of them. I had my own theories about being hurt. To my mind it was only the ego that could ever be hurt; and this was what the ego needed. It was an obstacle on the way to maturity, a kind of hymen that must be hurt once in order that it should never hurt again. Once wounded and having taken the wound, I said, you were grown-up. Grown-ups did not go through life being 'hurt'. You could only be that if you preserved your virginity of ego, thus becoming retarded and tiresome.

"Then you have no pride," was the accusation made by Marius.

"Well, possibly I have not."

"Then you can't be sensitive."

Sensitivity, in his case, focused upon himself. And from what I had seen of those who suffered similarly, 'sensitive' people *were* only sensitive about themselves. They were impervious to the inner workings of others. It was hard to make Marius understand that, where kisses were concerned, what I disliked was the act and not the person who performed it.

At this moment I might, had it occurred to me, have thanked God that love was so completely separate from the experience. I was in love and I loved being in love. I could have told you a great deal about love, under the impression that I knew all there was to know.

"Except the facts"? It was after Francis had read the portrait of my love in the English saga that he said that thing. He could not recognise the portrait; he had never met the man. When I asked his opinion of the character, Francis said, "He's two-dimensional. I only knew what the girl thought about him."

My love was a haunting; an enchanted slavery, a chosen bond. It was Heaven-sent, it was hopeless and my body had no part in it. Love meant that you wanted to be with the person all the time. You worshipped him as a hero, you would die for him, and the sound of his name spoken suddenly hurt you under your ribs on the left side. There were dreams of the companionship going on and on in some magic, impossible future.

A moment's indulgence of those dreams was now enough to make me ashamed for having allowed the horrid embraces.

"Down to the sea," I said.

I put the manuscript away in the Victorian desk that had belonged to the Duchess, one of those boxes in rosewood, like a small coffin, that opens on its hinge to form a slope when you lay it on a flat table. I set the coffin back on its shelf.

My bedroom windows open on to the terrace. I was coming along the terrace in my swimming suit, stepping lightly because the flagstones were hot, when I heard the jingle of bells. Now, at the top of the terrace steps, there appeared two silver-grey poodles, yoked together by scarlet, bell-ridden harness. They were without escort. They dragged a trailing leash. They came to me delightedly, sniffing my ankles.

I saw that they were exactly alike, small and cloud-edged, with very big eyes and elegant silk gloves below feathery bracelets, where their paws were trimmed. They began to dance and leap.

"Travelling alone?" I said to them as they spiralled about me on their hind legs. I stooped, and they dashed away down the steps. Beside the hydrangea bushes, they halted, challenging me to follow. I followed. This time they let me play with them. They gave me great pleasure. The difference in their characters became apparent. The girl-poodle was an extrovert,

a show-off; the boy-poodle had a melancholy wit like Jaques.
While one covered me with her kisses, the other lay low, then
pounced, stood off again and looked at me with his head tilted
sideways.

"Oh, you dogs, you'll be the death of me," came in a gusty
sigh from somewhere above my head. Crouching on the gravel,
I saw plimsolls—very new, very large, speckled plimsolls. I
looked up, past bony ankles and a grey linen hem, up a flat
incline to where the longest, saddest face imaginable peered
down palely.

It was a heavily-powdered face and a wide straw halo framed
it.

"Wait till her ladyship hears about you," the face said to the
dogs.

I rose and put their leash into her hand. "All the way down
to the sea they went," she said, "and in this heat too."

"It is warm today."

"It's terrible. Really it might be New York except one's
spared the humidity." Here she began to spin like a top. The
poodles, running around her in opposite directions, were tying
her legs together with the leash. She moaned and clutched,
"Oh-oh-*oh*, you naughty dogs." I turned them counter-clock-
wise, hoping that she would not fall and crush me. All the
time that I was unwinding them, the melancholy chant continued overhead, "Travelling with animals . . . just like a circus
. . . worse when it was the monkey . . . sweet in its way, poor
little thing . . . so kind of you."

"There," I said, "you're all right now."

No; she was not. "It's my head . . . I suffer dreadfully with
my head . . . always have. Migraine——" she added. "My
poor father was the same."

Uneasily, half-naked in my swimming suit, longing for the
sea, I wondered if my Wedding-Guest's doom were upon me
again. Francis had christened it. I would, he said, have been
the one of three, stopped by the Ancient Mariner, no doubt at
all. He saw the other two going fortunately by, myself detained
by the skinny hand to hear the story. It happened often; on

trains, in tea-shops, once in a ladies' cloakroom where a retired nurse had told me about her prolapse. Some people, Francis said, were natural Wedding-Guests, usually those with charitable eyes and attentive expressions.

"Only mine," said the sad, ultra-refined voice, "is more of a pulsing." I wondered what she had said before that. Now she glanced anxiously over her shoulder, then asked for two people whose names I did not know.

"They aren't staying here, I'm afraid."

"Oh, dear. . . . It's the Countess de Bretteville to see them. . . . You're quite sure?"

"Quite sure."

"But they *were* staying here . . . ?"

"I don't think so. Not lately, anyway. I can look in the register, but people seldom sign it."

She appeared defeated. "Well, Madam, I don't know what to say, I really don't."

Nobody had called me Madam before. From 'her ladyship' I had already identified her as a maid. Maids being on the decrease, a vanishing breed like buffaloes, I was interested. Equally, she had my sympathies; nobody would choose to be a maid with a migraine.

"I'm so sorry," I began, when, from the other side of the hotel, a light, hard voice yelled, "Boxer! Boxer!"

"Here, my lady! They aren't here, my lady!" she yelled back over the hydrangeas.

There was the slam of a car door, brisk steps on the gravel and she came into sight, the owner of maid and poodles. She wore a sailcloth shirt, faded strawberry-pink in colour, and blue shorts; gold bracelets in abundance, chunks of gold on the shirt, sandals with thick cork soles. Her skin was tanned nearer black than brown. It was a young body and a young stride, but as she came close I saw that she was not young.

The fairness of the hair was sudden against that tanned hide of a skin; thick, soft hair turning silver and cut short under her ears with a fringe across the forehead. It was the queerest face. The bones were boyish. I noticed the cleft in the upper lip and

the cleft in the chin, and these with the haircut reminded me of
Joan of Arc. Then she smiled. The smile was artificial,
treacherous, too quick and too wide. It made lines come on
the tan. It was a social smile and it was not followed up by any
light in the grey eyes. I have never seen such pale, blind-
looking eyes.

None of these details accounted wholly for her atmosphere,
so palpable and bizarre that it made me shy. She had hurt one
hand, I saw. She wore a white glove tied at the wrist with
tapes.

"Hullo. How d'you do. I'm looking for the Farringdons.
Johnny and April," she said in rapid staccato.

"I'm sorry."

She said, "Not here?"

"No."

"But they *told* me they'd be here. . . . Oh, *honestly*——" and
I caught a tinge of American accent in the voice. She stood
distractedly, rubbing her forehead with the palm of her unhurt
hand. The poodles fawned on her and so pulled the maid
Boxer forward at a Tower-of-Pisa angle.

"This *is* Francis Wells' hotel, isn't it?"

"Yes, it is."

"Would he know——?"

I explained that he was out and that I was his daughter.
"I'm Cara de Bretteville," she said, as if I should know about
that. "Well, there you are. No dice." She turned to Boxer.
"I've never really trusted April, anyway. She buzzes my right
ear, not my left one." To this obscure accusation, Boxer
nodded sagely and said, "Ah."

The grey eyes returned to me. "You wouldn't be in charge
here, would you? Oh, you would. Well, can I have a drink?
And water for the dogs? Have you bowls? Two bowls? The
bar's here? . . . Come along, Boxer. How's your head?"

"Still pulsing, my lady."

"A room where Boxer can lie down. Don't *argue*; go and
lie down. Wait——" She fished in the depths of a huge pigskin bag that was slung across her shoulder, found a gold box,

took two pills from it and dropped them into the large, dejected palm. "Going to be sick?" she asked threateningly. The maid denied it. "All right; now I don't want to hear from you for at least an hour."

I came back, having laid Boxer out in a room on the ground floor and found two bowls from the kitchen. Cara de Bretteville was studying the signed photographs beside the counter, a poodle under each arm. She was talking to the poodles, showing them the photographs. From the back, she looked like somebody of my own age, with the medieval haircut, the narrow waist and the bare brown legs.

"Only way to move Boxer is to give her an anæsthetic and mail her," she observed.

"She seems sad."

"Oh, she's always sad. That doesn't mean anything. Boxer can be useful and sad at the same time. She only becomes useless when in motion. Insisted on coming. Mustn't drive alone, says Boxer, on account of this." She held up the gloved hand.

"What have you done?"

"Oh, just set fire to it . . . no trouble," she said.

The bar was, as usually, cool and dusky with shadow, save for the bright panel where the french windows opened to the terrace. This woman sounded a note of disturbance in the peaceful room. No reason why; she seemed amiable enough. Now she put the poodles down on the floor, gurgling a little incantation over them; it sounded like gibberish. They appeared to listen.

On the counter there was a dish of lemons, some green and some yellow, some with their stalks and leaves. Cara de Bretteville eyed them and said, "Lemonade would be nice." No reason to resent an order launched into the air; I was serving here, after all. I filled the bowls from the tap and set them before the dogs. The girl-poodle sprang forward to drink and the boy-poodle stood still. "Don't watch him—he won't drink if you watch him," the brittle voice snapped.

"What are their names?"

"They vary," said Cara de Bretteville, "I don't know what they're called today."

This confounded me. "Well, dogs needn't have the same names all the time. Come to that," she said, "people needn't either. Except for signing cheques." She looked quite cross.

"Would you like me to make you a *citron-pressé*?"

"M'm—I think so. Thank you." She climbed up on a stool and bowed over, resting her hands on the bar and her chin on her hands, blinking at me while I made the lemonade. It was like being watched by an animal and not offensive, although it made me jump when I turned round from the shelf where the sugar was and found her still doing it.

"Live here? All the year round, I mean?"

"No. I'm at Oxford."

"What I ought to have done . . . many years ago. Pipe down, my loves, pipe down. Excuse me." She carried the dogs over to the window-seat and arranged them there, pressing them into a neat mould, head to tail. "Stay, now . . ." she warned them, climbing back on to the stool.

"When do you——" she began. Then she suddenly cried, "Ow! That's a loud one" and clapped her hand over her left ear . . . "*And* long, too . . . Goodness. . . ." She kept up a listening pose with the ear still covered. "Think I know who it is." She gave a tender, secretive smile. "Ever get it?" she asked me.

"Get what?"

"A telepathy-buzz. In your ear. A bell ringing."

I shook my head.

"When somebody thinks of you, I mean." The brittle voice had done its trick of turning slow and American. "A ping. In your ear? Don't you?"

"Well, no; I don't."

"I *always* do." She seemed a little aggrieved. She left her lemonade untouched, blinking at me again. I said, "Would you see if that is sweet enough?"

"It won't be."

I advanced the sugar-sifter, but she was once again deflected, scrabbling in the pigskin bag, muttering, "Where the hell are my glasses?" There were two pairs of glasses, with heavy rims of tortoise-shell, on the counter beside her. "Not *those*," she said impatiently, "those are long-distance and bi-focal. I want the middle range. Hell . . . What *is* that on the shelf behind your shoulder?"

"One of the bottles?"

"No. It looks like a bubble on a stand."

I shook it and set it before her. It was a German toy; a cheap snowstorm paper-weight, with a papier-mâché rabbit walking through the snow. Cara de Bretteville put on one of the pairs of glasses.

"But it's a *rabbit*——" she said excitedly. "A rabbit in a red coat and boots. . . . I couldn't love it more. Whose is it?"

"I don't know, really. It has always been there."

"I'll buy it," she snapped.

"Buy it?"

"Yes. What'll you take for it?"

I was bewildered. "I couldn't sell it to you without asking Francis."

"Your father? Is he fond of it? Does he play with it?"

"Well, no . . . never, in my recollection," I said truthfully.

"Do *you* play with it? . . . Does anybody? . . . then why can't I——?"

"Because it isn't mine to sell."

"But if it just *sits* there."

She was as obstinate as a child, I thought. I said, "Sorry——" and held out my hand for the paper-weight. After a moment she gave it back. She exchanged one pair of glasses for another. "A lorgnette," she said, "is the solution. A lorgnette in triplicate." She scrabbled in her bag again, found a notebook and a pencil and wrote LORGNETTE on a blank page. Then she smiled at me again.

"Oxford," she said . . . "When do you go back?"

"On Thursday."

"Wonderful. Like to help me?" The smile widened. "You'd be just the person. Much better than that ass April.

Oxford student; *sans peur et sans reproche*, d'you see?"

"I don't quite see, no. Just the person to do what?"

"Take some dollars in."

"Smuggle them in?"

"No. Heavens, no. They won't ask you any questions, just take them in." The smile held. She fished again in the pigskin saddlebag, drawing up two leather wallets. Solemnly she rifled them, laying their contents on the bar counter: a passport, tickets in a travel-agent's envelope; old letters, snapshots; travellers' cheques and an ordinary cheque-book; something that looked like a pawn-ticket, a vaccination-certificate and in due course a thick envelope, sealed.

"Don't lose it . . . not that it's the end of the world if you do. I *can't* worry about money because it never seems to belong to me . . . nothing ever does seem to . . . in fact I'm never quite sure that *I* belong to me—what d'you think about that? Do we—or don't we?" She was blinking again. "Oh, and this——" she slipped some ten-dollar notes from one wallet— "I'd like to change some into francs. What rate d'you give?"

I was feeling a little dizzy. I said, "Do you mind my asking why you want me to take dollars into England?"

"Well, because I'd have to declare them. I'm an American resident but I'm still a British subject."

"Is there anything against declaring them?"

"Oh, yes. They're nosey, at the Customs. They'd want to know why I'm carrying three thousand in cash instead of traveller's cheques." Here I was prepared for her to add that she was psychically allergic to traveller's cheques, but she said, "I want to give the dollars to somebody, you see. Swop for sterling. Somebody in England who needs dollars badly for a trip to America."

"But isn't that illegal?"

The smile widened still more. She nodded vigorously, reminding me now less of Joan the Maid than of Harpo Marx.

"Then it would be illegal for me to do it," I said.

"Look, babe, they wouldn't *ask* you about dollars; why should they?"

"Even so, it's an offence against currency regulations."

"Well, of course it is," she agreed, "what else can one do when they *make* these stupid regulations?"

Then I laughed. She laughed too, but I did not think that she saw how funny the line of reasoning was. She said, "They came through the French Customs in Boxer's stays. But it does make her so nervous . . . and I've been caught once before. Do do it for me, won't you, please? . . . I'll give you a walloping percentage."

According to the Duchess, the quickest way to make an action look honourable was to get paid for it. I awaited this effect of the bribe. It did not come. I said, "I'm sorry to say No again, but I couldn't do that for you."

She didn't look angry. She looked baffled.

"Really not?"

"No, really not."

She put on her glasses. "Strictly from disapproval?"

"Well—strictly from not liking to break rules."

"Holy mackerel——" she said softly. "How old are you—mind?" The smile flashed again.

"Of course not. I'm nineteen."

"And when people make rules, you keep them?"

"If the rules are right, yes."

"You really do? Do what you're told?" She rocked thoughtfully on the stool. "Mean that? But how d'you know they're right? I mean——" she said, "doctors have been telling me for twenty-five years that I ought to have my appendix out."

"Couldn't they be right?"

"Can't be. I'd have blown up long before this." She shook her head. "No, I just don't get that point of view," she murmured. I gave the envelope back to her. There was no reason why I should feel ridiculous. The feeling came from the look in those blind, dove-coloured eyes. It was she, I said to myself, who was ridiculous. Trying to buy other people's paper-weights and getting telepathy-buzzes in her ears and not having her appendix out.

"And which of us is the fool? That's the question, isn't it—
or isn't it? Tell you what it *really* amounts to——" she lit a
cigarette. "All the trouble, I mean. Not being able to live
inside the other person's head . . . That's it, isn't it? Half an
hour inside the other person's head and you'd be fine. No,
I'm wrong. You'd be sunk, of course."

"Sunk?"

"Well, of course you would. Never be able to disagree
again. *Or* hate. Love everybody then. Most inconvenient,
come to think of it, wouldn't it?"

I wanted to tell her that I was not in the habit of hating, but
I thought that she would take it as further evidence of priggish-
ness.

"Shall I change these for you?" I asked her, touching the
ten-dollar notes.

"Black-market rate?" she snapped.

"Well, no—current rate, I'm afraid."

"Sorry," said Cara de Bretteville as firmly as though I had
begged a favour. She whisked all her possessions back into
the saddle-bag. Then she looked at me and laughed. I tried
to laugh too.

"Poor baby—you want to swim, don't you? Let me pay for
the lemonade. Can't swim with this hand. I'll just sit here till
Boxer and the dogs wake up."

"That'll be forty francs, please."

"Bistro prices? Two hundred at Eden Roc, tell your father.
What about Boxer's room?"

"No charge," I said.

"Well, thank you kindly." She slid off the stool and strode
on to the terrace. The sunshine made her hair white-gold and
the tan almost negroid. I often remember her at this corner of
the terrace, seeing the exact pigment of each colour, the pink
shirt, the blue shorts, the dark-brown skin and the gold nuggets
glittering.

"Sit out here—may I?"

"Can I get you something to read? There are new magazines
in the *salon*, English and American."

"Thank you. But I think I'll just sit and talk to my Familiar. It's a frog," she added brusquely as she sat down at the end table in the shade of the palm tree. Her eyes met mine, unsmiling.

For a moment I was sure that she was not merely eccentric, but certifiably insane. Then, as I went down the garden to the rocks and the sea, she lost her obsessive quality. By the time that I had swum across the pool, she became classified. She was one of the routine oddities in this place. With the quieter end of the season, I was a little out of practice, that was all.

I had not been in the water for long when I heard her car drive away. This surprised me. I had pictured her still there when I came back, with Boxer soundless in the room along the passage and the silver poodles sleeping head-to-tail. Her departure was, inexplicably, anticlimax. It was not that I wanted to see her again, but that I had expected to.

After the swim I lay in the sun and presently returned in search of luncheon, going by way of the bar. I meant to fetch the bowls that I had taken for the dogs. But Boxer, headache and all, had doubtless been ordered to replace them in the kitchen. They were gone.

So, when I looked on the shelf, was the rabbit paper-weight.

"Well, if *that's* all she stole," said Francis. He made a quick examination of the money in the till. "And it appears to be. Not that I am ever entirely certain how much we carry."

"She didn't need money. She was loaded with money. To the teeth."

Francis poured himself a Pernod. He said, "You could have given her that paper-weight, you know."

"Indeed I could not. Nor would you, if you had seen her."

"Sometimes," said Francis, "you remind me very much of a child I used to know, called Penelope."

I made a face at him.

"What have you against the poor lady?—apart from her being a thief, which," said Francis, "you didn't know at the time. . . ."

I thought about it.

"Chaos came in with her," I offered. "It is my least favourite thing."

"Here we have it frequently."

"Not that sort. Our sort is predictable and consistent. It has its own rules. In fact it isn't chaos; it is more a social *laisser-faire*, or do I mean *laisser-aller*?"

"Do not ask me what you mean," said Francis and added, "For example, money."

"I don't mind being poor at all."

"But you mind rich people."

"She wasn't rich."

"Oh? I thought you said she was loaded with money to the teeth . . . And a maid," said Francis. "What about that?"

"It wasn't the cause of mistrust, I mean."

"What was, then?"

"She gave me a hot feeling in my head—the feeling that a lot of parcels would come for her after she had gone. Oh, and there was a kind of out-of-date aura, like motor-veils. And she'd set her hand on fire. And I would never know what went on in her mind."

Francis was giggling by this time.

"But did you *want* to know what went on in her mind?"

At least, I thought, I knew what went on in his. He was wholly consistent. I knew him right through, even to the agonies far down which everybody has and which, in a parent, a child might not guess. Francis had, I thought, fewer agonies than most people, but they were there.

"You, who are so tolerant in theory——" he thrust at me.

"But don't you see, I'm *everything* in theory? At my age one doesn't get practice."

Francis had no answer to that. "There was," he recalled, "a displeasing circumstance named Count Anthony de Bretteville who gave rather more than the usual number of bad cheques along this coast. I believe he got himself killed in a motor accident in Florida."

"This would be his widow, perhaps?"

"De Bretteville," said Francis, "would have more than one widow."

And he departed to take a bath, warning me as he went that Father Lasalle and the two architects from the villa on the point would be here to dine.

I sat on the balustrade and swung my legs. There was the smell that hung about the garden at evening: pine-needles, tobacco-plant, a touch of garlic. The sea was whitening and the setting sun dazzled all the immediate horizon, with the Estérel mountains flat and inky to the west. It was the hour of pleasurable melancholy; the hour of wishing that he were here. I signalled to him in my mind. Perhaps I could make a bell ring in his ear, but more likely not. He was the last person, I thought, to be endowed with the chaotic woman's extra-sensory equipment.

Where would he be?

At Whiteford, most probably. In the Dower House where he lived. But I could not see him there; my imagination set him perversely in the Manor itself. And since I knew the library better than any other room in the Manor, it was there that he sat now. I could see him at the long table, in the tawny-hued room with the bookshelves going up to the ceiling and the white, supercilious busts of his ancestors looking down.

"Hullo, Livesey," I said to him softly.

A car came sweeping round the gravel from the front gate; a long black car with the hood rolled down and the luggage piled in the back seat. A man got out.

These things did not happen.

II

Livesey's Voice

I WAS running like hell. I was running from Cara, and this time, I told myself, it was the last time. It had shocked me to find what she could do. All her old tricks were there. She could still make me feel, at the end of half an hour, as though my head was a bird cage full of budgerigars. She could still knock plans sideways, for the sake of knocking them sideways; still lose me a whole morning, make me late for lunch, bull-doze me out of a dinner-date, make me drink too much, eat too quickly and drive miles to meet people in whom I've no interest. It's a special gift for disorganisation. I have never, thank God, met anybody else who had it.

And she could do more to me than that. Much more.

All the worse, too, because I wasn't expecting it. I hadn't seen her for five years, not since de Bretteville was alive and she effectively torpedoed a business trip to Charleston, South Carolina. That meeting was pure accident; I ran into Cara and Anthony at the hotel where I stopped for lunch; she caught me unawares. Of this meeting, at Antibes, I was forewarned. It would, I told myself, be firmly handled and quickly over. I had other anticipations than Cara. I rarely took a holiday at this time of year and I drove down the French roads feeling free and gay. One evening would see her problems settled. With unusual restraint she asked only for my advice. A blotted scrawl at the end of the letter from New York looked as though it tried to say 'I am all right for dough'. Most improbable, I thought; Anthony had left debts behind him. Cara the widow, returning to Europe 'to settle down', would already have involved herself in enormous expenditure. She always did.

But—for once—I wanted to see her. Because of our daughter, Gyp. Since I let Cara divorce me, she had the custody of the child. I was always vulnerable here. And at the moment I passionately wanted to see Gyp, to argue with her and persuade her against the convent. It was a new kind of worry. All my worries for my child until now had been based on the belief that she would turn into a bad girl, a Riviera-cum-Palm Beach girl—never into a nun.

Cara, I was sure, would have little sympathy for the convent. All the same, she appeared to have left Gyp behind in America with a lot of nuns. It wouldn't do. And it was Cara's job to put it right. That was her only significance in my mind at this moment, a mother with a job to do. Cara my doom was, in theory, exorcised. It had been a long, long process, but I was quite sure that it was complete.

I had asked her to get me a room at the Cap Hotel, not fore-seeing that she would promptly move up from the villa where she was staying with some of her avoidable friends. Bringing Boxer, the melancholy lighthouse who had never deserted her; and the two poodles that were the latest in the long line of dogs, monkeys, lemurs, cats—the Noah's Ark procession. (I've always been thankful that the white Angora rabbits came in de Bretteville's time. Cara's rabbit phase, according to reports, was one of the worst.) I love animals, but I have never seen them as primarily portable, the way that Cara does.

It began at once. The bellboy had just set down my luggage on the floor. Dusty and tired from the long day's drive, I stepped out for a moment on to the balcony to blink at the Mediterranean before I took a bath. The telephone rang. I said I was going to have a bath and a drink. "No, don't do that . . . Come and have a drink here first . . . *Here* . . . Two rooms away, don't be silly . . . come along; I've got a bottle of champagne on the ice . . . Livesey, don't be such a *sissy* . . . You've got the strength to walk six yards, no? . . . What?"

That evening I got my bath at ten and we dined at eleven. The only strength of character I showed was in refusing to go to the Casino with her at a quarter to one. We settled no problems that night. In trying to discover why not, I can only see that people with pet names kept coming in and Cara went on ordering champagne; and there were other interruptions like feeding the dogs and unpacking a whole case of china that she had bought for a wedding-present that morning in Toulon. There was also a telephone-call from New York that was practically continuous in its threats and coy withdrawals and was finally there, but inaudible owing to weather conditions. The rest of the time she was telling me stories and making me laugh.

I lay down to sleep with a violent headache for company. I

mulled over our talk about Gyp. There had been little satisfaction there. Cara had said, "We can't discuss it intelligently
when we're buzzed like this," and then went on defending
Gyp's decision.

"Let her *try*, darling. If she hasn't a vocation, she'll find out
faster than light. I told her that, at the beginning."

"Did you put her up to it?"

"I should say not."

"She could have waited, couldn't she? I can't think why you
didn't put your foot down and make her wait until she's
twenty-one."

"None of my business."

"But, damn it, you're her mother."

"Well, you know, I sort of sympathised." She blinked at
me: "Had more fun with that than with anything else in my
whole life, after all."

"Fun?"

"With the Church." It was too robust a comment for my
taste. It was typical of her slightly indecent approach to everything. And it wasn't true. I could remember the frail tenure
of Cara's Catholicism. I always thought she copied it from
Crusoe. I said, "Listen, that's nonsense. You threw it away.
You haven't done anything about it for years. It was just a
phase, like that yoghourt and black treacle diet."

"Only more fun," Cara repeated. And now, because of the
drinks, I could see her religion like a toy, a ball that she had
tossed over lightly, unseeingly, into Gyp's hands. It made me
very sad.

The next day (the day of loss and ruin) Cara told me that she
was coming back to live at Whiteford. When I laughed, she
did not. When I told her that I was selling Whiteford she said
that she would buy it. When I said "What with?" she slapped
my face and said that she had accumulated an enormous nest-
egg by not paying any of her debts. "Not *bills*," she explained,
"I don't *have* bills any more. Just debts. And the people are
all so rich that they don't care. They came across in *dozens*
when Anthony died."

I paced the floor. She was still in bed, with the poodles on her feet, claiming a fatigue of which I saw no sign. Why she had decided upon Whiteford did not emerge. She said, "A base, after all, is what one needs. I feel tired in my head . . . know that one? Feeling out of step; precarious; nice to put one's feet up on something solid." Then she added outrageously, "You know I've always loved it. More than anywhere." That for all the years wherein I had waited for her to come back to it.

"Getting old, too——" said Cara, looking, to my eyes, not more than thirty. She sprawled on the pillows, with the nightgown slipping off the bronzed shoulders; ("The Riviera tan on top of the Florida tan is almost too much, wouldn't you say?") unconscious of her body or my eyes; lighting another cigarette, ringing for Boxer, forgetting why she had rung: "I'll ring again when I remember . . . Old, now . . . Time to settle down . . . Don't want people any more . . . just a lot of animals and some peace . . . Battered, I am . . . Poor darling Anthony, he couldn't help being a stinker . . . What's worrying you, Livesey? . . . You needn't *be* there . . . Well, but you can go on living in the Dower House and we can dine with each other once a week; a most gentlemanly arrangement." She dived for the telephone. "No, don't go; it won't take a minute. Just remembered I said I'd call Bruce." Then peals of laughter and: "More. I insist . . . Tell me more . . . *No* . . . she didn't? . . . Not possible . . . I don't believe you . . . Naked except for a tricorne *hat*? . . . Boots? What sort of boots? . . . I want a clear picture . . . Oh . . . I didn't see them like that, at all . . . I saw tassels. Livesey's here. Yes, I'm bringing him."

"No, you're not," I said.

"Yes, I am. Not till this evening," she added in a tone of infinite reassurance. She hung up. "Now, what would be nice to eat and drink? Send for a menu, shall we?"

"I'm going out to lunch."

"Well, you needn't go yet . . . Must eat something. Only coffee for breakfast . . . Hollow inside."

"Cara, let's get this straight about Whiteford. . . ."

When I arrived at the villa where I was expected to lunch, my host and hostess had given me up; the party was already at the table. My conduct was neither polite nor intelligent; he being the director of a company in which I'm interested. And the moment was exasperatingly familiar; coming in late with unconvincing excuses; the sense of having been in prison in that room, of having left a bit of me still there. I had had it before, many, many times before. It was just one of the tiring little agonies from which, I thought, I had freed myself for ever.

Prison in that room . . . an amiable prison, scented and cool and echoing with laughter. Watching the sun on the water, and down on the terraces under the palms the people who were not prisoners walking free.

Cara was still there when I went back. I had hurried back; she was half-dressed; "Be ready in five minutes." Twenty-five went by. (Caught in the web again, watching the clock, being made to laugh, having a drink I didn't want and playing with the dogs.) Out into the sun, still imprisoned: "But of course you're coming to Monte Carlo." She had a date with a dressmaker; it would take no time at all. And afterwards we would drink with these at Cap d'Ail and dine with those at Villefranche. No, I said, we wouldn't.

"Well, come to Monte Carlo, anyway. Fun. I'll drive."

"Your car?"

"Not so much mine as André's. He's got two."

"I'd rather we took mine. I've a dinner-date."

"I'll get you *back*, Livesey. Don't fuss."

We took André's car.

"Listen," I said. "Once and for all—about Whiteford."

"Oh, *look*—funny dog . . . sort of sawn-off lion, d'you see? . . . Whiteford? I'm buying Whiteford—shut up."

We were a long time in Monte Carlo because she had come on the wrong day for the dressmaker. "But if Madame will return in forty minutes . . ." The forty minutes gave Cara opportunity to change some dollars at the black-market rate and choose a birthday present for André's baby niece. By the time that she fell upon a mechanical cat in white fur that walked and miaowed and cost twelve thousand francs, she was late for her fitting. Then I sat in a tiny, smelly room full of lace and depressing little ornaments; the window looked out on a blank wall.

Cara emerged, limp and martyred. "I don't think I've ever been so tired; I feel quite sick. We must have a drink immediately at Caramello's."

"My dear, it's a quarter to seven now. What time are you supposed to be at Cap d'Ail?"

"I said about half-past five; you can drop me there. Don't fuss, darling; I can't take it."

She revived on the second drink which the owner of the restaurant, who was a friend of hers, insisted upon standing us.

"Well, darling Livesey, if you don't *want* me at White-ford——" (That blink of the eyes and the laugh) "Then the hell with it. . . . I just thought it would be nice." She could still perform a trick that had the effect of plucking a violin-string somewhere inside me. "Come on, let's go"—with a sudden scramble that took no account of my unfinished drink. And walking ahead of me, whistling a tune I didn't know; that extremely youthful walk.

"You don't have to come in and play with this bunch," she said at the gate of the villa: "Somebody'll drive me back. Just leave the car where I can find it. . . . Keys with the concierge, yes?"

"Oh, I'll come in for a minute."

And now, in the villa, the other feeling began. It was the exact reverse of the imprisoned feeling. I had not thought that I would have it again. Here, I stayed on the outside, watching her with André and Bruce and the rest, watching her absorbed by them, loved by them, making them laugh.

The whole look of her changed for me then; I was back at my youth, at my private pain; shut out, deleted, while the laughter went on with Crusoe.

How little, I thought, I had valued her in all these hours.

She had put herself into a different perspective now. She was like something in a shop-window, that I longed for and couldn't buy.

This was the worst. I had another drink; then I went to the telephone and cancelled my appointment for dinner.

Towards eleven o'clock we were keeping the date at Villefranche. In the sense that all plans had changed, apparently to everybody's satisfaction, and the people from there were coming to join us here. 'Here' was a restaurant on the outskirts of Nice, a long, low, glass box facing the sea. We had finished dinner, Cara, myself, André, Bruce and a girl called Bingo who was a carry-over from the villa at Cap d'Ail. Coffee and liqueurs were on the table. Since Cara's lighter needed filling and at once became an emergency in the way that all Cara's needs become emergencies, a *chasseur* had been sent out for lighter-fuel.

"No, I'll do it," Cara said, taking the lighter away from me. She overfilled it. When she flicked it open she dashed a shower of blazing drops down over her hand and on to the tablecloth. She raised the hand quickly towards her mouth, lighted her cigarette from one of the separate little flames burning on her skin, looked at me and laughed. There was the usual chorus of "*Cara——*" and the others laughed too.

"Livesey doesn't think it's funny. *Why* don't you think it's funny, Livesey?" Now she was smearing butter on her hand, wrapping it in a table-napkin. The talk and the laughter went on.

I watched her. I saw her changing colour and growing quieter; presently she said, "I'm so sorry. It really does hurt. I'll have to go. Nobody else need."

So, she aroused the last of my private demons: my impulse to protect and look after the person who is hurt or ill. It is as sharp when it comes as sexual desire and, in her case, shamefully linked with it.

The physical appeal to pity made me jealous and savage as a dog inside, while André fussed over her, wiping her forehead with a handkerchief dipped in ice-water, Bruce tried to make her drink his brandy and the girl Bingo recalled a terribly good doctor who lived in Nice.

I paid for the dinner; registering as I did so the fact that the cost of it was twice the sum that one of my labourers at White-ford earned in a week. I took Cara out, holding her arm until she pushed my arm away. I drove her home.

She was very quiet. The gesture stayed on my eyes, the little deliberate gesture of silliness and ruin as she lighted the cigarette from the flame on the back of her hand. It became enormous in my mind. Pointless bravado, sheer asininity, I said to myself as I raced the car along the sea-road. And still there was the ache of my body.

"Are you all right, Cara?"

"*Yes*," she said impatiently, but it was a thread of a voice.

At the hotel I got a doctor who dressed the burn and chose her a sedative from the considerable collection on her bathroom shelf. Boxer helped her to bed. I sat on the bed, having a last drink. She was in better humour now. She said, "Thank you for being kind to me. . . . But it *was* funny, no?"

"No; not really."

Her eyelids drooped. The sleeping-pill was beginning to take. . . . "*I* thought it was . . . Oh, my God, I meant to call April—— Will you do it for me, Livesey? It's important; she'll take those dollars in."

I didn't know what she was talking about. I said, "It can wait."

"Yeah, sure," said Cara sleepily.

I drained my glass. I looked at her, lying there with the poodles pressed against her hip, the lamplight on her hair. All that had wrecked my life was in that line of neck and shoulder. Her scent was in my nose; the scent that she never changed, that was like a doom, reminding me of everything. I was tired to death, but my body wanted hers as badly as ever.

She opened her eyes and smiled at me, looking as though she knew. Then she said, "Good night, darling—*must* sleep," and blew me a kiss.

I said, "Good night, Cara. May I steal a sleeping-pill?"

"Mm . . . help yourself—didn't know you used them," said the drowsy voice.

The pill didn't work for a while. I don't believe that I wanted it to work. I was on the edge of surrender. I had said that I would never go through that again and now I knew most certainly that I must have it again. With all that went beside. She was in my bloodstream. I should have known better than to come here. You don't, at my age, escape from an obsession unless you find another to put in its place. And I never had. And now I didn't care. Anything would be better, anything, than the sense of desolation when I watched her with the others, as though I stared into the shop-window and longed and marvelled and could not buy.

She would come back to me. That was proved. By the tiredness and the need for Whiteford, by the gestures of friendship today. She had always signalled to me when she was in trouble. She always would. "All right, Cara," I said, "you win." I went to sleep still wanting her.

It was a dream of Whiteford that awoke me; nothing to it, just the house and the trees and the lake; the feeling of solitude and peace. I sat up and saw the sun blazing into my room, the room in the Riviera hotel.

It was late. I rang for my coffee. 'Lord,' I said to myself, 'that was a close shave. Out of here. Today.'

Sanity had come back. I saw her for what she was in my life, a taste like a drug, a taste that I'm ashamed of, a taste that I have conquered.

I packed my bags while she was over at Miramar, chasing her friend April. The fear of her invading Whiteford was the only real fear left. I took care of that. I re-read the agent's last letter, then sent him a wire telling him to clinch the sale.

("I just thought it would be nice," her voice echoed.)

I wrote to Gyp at the address Cara had given me; a gentle letter, asking her the questions that Cara had not answered. I begged her to write to me soon.

I waited for Cara. She had said that she would be back for

lunch, but she did not come till half-past five, when I was in the courtyard and they were putting my luggage in the car. She wore a glove on her burned hand. She was in high spirits, having bought new collars for the poodles and met a number of people whose names I didn't know.

"Where are you going? . . . That's rather violent of you, isn't it? . . . We haven't settled anything . . . You were thinking about me, weren't you? . . . You buzzed my ear. Well, if you're going straight back to England, you can take my dollars in, can't you? . . . April wasn't there and Francis Wells' daughter had scruples . . . odd at nineteen, no?"

"Francis Wells' daughter," I said slowly. "You mean Penelope. . . ."

And so it happened, the small, unforgivable adventure of peace and magic that lasted a little more than a day and that is lost for always. And yet in my mind it stays for always, because if you do a wrong thing, it must stay. I'm not clear in my mind with the thought of eternal punishment. For me, punishment is here. All the punishments that I've ever had for wrong-doing have been immediate. And they go on. Cara has teased me many times about my conscience and has claimed on occasion to be able to hear it ticking like a clock.

III

Penelope's Voice

It was entirely impossible that he should be here. As he came to the foot of the terrace steps I was prepared to see that he was not Livesey Raines at all, but an illusion of Livesey, conjured by my thoughts. I would see straight through the phantom to the hydrangea-bushes behind it.

No; he was solid. Certainly his clothes were white, suitable to a ghost, but these were a white sweater and white linen trousers, normal Riviera uniform at evening. His skin was at the earliest stage of tan; the reddish stage; he was too fair to turn brown at once. Always large, he now seemed larger. Always, to my eyes, free and placid, he now seemed gay. He came running up the steps. I looked into his face. I saw that the lines upon his forehead were almost smoothed out, or perhaps the sunburn made them less obvious.

"There you are——" he said, as though I had arranged to meet him on this spot. He did what he had never done before; he took both my hands in a protective clasp, squeezed them and let them go. He stood, looking down at me.

"Well, good evening, Penelope. Did I frighten you?"

I realised that I had stared for too long. "The *last* place where I'd expect you," I said.

"I know," said Livesey.

"I am adjusting," I explained.

He said solemnly, "I won't interrupt the process."

"Out of your context, you see."

"Yes, aren't I?"

"And I was just thinking about you, which makes it all the odder."

"Were you? What put me into your head?"

"Oh . . . well," I said, groping, "Aunt Anne is here—at least she isn't, not at the moment, but she'll be back tonight."

"Clear as mud, that makes it," said Livesey, "why you were thinking about me."

"Well, you know what I mean. . . ." I meant that he was not my friend, but Aunt Anne's. In the old days when I stayed with her, he was seldom at Whiteford. His crippled brother Crusoe lived there and Aunt Anne used to leave me at home when she visited Crusoe. It was only since Crusoe's death that Whiteford Manor had opened up to me. And that was when Livesey began. And the secret that I had made a hero of him was shared with none. And I felt that—by this disconcerted burbling—I exposed the secret now, to the hero himself, the last who must ever know.

"You look so gay," I hurried on, making it worse. "Perhaps it is the clothes."

"Can I take them off? I mean I'd like to swim."

"It won't be warm. People catch chills at this hour; I warn you."

"Let's go and look at the water, anyway."

Really, I thought, there was no accounting for this. As a haunt, he had accompanied me so often down these steps that his physical presence here was almost absurd. I looked at the car with the luggage and said in a timorous voice, "Have you come to stay?" The prospect was alarming. It would bring my two worlds into collision; collision, certainly, not fusion. Aunt Anne fused where Livesey would collide. I could not imagine his blending with this background. *Chez François* was the antithesis of Whiteford.

"Well, I don't know, bless you . . . I ought to get on. I'm aiming for Paris. And London." As he said it, the frown came back. "In fact, I'm running like hell," he added.

"From what?"

"From a lot of rubbish." He spoke crossly and then we went on down the garden. I asked no more. His private life was always a mystery to me. The path grew steep here and this must be why he took my hand. But the clasp made for companionship and he was only my companion in the dreams of the magic future that could not happen.

For nearly two years I had been resigned, burning and humble about Livesey. I must go on being that; it was the only thing to be. Ours was not a relationship; it was merely an intermittent rendezvous, made by Whiteford Manor, the far, shuttered house with the threat of sale hanging over it. When Livesey found that I cared for the house and its treasures, he had given me the freedom of the place. I had written whole chapters of my book in his library. Often I went there without seeing him; and although there was always a small pang, desolation in miniature, when I did not, the house was second-best, bringing me close to him.

Nothing else could bring me close. There was the difference

in our ages, the difference in our lives. He moved at speed in places where I could not follow. His large car rushed him to London. Aeroplanes rushed him all over Europe and across the Atlantic. My aunt said that his work was a palliative, a retreat from an old sorrow. I did not know how she knew this. Livesey's wife left him long before Aunt Anne came to Whiteford. There was one daughter who stayed with him on a brief yearly visit. I knew nothing of any of it; Aunt Anne wrote the slick epitaph; and made it sound like the synopsis of a serial in a magazine. I was certain that he was not unhappy now. Perplexed a little, yes; that was visible on his forehead. I thought I knew what made the perplexity. One explaining gesture was hoarded in my memory.

I had met Livesey by great good fortune at Paddington Station. I was on my way back to Whiteford. I only had sevenpence-halfpenny and I had lost the return half of my ticket. Livesey, dressed as a magnate in a blue overcoat and bowler hat, bought me a ticket and we travelled in the unfamiliar splendours of the first-class Pullman. Suddenly he had pushed his wallet across the table, "Here, help yourself. You *can't* go about with sevenpence-halfpenny."

I remembered the lines deepening on his forehead, the baffled look in the blue eyes when I refused. One mood of Livesey was set for me for ever by that moment. I saw him often in imagination, flying around the world, holding out the wallet to unfortunates in far places, saying, "Here—help yourself." Innocently rich, ashamed and worried by other people's poverty, that was the magnate version.

There was another; the squire, in a tweed jacket patched with leather, carrying a gun on his arm. I had met him in the lower field by the lake.

"Hate shooting rooks," Livesey had said.

"Why?"

"Because I like rooks."

He was too kind. That, I thought, was his only trouble. I did not know his loves nor his friends. I got glimpses of his week-end guests, crowding the narrow village street with their cars. Aunt Anne (blasphemously) found him dull. She had loved the eccentric Crusoe and she talked about him, not about Livesey.

I had my own talks with him—casual, trusting, all too few. I treasured them; months would elapse between them. Once he had wandered into the library to ask whether I wanted tea. He was up at the Manor because prospective buyers had come and there had been tea for them in the peacock-room; a ridiculous little jewel-case of a room on the first landing. Livesey and I had sat there among its silks and rainbow-colours, drinking the tepid tea and discussing Whiteford's future. If it must go, I wanted it to be a Workers' College. That led to politics, on which we were not agreed, though we could argue without anger.

I respected the lights he steered by; the orthodox lights of Christianity, Toryism, Eton and King's. By these lights, I would say that if the village green had to get mislaid, its most fortunate destiny possible was to turn up in the squire's back-yard.

Livesey the squire, Livesey the magnate, Livesey the furiously active absentee in the airliner, these were accustomed aspects of a hero who remained far off. What the devil did I do about Livesey the intruder in this garden, still holding my hand, swinging it lightly, as we came down to the water?

Well, obviously, turn the talk to Whiteford. But the question brought the frown.

"I really am selling, this time. One of the reasons I want to hurry back." He looked at me ruefully. "Sorry, Penelope. Think it makes you sadder than it makes me."

"It is the sensible action," I said. "One can always, despite one's feelings, approve the sensible action, *Deo gratias*."

He gave a roar of laughter, a lion's laugh; I had provoked it before.

"One can, eh?" said Livesey.

"Shut up. Any hope for the Workers' College?"

"Not a hope. . . ." He squeezed my fingers: "Poor Penelope."

"I am not poor Penelope just because I happen to have humanitarian impulses."

"You wouldn't like to see it as a shabby barrack full of strenuous oicks, you know you wouldn't," said Livesey placidly.

"What I like doesn't count. Selfishly I want it to go on being what it is. But that's the short-term view. In the long-term view"—I hustled a shambling crab with the toe of my *espadrille*—"the Workers' College should prevail. Mark my words, Livesey; that's what ought to happen. The fact that I'm a martyr to moral inconsistency has nothing to do with the case."

Livesey said with a groan, "I can never believe that your conversation is true until I hear it again."

"Ah, well," I said, finding nothing else to say, but being pleased all the same.

"Nobody aged nineteen should have your powers of detachment. It simply isn't fair."

(Marius had said, "What is so indecent about you, Penelope, is that you have a wholly middle-aged sense of proportion.")

His blue stare made me self-conscious. Besides he was looking at a place full of my own secrets, the place where I began. On that rock, for example, in my misanthropic childhood, I had sat for long hours, hating. And there, above the orange trees, was the next-door villa, 'La Lezardière', the shrine of a lost devotion, the villa of the Smugs.

Remembering the connection, I explained it to Livesey.

"That," I said, "is the villa that his family had, when he was quite a small boy."

"D'you see him ever?"

"Oh—just occasionally."

"Queer thing, this religious vocation," Livesey said. But the frown had returned. "Don't know why kids do those things." And he gave a short, sharp sigh. I went back to Whiteford; "You will let the National Trust have it, at least?"

"Nothing doing," said Livesey, "they've got more than they can handle."

"Alas. I could have been the caretaker."

He grinned. "What about that Degree of yours?"

"After I come down, I mean. A delicious life. Living in somebody else's beautiful museum and writing my books in the evenings."

Livesey shook his head as though this were the last folly. He sat down on the nearest flat surface, which was the step of the diving-board, and began to fill a pipe.

"According to the Duchess," I explained, "one should be scrupulously careful in youth not to acquire possessions. And I subscribe to that. Provided I can look at things I like, I don't want to own them. Moth and rust," I added—"to say nothing of the pangs on leaving them behind."

"You and your Duchess," Livesey said, as though I had invented her.

"Who is the buyer, Livesey?"

He hesitated before he answered; his voice sounded a little abrupt: "Don't know yet. Agent told me before I left that he'd had two good offers and this morning I wired him to clinch the best."

"Only this morning . . . ?"

He seemed to challenge questioning as he stared at me across the flame of the match held to the pipe. I felt insecure, frightened, about to walk on new, treacherous ground. I was relieved when he got up quickly, saying, "Look. I must have a drink; is that all right?"

"But of course. Come along."

The lights were lit in the bar. As we came up the steps, Francis moved out of the bright cave on to the terrace and stood below the palm tree, waiting for us. I remembered that these two had not met. Their acceptance of each other became suddenly, painfully, important; I felt a tremor inside. My nerves, of which I am not usually aware, dazzled the moment. I made the introduction and got away. To my room, to the looking-glass.

Marius said that my face blended Madonna and monkey. Francis said that I looked like a bush-baby. I tried to see. I had the family long neck; my hair was brushed back behind my ears; the tops of my ears slanted up and my eye-sockets went up at the same angle. The cheek-bones were bumpy, with hollows beneath. Javanese-looking, was I? My nose was small; my lips stuck out a little. I made a sudden hideous grimace at the reflection, despising me because I had been anxious to know how I looked to Livesey.

'Perhaps he will go now, without saying good-bye. Yes, I would rather he did that. Looked at his watch and swallowed his drink and went . . . Oh, *would* you?'

The expression of my face was now so arch that it positively sickened me. I put on a white dress that had a pattern of brown leaves.

They were all in the bar; the two architects, the priest, Jeanne and Francis and Livesey. Aunt Anne said that he was shy, but the proof of shyness to me is awkwardness and Livesey was well co-ordinated, even in silence. Was he—possibly—the kind of Englishman at whom Francis poked fun? I could not be sure yet. He seemed to be staying to dinner. I watched him like a cat.

I had not heard him speak French and it came as a dis-proportionate relief to hear him speak fluently, with a passable accent, talking to Father Lasalle. A danger-signal, this relief? Oh, stop fussing, I said to myself; as far as Livesey and you are concerned, the situation cannot possibly get worse. There *isn't* a situation. And this you realise, and with this you are content.

The blue eyes met mine across the table. Emboldened by half a glass of Dubonnet, I let myself stare back. The face, I thought, has regularity of feature and breadth of forehead; no outstanding beauty, yet a completely satisfactory arrangement of lines. The same pleasure that I get from looking at Georgian architecture, I get from your face, Livesey Raines.

I found myself collecting details: the cable-stitch pattern of the sweater, the wrist-watch with the complex dial, the exaggerated curve of the pipe-stem. In company, a game of pleasurable spying. 'And oh,' I said to myself, 'you have played it before; it is not your first knowledge of the moment when another's possessions become lit with importance. It happened for half a week at the beginning of Marius; in memory there is the same halo around a pencil-box lying on a school desk higher up in the class than yours; far back, the shimmer touches a butterfly-net, a camera, the water-skis, belonging to the Smugs.

'He has come a step nearer, that is why it is happening. It is entirely logical that these small things should have been invisible until now. Always you have seen him in distant, heroic proportions.'

"You are not getting on with your drink," Livesey said, leaning a little towards me, the talk around us leaving us for a moment safe and alone with each other.

"I'm not much of a one for drink."

"Aren't you, darling? Why not?"

He had not called me darling before. My mind stopped at it. My lips went on talking. "Nothing to do with moral disapproval," I said, "but because it blunts and blurs."

"Yes, it does. Thank God," he added, draining his glass and looking at me now with a bright, friendly curiosity that was new. The man of heroic proportions had never worn this look; he was a man in another time and I saw that that time was over, that my boats were burning.

Now I was afraid. I was crying to God inside my head, 'Oh, don't . . . please don't let it change. I have been so happy.' And then I was making my own exultant reply to the fear, 'But, fool, it is the beginning of adventure. The lights are going down and the three knocks sound for the rise of the curtain.'

The waiter brought the candles and we dined in the bar, at two tables placed together in front of the french windows. Nothing new here, I thought. I looked at them: at Francis, Mephisto behind the candlelight, at Jeanne as sleek and lively as an otter, at the sculptural beard of the architect called Sigrand, and the amiable roundness of the architect called

Brice. Then Father Lasalle in his black robe, source and focus of the question-mark. Nothing new here, my mind repeated; the glinting of the candle flame on bottle and glass, the panelled length of the bar stretching away in shadow; around the bar's curve, the small bright glimpse of the *salon* where the Duchess had died.

I was among my own; but I was taking a far, a fatal walk away from them. The face with the lined forehead, the flushed skin, the eyes made larger and more brilliant by drinking, was the only face that I could see.

And now we were at the end of dinner. Soon he would glance at the watch with the complex dial, and rise and go. And the salt would lose its savour on the instant, and all the lights would go out. As it was in the beginning; Livesey the absentee. But this time I would mind much more.

Now, as we rose, he said to Francis, "Would it be too much to ask which room I've got? Point is—I'd like to get my luggage in and do a bit of telephoning."

"There are six rooms," said Francis, trying to disconcert him. "No, five. I'd forgotten about my sister coming back."

"Thanks, just the one," said Livesey, unperturbed.

"He'd better have Number Three," Jeanne and I said together. It was the best of the rooms, I thought, through the rainbow-arc of the minute.

"Show me?" Livesey's look in my direction was truant and conspiratorial, wholly out of character. "I'll just get my bag." In the general movement there was no difficulty in walking out on to the terrace with him. We did not speak now. We went down the steps and stood beside his car. For a moment his silence seemed as profound, as significant, as my own. The lights from the terrace did not reach as far as this and I could not see the expression in his eyes. Then he said abruptly, "We might go for a drive afterwards. Moon's coming up."

"That would be nice," I said in a prim tone.

"Would it be nice?" There was a chuckle behind his voice.

"I'm glad you're staying," I said formally.

Without warning he did what I had never, consciously, wanted him to do. The embrace was violent, not gentle, as rough and hard as the others had been. But I thought that I could feel its reluctance, its compulsion, all that in his mind must be unforgivable, and I expected him to swear at himself when he let me go. He did not. I stood there, dazed, being sorry that I hadn't responded to it. Everything was, for an instant, spoiled and sad.

He put his fingers below my chin, raised my face and kissed the tip of my nose very gently.

"Sorry——" said Livesey. Now Jeanne had sent the valet to help carry his luggage and we were stranded. "See you," he said. "Couple of telephone calls to make."

I went to my room. I didn't understand. He had broken his old image and left me with a new image that I dared not define. Bemused, I went back along the terrace to join the others.

To their eyes, I thought, I must be changed. Nobody remarked upon my absence or my return. They were in a comfortable circle, talking.

'Conflict' was the first word that I heard clearly. Father Lasalle said it and I had a second's wild hope that he might be talking of dualism, his stock-in-trade. Which showed that I was delirious; his preferences in talk were wine, rock-plants and local history.

"Conflict—in that face," Francis said musingly, "I didn't notice it." Was it my nervous state alone that made the comment sound disparaging? Perhaps, I said to myself, they are not talking about Livesey at all.

"The forehead disquiets itself, but the eyes are calm," said Father Lasalle in French.

"He's as rich as Croesus, don't forget."

"What's that got to do with it?" asked Sigrand.

"Riches always furrow the forehead and harden the arteries," said Francis.

"While poverty," murmured the priest, "performs the same functions, have you noticed?"

Francis called to me, "What about him, Penelope? You're the one who knows."

"About whom?" I asked deviously.

"Your gentleman-friend . . . Raines."

I must talk about him as though this evening had not happened. It should be possible; it was two years' habit after all.

"No gentleman-friend of mine, I assure you." Yes, it was easy enough. "I only know him through Aunt Anne."

"Has he a rendezvous with her, d'you think?" Jeanne didn't say it seriously. But still, I thought, I don't really know why he came.

"If he married her, now," said Francis, "we could all be kept in luxury."

"Which you would dislike," said Father Lasalle.

"Aunt Anne doesn't care for Livesey," I said. Here I was at pains to extinguish the small, licking flame of indignation inside. How dare she not?

"Is that why he frowns?" Brice asked.

The idea of his cherishing an unrequited love for my aunt made me giggle. I giggled too loudly and suddenly; they all looked at me.

"I think," I said, sounding what I hoped was a note of cool detachment, "that it's his conscience that makes the frown."

Here I glanced towards the *salon*; I was uneasy lest he should return. Francis saw me do this. "It's all right," he said, "I can hear him in the office, fighting with the telephone."

"His conscience troubles him—why?" It was the priest who asked the question. With all the bewilderment, I thought, of one who knew no reason for a troubled conscience.

"Father, I think it is because of being a thriving industrialist in an impoverished world."

"Cause for congratulation, more," said Father Lasalle.

"Not for Livesey. He's made to a medieval pattern," I explained. "He would be the kindest liege-lord in the feudal system. What he can't accept is the fact that the world's population has grown too large to be coped with in small communities by benign squires."

"H'm. You try to put the poor fellow right from time to time, I hope," said Francis unkindly.

"Of course I don't. It's no business of mine. That is just my diagnosis of the situation."

"Give Penelope a crème-de-menthe. She's in her most pompous mood."

"*C'est curieux*," Jeanne told him. "You are the only person in this house permitted to be pompous."

"Fluent, in my case, darling. Pompous in Penelope's."

"Quite a sad thing for a rich man to be born without the proper instincts of a thug," said Brice.

"What's the solution, Father?"

Father Lasalle, refusing to be drawn, suggested courses in thuggery.

Over the sea the moon was rising. Now I heard his footsteps coming through the *salon*.

"We could put some good money on a green table," Livesey mused; "Casino at St. Raphael, isn't there?" He had headed the car instantly for the west, when I had expected him to go the other way, towards Cannes and Juan.

"Rather a sad one, they say . . . I'm under age for Casinos."

"So you are," said Livesey. "Never mind."

"Do you like to gamble?"

"Sometimes. Out of bloody-mindedness." I got another disturbing hint; the hint of a coarse and private mood; wholly masculine, nothing to do with me.

It was the last, for the moment. He reached for my hand and held it. When he did that earlier I was ill at ease, not knowing whether to hold on or let go. This time it was more close, more comforting than any embrace. It made silence easy. In the path of the headlights, on the road's watery surface a rounded clumsy shape lurched slowly.

"Careful," I said. "A toad."

"I won't hit him. Enormous, isn't he?"

"And full of pathos; I don't know why. I like toads."

Livesey turned his head for a moment. "I've yet to hear you say that you *dis*like anything. . . ." He sounded puzzled. Then he said, "One thing you don't like, though, isn't there?" His fingers shook mine gently.

"And what is that?"

"Being kissed by gentlemen—who aren't gentlemen or they wouldn't have done it." It was an unwieldy way of saying that he was sorry and my skin went hot; for him as much as for me.

I said, as steadily as I could, "Please . . . Perhaps I ought to apologise too. I mean for not taking it lightly. I believe I am exceptionally retarded in those ways."

"Oh, darling, please go on being exceptionally retarded. No, don't; hell, I don't know——" said Livesey.

Silence came down on us again. We were circling the bay of Agay and the moon was high. Lovely, and a little battered and above all peaceful, I thought, this stretch of rocky land under the moon, with the trees as still as the sea.

"Incredible—" Livesey said—"the sense of peace I get when I'm with you. I'd forgotten."

"Well, I am glad that you do."

There was a small café at the end of the street; it looked like stage scenery; a frail lighted porch with a trellised vine, two little tables and the coloured backcloth of the bar inside. I had seen it often; tonight it was different, important. "Let's stop here," I said and already he had seen it and braked the car.

"Wish I could make up my mind what little animal you remind me of. Crusoe could have told me. All his people were animals. Is it a flying-fox? . . . No, too pointed. Only your ears are pointed."

"Francis says a bush-baby. Marius says a monkey." I left out the Madonna from what Colette would call a *pudeur civilisée*.

"Who's Marius? Smack his face for him," said Livesey lazily.

It seemed a waste of the moment to talk about Marius, but I gave what description I could. At the end Livesey said, "Sounds like hell to me."

"Well no, he isn't. It is just that he fights wars inside."

Livesey was silent. The shadow of the trellised vine was making an odd pattern on his temple and cheek. Over his head, moths blundered against the coloured electric-light bulbs and one fell down with heavy wings beside his glass.

"Wars inside . . . Fair enough. Everybody does that," he said at last.

"Do you?"

"I suppose so. Don't you?"

"I think not."

He turned to stare at me; a stare that I could not escape, deliberate and searching, and, I thought, loving, though there was a twinkle about it suggesting that he wanted to laugh at me.

"You are so very sweet—d'you know that?"

I was dumb; I could say nothing that would not sound coy, or alternatively too serious.

"Much too old for you, aren't I?"

"Age," I said, "has nothing to do with anything."

Livesey said, "Oh, hasn't it? Wait till you're forty-six and you'll know. . . ." He leaned across to me and touched my cheek. "Past the half-way mark . . . Long way past." He growled, looking straight ahead of him, " '*Time's horses gallop down the lessening hill.*' "

It is my habit to think and talk in quotations, but Livesey is not the sort of person who does; and somehow the line sounded all the sadder for that. Again I was dumb. I could think of no consoling rejoinder.

"When you've spent more than twenty years of it in hating," he said.

"Oh, not hating. Not you. I don't believe it."

He met my eyes again. "Is it so very bad?" he asked innocently.

"Well, yes. It is the worst thing, surely."

The fat woman came out from the coloured backcloth to know if we would like something more. "Don't think so—" Livesey said—"And you haven't finished yours. . . . But— haven't you ever hated anybody?"

"Oh yes. When I was young I hated everything in sight."

"People too?"

"People too."

"But you grew out of it?" His tone was teasing.

I said, "Yes——" and I looked back upon the revelation as I remembered it; the mood following Violetta's death; the tearing of the Anthology. A preliminary eye-opener. One step forward; one stage of a climb completed, a first foot-hill with the whole range of mountains still ahead, but the plain at least left behind. That was what it had been.

I dared not ask whom he hated, because I knew. It could only be his wife. And I was a little cold and cross inside, because Aunt Anne's magazine-story view of the private sorrow, her cliché summing-up, had been right; and all my fine theories wrong.

"Mustn't hate, ever," I said in a grumbly, governessy tone.

Livesey now seemed suddenly in high good humour, laughing the lion's laugh. "How about wishing somebody were dead? That not allowed either?"

"*Livesey*—that's worse. I mean it's the same thing. Unless, of course, you want them to die because they are suffering."

"No, darling. Because they make you suffer—one suffer—*me* suffer."

"Even so." Now I was shocked. "I *couldn't* want somebody to die," I said limpidly.

"Well, having blotted my copybook all round," said Livesey, "shall we go?"

At once I began to be sorry for him. And as he took the wheel of the car he came back a little into his former perspective; large and remote and competent, doing a thing that I could not do.

"I wish I could drive a car."

"I'll teach you."

They were comfortable words, hinting that we had time ahead. Under the shadowy tunnel of the pines, beyond the bay, I said, "I'm sorry you're unhappy. I always thought you were all right."

"You did, eh?" He slowed the car and took my hand again. "Well, pray for me, won't you?"

"I always do." My heart beat hard. I said, "I love you very much, you see——" and there was satisfaction and peace in saying it.

He took both my hands and drew me towards him. At first the kiss was gentle and different, taking away the other memory. Slowly it changed; becoming at last the fury that I had never liked nor wanted. But this time I began to understand. I went to meet it instead of drawing back; and presently I found the clue to it in the rest of my body. This was, beyond all else, exciting; and it was true closeness, as the books said. It was Livesey who broke away. He held me against his shoulder, looking down sadly.

"Oh no," he said, "it isn't fair."

I said the thing on top of my mind. "I am so happy." And he hugged me close.

"You have no idea how curious I have always been about all this."

"All this has got to stop. And now."

"I see it has. It's all right, Livesey dear. Not to worry, please."

He looked at me almost shyly, starting up the car. He said, "You are the most astonishing kid," and sounded a little like a Smug, but I found the phrase endearing.

"We should swim now," I said, looking at the lit water, and Livesey replying, "Good, practical suggestion——" made me blush.

"I like to swim when there's a moon. Very quickly in and very quickly out," I said, loftily, letting it go.

"From the hotel?"

"Of course."

"All right. Let's do that."

A note left by Jeanne told us that the company had gone to Sigrand's villa on the point. From the terrace we could see the lights of the villa and hear the gramophone music coming across the water; Lohengrin. "Well now, there is a thing I do not like," I said to Livesey. "To wit, Wagner."

Our mood had changed; we were frivolous and giggly. It was what I imagined a drunken mood to be; as far as I was concerned it felt like the most agreeable stage of a fever. And I think for him too. It is very clear in memory, the look of his face, laughing, the wet spiky hair, the body with the marble curves of muscle and the water no longer black but silvered, bubbly all around him. (And the things that were funny only for us; the small jokes that would not sound amusing if you told them to anybody else. In drunken optimism I saw them becoming key-phrases for the future, a code that we would use.)

Cold and weak, we came out of the water. It was not late. The music still sounded from the villa on the point. At one moment when a fishing-boat glided in, with a lamp at her prow, close to the rock-horns that circled the pool, I thought that they had come to look for us. The questing light moved on, trailing its flakes of fire on the water.

"Bed, I shouldn't wonder," said Livesey; his hand, large and cold, caught mine.

"Oh yes. I'm sleepy, too." A lie. I wanted to be alone and to remember. It seemed a most perverse contradiction to the enjoyment of his presence, and still it was there.

On the terrace we turned to each other. This again was different. I felt the protection of him; it might have been the huge, kind hug of a giantess Nanny in a towel robe. Never, I thought, have I been so safe.

"Good night, my darling," I said to him.

"Good night, bush-baby."

"What time would you like to be called?" I asked, remembering that he was a guest in our hotel—"And with tea?—It is quite simple," I added, because this appeared to worry him, "I'll just write it and leave it on the kitchen table."

Even so, he came after me into the kitchen and there again we hugged and kissed each other good night. The door was open.

I had not been in my room five minutes when I heard the quick footsteps and the knocking. Still dazzled, grinning, I opened to Aunt Anne. She was wispy and sunburned from her picnic. Her expression was quite inquisitorial:

"Where is everybody, I should like to know?"

"Over at the villa with Brice and Sigrand. Have you had your dinner?" I asked, wriggling into my dressing-gown. My wet swimming suit lay on the floor.

"Yes, thank you; a long time ago. It's after eleven o'clock."

"What is the matter?"

"Who was that—with you?"

"Where?" I asked her craftily; I still felt the way that drink ought to make one feel.

"On the terrace; and in the kitchen; you left the door open, you know."

"Well, all right." I picked up my comb and hairbrush. I made a neat savage parting with the comb in the middle of the wet hair and, unintentionally, splashed my aunt's face. She stepped back, and began to dab with a handkerchief in an affronted way.

"I'm sorry. . . . Been swimming. It was Livesey," I said— "Livesey Raines."

"I thought so," said Aunt Anne.

I combed my hair back behind my ears. Over my shoulder her face—in the looking-glass—was distorted, flushed.

"What's he doing here?"

"Staying here."

"Well——" she said, "it seems very odd."

Against my will she was scoring a victory over my nervous system. Or perhaps I was only cold from the swim. At any rate I had begun to tremble violently and I dropped my hairbrush.

"Just turn on my bath," I said, "excuse me."

When I came back she was sitting on my bed; she opened her bag and adjusted a cigarette in the long amber holder that is the only outward sign of fidelity to her dated dream. I sat down in my arm-chair.

"It really is rather strange, isn't it?" she said.

"What is strange?"

"His coming all this way."

"I don't know where he came from, I'm sure."

She tried another line, "What did Francis have to say?"

"About what?"

"Well, about Livesey, of course."

"We haven't discussed him yet," I said sweetly, kicking one foot up and down, so that my slipper flapped and presently fell off.

"Penelope . . ."

"Yes, Aunt Anne?"

"You—you didn't invite him here, did you?"

"Indeed not. He just walked in. But if I had," I said—"why would you mind?"

She looked disconcerted. Drunk with power, I repeated the question. I would not make a concession to this hectoring until it explained itself truthfully on the basis that she had seen us in each other's arms.

This did not emerge. She crumpled a little, "Oh don't be so difficult and spiky, darling. I was wondering, that's all." Then she suddenly wailed at me, "Penelope—you *can't* want to be the same as everybody else. You, of all people."

"Turn off the bath," I said. "Excuse me."

When I came back she was blowing her nose. "I mean," she said—"You *don't* just want to fall in love and marry and settle down—like other people."

That touched my heart, though I thought it silly. "In my youth," I said, "I had an overwhelming passion to be like other people. Other People were a whole romantic race, miles beyond my reach. Not now. I don't really think that they exist, except in the eye of the beholder. . . . Just as somebody has indicated that gangs do not exist, unless you create them out of your own sense of separation. Nobody has ever been conscious of belonging to a gang; only of *not* belonging. Proust, now, saw desirable gangs everywhere—to which he was not admitted."

Aunt Anne had risen from my bed. She looked as though she would scream. She nearly did. What came out was a whinny, "I don't understand a *word* you're saying. I'm not asking for a *lecture*. . . ."

"Oh dear. Well, what are you asking for?"

"He's so dull and his wife was a wonderful person."

Colder than before with sudden rage, I said, "Was she indeed? I'd no idea you knew her."

"I didn't know her," said Aunt Anne, on the edge of tears again.

It was idiotically mysterious. I patted her and said, "You won't mind if I have my bath now because it is getting cold and so am I." She hung at the bathroom door like a doom. "Your body's quite beautiful," she said—"Do you know?"

I lay down in the water from crossness.

"Crusoe was in love with her . . . she must have been wonderful."

No arguing that one. I tucked the sponge under my chin and said, "Is she dead? And if not why are you embalming her in the past tense?"

This question appeared to annoy her profoundly: "*Dead?* Why should she be dead? Of course she's not dead. She left him—and who wouldn't, the dull dog?"

I prepared to throw my sponge at her. But she ducked out of the bathroom quickly, saying, "Well, I don't know why I stand here talking. It's very late and I want to go to bed."

'All that,' I said to myself, 'was most unreasonable.' But according to the Duchess there was no common denominator of reasonable behaviour and I had better things to think about than the confusions of Aunt Anne.

There was the whole evening to be lived through again. From the first moment when the car came sweeping on to the terrace and I could not believe in the sight of him. Presently I found that I could recall every minute and every word that we had spoken. But I was little the wiser. When I tried to think what it proved, I could see only that it had put a change upon the face of my world.

.   .   .   .   .

"I am not going to work," I said, "because it is the last day."
I took the manuscript out of the rosewood coffin and enclosed
it in a folder. Livesey watched me.

"All that handwriting . . . you don't type?"

"Alas, I have no typewriter."

"Good lord, I'll give you a typewriter. Dozens of them
idling their time away in my office. Remind me . . ."

"And these," I said, picking the albums up from the table—
"must go down to my room. The rain will come in here."

"What are those?"

"The Duchess' letters."

We sat on for a little while in the summer-house, turning the
pages. He had come into my kingdom. Always before, I had
come into his; the visitor at Whiteford. I liked the change of
role.

" '*The prideful gusto with which some people assert their dislikes,*' " Livesey read aloud. "She's fun."

"Well, but it's true, isn't it?" I read on, " '*For example*: "*I
simply hate caviar.*" *This is the mark of the vulgarian, of the
unimaginative and of those who find it difficult to make impact
on society by any other method.*' "

"There's something about her," he said, "that reminds me
of Brother Crusoe. Oughtn't you to wear glasses?"

"I don't know; why ought I?"

"You bend your head so close when you read."

He has a daughter, I reminded myself, and he would notice
those things. But the solicitude was sweet to me. Marius said
that I bristled with independence, that he was aware of
porcupine-spikes protesting when he tried to help me on with my
coat. All that I asked now was to be looked after by Livesey.

We carried the heavy books down to my room. "You don't
want to pack? You're very placid about this departure, aren't
you? I thought girls always fussed."

"It is routine," I said. "And I have so few things."

We came out on to the terrace. "Let's have a picture," said
Livesey. "Sit on the balustrade; the way you were sitting when
I got here last night."

As he lowered the camera and slung it on his shoulder again, my eyes were taking a snapshot. His physical image came sharply into focus; the new Livesey of today, bare-throated and ruffle-headed in the sun. I looked back in my mind at the other, the statue in the niche at Whiteford, whom I had been content to love distantly and in silence. A bloodless kind of worship, I said to myself; the long unnecessary prelude to this moment, when all I want is to take hold of that hand and feel the pressure of the fingers, and the skin of the bare arm against mine.

He took my hand as promptly as though he had received the message. We went to the car.

"Don't they want you around? As it's your last day?"

"Oh, no. Tonight the dinner will be *un peu gala*," I said, "that is all."

We drove into St. Raphael; the road was changed, red rock and blue sea and green pine glittered in the confident sunlight. We passed our café, bleached and undramatic with morning, still making a signal as though it raised a hand.

In St. Raphael I bought some more foolscap paper and a new toothbrush. We drank iced coffee at a table in the street. We drove on around the harbour and he took another photograph of me, standing with my back to the water. We swam from Fréjus-plage. On our way back to the town we found a stall; a miniature shooting-gallery with the owner of the stall half-asleep beside it. Livesey took a rifle and shot down improbable prizes. There was a small replica of one of Mistinguette's legs in plaster with ostrich-feathers round the top; a black wooden ship with pink celluloid sails and an ashtray shaped like a mermaid. I insisted on keeping them. I put them in the back of the car with my parcels.

We ate our lunch on the waterfront and then prowled through the golden, dilapidated town. It was silent with the end of the season and the early afternoon, the stranded hour. As we passed a little shop whose façade was hung with large straw hats, I was reminded of Aunt Anne. Seeing an identical coolie's hat, I saw also her cross perplexed face below the brim.

At the end, like this, when autumn is beginning, I have had enough of the sea; I want the mountains and the inland roads. I said this to Livesey; and we went up by the hairpin-bends to Gourdon. At Gourdon we bought a white, polished ram's horn slung on a cord. I tried to blow fanfares on it as we came down, but I could only make frog-croakings. Those echoes and the sounds of our laughter still stay, I think, on the road above Auribeau and I could hear them again if I went back to listen.

It was late afternoon now; the beginning of sunset dazzled us and the wind blew cold on our baked foreheads.

"Home," I said to him.

It was almost dusk when we saw the bird. It fluttered down into the road, looking pleased with itself; a fairy-tale bird, reddish-gold of body with heraldic wings and tail in black and white, and a crested head. It strutted for a moment and flew off.

"A hoopoe," Livesey said. He puzzled about the hoopoe, saying that this was the wrong time of year and wondering how it had got off its course. To me the bird was the day's crowning magic. In memory it would be there.

Now there was the moment of whitened sea and sky, darkening rocks and trees; the car slowing at the last bend of the road before the railway line. And his face looking down, half-sad, half-laughing.

"Oughtn't to do this, ought we?"

"Oh, why not, why not? We have so little time."

"Wish I could drive you back to England."

"There," I said, "we should be faced with the inescapable mathematic of two nights in hotels upon the road."

"*Inescapable mathematic*," Livesey echoed.

"Well, it is."

"Darling bush-baby . . . This won't do."

"Your conscience," I said to him.

"Ticking like a clock?"

"Oh, but one's conscience *is* like that, isn't it?" I said, pleased because he was not usually so imaginative. "I've always thought so: I'm glad you do. Mine, I think, is a grandfather clock, just audible from downstairs. What sort is yours?"

"In fact," said Livesey, "that was my wife's description of it."

"Oh . . . Oh, I see. Well, she must be nice if she thinks things like that," I said, hearing my temperature drop in my voice.

"*Nice*——" He made a snorting noise.

"She is the person you hate?"

He gave an assenting grunt.

"But why?"

"Don't know. . . . Yes, I do. . . . Seems so bloody silly and wasteful—all of it. I just wanted a quiet life."

"And she didn't?"

"No, she didn't." He chuckled suddenly; I was disturbed by the chuckle; its reminiscence shut me out. "Devil of it was she could always make me lose my temper. Nobody else ever has."

"I cannot imagine your losing your temper; I seldom lose mine. We are placid types, I'd say. Did you hit her?"

"I came damn' near it sometimes. Don't know why I didn't. Or strangle her. But then she'd make me laugh," he said—"Just as I was really ready for murder. She could always make me laugh."

This, for the first time in my life, was true, authentic jealousy. The green-eyed monster of fiction and fact; stabbing at my vitals so suddenly that I put my hand on my stomach.

"What's the matter?" said Livesey.

"Nothing . . . nothing at all."

"Oh yes there is."

"Well, perhaps I have a chill. I feel a little odd inside."

I must remember, I thought, that here on the last *lacet* of the road above the railway line I learned the meaning of jealousy.

"Feeling awful?" Livesey asked, with his arm around my shoulders.

"Not awful, exactly. Just odd."

"Well, home we go. Get you a drink."

And nothing else, I thought, could have provoked the jealousy; no other words could have had this lethal power. He could have told me that she was beautiful, that he still desired her, that she was a saint. No grandiose claim for her could have spiked my guns in the way that this small horror had—the fact that she could make him laugh.

I suffered Livesey's drink, a *fortifiant* made from brandy, sugar and the yolk of an egg. I could not enjoy the solicitude, which was sad. I promised to lie down. As soon as he was gone, I got up and presently found Francis in the dining-room that was prepared, with flowers, for the dinner *un peu gala*. He was laying the table in an absent-minded way.

"What's taken your Aunt Anne?" was his greeting. "She just telephoned to say she won't be back till late."

"Oh? Well—she doesn't like Livesey being here."

"That, in the French idiom," said Francis, "sees itself. I wondered why not."

"I told you——" my voice was listless. "She finds him dull. Look," I added, "no forks."

"Do *you*?"

I was at the sideboard getting the forks. I repeated, "Do I . . . ?"

"Find him dull?" I saw the Mephisto lines crinkling upward. "I mean," he went on, "last night I could be sure you didn't. You now look a little as though you'd been eating ashes."

I set the two candelabra on the table.

"Not that I mean to pry, Penelope. You know that . . ."

I dodged it, saying, "What do you make of him? . . . I'd like to hear."

"Of Raines." He hesitated, looking down, the face with the delicate bones turning shadowy, as always when he thinks hard. "Well . . . he's your type, isn't he—a little? . . . English viking . . . English orthodox. I can see the façade—and the reason."

There was a little smile now beneath the pointed silvery moustache and this hurt me.

"But—as in your book," he said very gently, "the man is less evident than what the girl thinks about him."

So he had guessed when he read the book. I didn't know

why I should want to cry. I laid the best table-napkins carefully on the four plates.

"So—darling—as far as an opinion goes—" he paused—
" 'Ask me no more for fear I should reply.' "

The little smile stayed. I never quarrelled with him in these days. I was near it now; I could feel a carillon of discordant bells jangling inside.

"I'd rather you said what you thought, Francis."

"Quite sure?"

"Quite sure."

We faced each other across the flowery table.

Francis looked as though he were calculating a risk; he took a Caporal from a crushed packet and lit it carefully. "Well, in my view he's a nice, stupid fellow. And nice stupid fellows can do a devil of a lot of damage when there's fragile stuff about. Like Charlemagne wagging his tail in the *salon*."

I had not thought that I could be so angry. I could see the look in his eyes saying, 'You asked for it.'

"In fact," I snapped, "you don't see any more than Aunt Anne sees—is that it?"

"No—on the contrary. Unlike Anne—with her passion for freaks—I like simple people. People who are all of a piece. I mean," he added, "one of the troubles with your poor friend Raines is that he *isn't* all of a piece."

I stared stonily at the flowers.

"He's mixed up somehow," Francis said. "It's all over him. And I don't think, if you'll forgive my saying so, he's got quite the mental equipment to straighten himself out."

My mouth seemed to turn into a stiff muzzle as I forced the words through, "Francis, you were right. . . . It's better that we don't talk about Livesey."

On his face I saw—for the first time in many months—the reflection of one of the agonies down below. I saw my father not as the person troubling me, but as the separate person who lived—like everybody else—alone. Francis has the integrity that belongs to poets. It was easy to know in this moment that he was stricken because he had spoken the truth, his own truth, when it might have been wiser to muffle it and spare me.

And I saw, in a doubly refracted image, myself in his own eyes; the source of worry and fear; the child who must be, and could not be, made safe.

I remembered the pleasure that some of my achievements had given him. Prizes and certificates, I thought, scholarships; these were all very well. What pleasure would he get as I climbed the imponderable hills . . . the cliff-sides of experience? None, perhaps. Only pain.

I wished that he had other children, so as to take the pang out of me. Because of the war-wounds that crippled him, he couldn't father another child.

So I stood, with my anger deflected by knowing what it was like to be Francis.

As he turned, limping, with a courteous nod and a gesture of apology, to leave me, a most unwelcome voice echoed out of yesterday, 'Half an hour inside the other person's head—and you'd be fine. No—I'm wrong . . . you'd be sunk.'

The chaotic woman was the last person whom I wished to remember at this hour when my boats were burned. I went on to the terrace. I found Livesey talking with a greyhound of a man called André, who had stopped here for a drink.

IV

Cara's Voice

IT was four in the morning when we stopped playing. They kept the last table open for us, long after everybody else had left. I was too beat and hazy to take anything in. I did find a plaque in my pocket, while I was undressing; one of the square ten-mille jobs. It gave me a kick; it was the second lucky thing.

The fact that Livesey was still on the coast was the first lucky thing. I'd been hanging on to that for the last three hours, hadn't I? From the moment that André (was it André?) said, "I saw Livesey over at Miramar," I had hung on to that. Even the cards took a turn for the better, didn't they? . . . Not for long, though. What a bloody bank, that last one; must have run twelve times after I passed it. . . . *Banco suivi* to you, pretty creature—next time and every time.

I was still buzzed, so none of it got through, except the two lucky things. I swallowed the sleeping-pills down with Alka-Seltzer. I climbed into bed and my hot-water-bottle was cold, so I pushed the poodles over to one side and rested my feet on the warm patch that their bodies had left. Never know why gambling hurts one's feet.

Now . . . keep on thinking the lucky things, till the pills work. What hell these heart-thumps are; frightening, a little; and the singing in my ears. (*Banco . . . Huit à la banque.* Oh stop.)

You didn't. No, you didn't. You couldn't have. . . . Not the lot . . . and cheques . . . remember the cheques? . . . No, not really . . . I really don't. . . . Come on . . . get it all back now. . . . *Banco . . . une carte.* . . . *Huit.* . . . There you are. *Neuf à la banque*, would you credit?

No, no; I'm not still doing that; thank God. It's getting better, too; it's dimming; the edges are rubbing off. Anyway it's all right. You're safe, you fool. Livesey's here.

That *was* better. My heart had stopped taking its rhumba-lesson and the beautiful drowsiness moved in. I needn't be frightened any more. This was sleep.

The dreams began at once. They were the old dreams, every darn' one of them. I began at the long road beside the river and that's a gay one. It's summer and you leave the road and cut across under the trees, and the road and the river catch up with you.

I didn't walk on the waterfall; that only makes trouble, though it begins beautifully, on the wide lily-leaves. . . . Out beyond the lily-leaves there are more and more waterfalls, and fountains and stone arches and nowhere to stand. I know about that now. I went on down the grassy path and the field sloped up on my left to the place where the hills are dangerous.

That's where the giants looked out when I was a child and there aren't giants any more but I don't go there, I just look at the dark trees on the hills and remember.

It's a queer landscape. Usually at the end of the road by the river you get to the house that has two ways in. I didn't, this time. The road led only into the town and that bothered me. You come *out* of the town before you reach the river. Why was I back here again?

Come to think of it, I hadn't been in the town for a long time. It is just one street of houses, as it was in childhood. Nobody there. Now the last houses and the wall with great mossy cracks in it and the giant's footprint on the pavement; then the place where Shady Lane used to be. Shady Lane was the little dark turning that sloped downhill to the right. And you hurried on . . . or tried to.

Here *was* Shady Lane, though. . . . That was a queer one. A horrid one. I ought to have known better than to make it come. It was as dark, as menacing, as I remembered it, the black tunnel. "*Don't go down Shady Lane.*" That's what the voice used to say. No good. There was the bright road ahead, but you couldn't follow it. You went down Shady Lane.

Oh, and it was terror even now. There were spiders here, great webs across the road. When I saw the first I tried to turn back, but there was a web on the other side too; barring the way that I had come; the web and the crouching monster in the middle.

"*You can make them into leaves.*"

So the mercy was still there; the kindly voice from long ago. I never did make them into leaves; I didn't know how, but the voice broke the spell of Shady Lane and brought me out into the clearing. . . .

Good God, I said to myself, *not* the clearing, it's a hundred years since I saw it. And it still has the furniture of the child's fairy-tale; bright red toadstools and Arthur Rackham trees, and sparks among the trees that must be fireflies. (Of course the clearing is always here. It is just that you don't come and see it any more.) I'll wait though, I said, because of the diamond ship. You always waited for it and it slid in like a train on invisible tracks, the lighted ship coming into the clearing. It blazed with lights and toys, and it was all of ecstasy.

"*Here it comes. . . .*"

Oh, *too* good, I said to myself, so pretty—and I've never known where the shouts come from. They used to wake me up while I was trying to get my hands on the toys. They didn't now. I saw it come to rest, shining and splendid, and then I was away, comforted, because it was the luckiest thing. By this token I should get through to the last sea, to the lonely shore and the crumbling Eastern palace with the yellow arches. It is so old in your mind that you cry for happiness at seeing it again.

But I didn't get to the last sea. At first, because there are always two ways in, even to the palace, I fooled myself that this was the courtyard entrance. As soon as I stepped over the threshold I knew that I was wrong. This was the damnable place; the place where they despoiled the altar.

They were at it now, the mob, in the room that had been the chapel. Not a Carmagnole mob, but a cheerful Bank Holiday crowd with stupid red faces. I could smell their clothes. They had taken down the tabernacle. The Cross was gone; and they were setting their beastly plates of food all along the altar-cloth. They had torn up the pews. There were little tables all over the floor and a juke-box playing. It was worse than I have ever seen it. And the noise was terrific, all of them swarming around shouting, so happy and stupid and repulsive.

Would nobody help me fight them? No, there never was anybody. I called aloud for Gyp, but I knew that was no good, she was miles away somewhere else; she wouldn't hear me. Then I was shouting into the crowd, "Damn you—all of you—I won't stand this . . ." and scrambling up the steps and hurling the plates of food down off the altar, but they went on laughing. . . .

I said, "You bloody fools—the Sacrament was here—the Sacrament——" But on the cloth there were only the crumbs of their filthy cakes and I began to sob with rage.

.   .   .   .   .

It was the sobbing that awoke me. I was crying in my sleep and I hadn't done that in years. For a few seconds I thought that it was only the nightmare that made me feel so awful. I sat up and met my hangover in person as you might say.

It was a stinker. I was shaking all over and my head was made of marble; nothing I've found aches as much as marble at early morning. My heart . . . well, it wasn't there; and the less said about the bouncing, fluttering substitute the better. Oh, what the hell was I thinking of, at my time of life? What was the bat all *about*, anyway?

Then I remembered.

Oh, no. . . . *Oh, no.* Oh, no, no, *no.* . . .

No remorse to touch it. There never is.

I threw away the pillows and lay flat. This made me dizzy, so I put them back again. I drank some water. It gagged me and I lay clenching my hands, rigid with the fear that I was going to be sick.

As this subsided, the other terror walked in. Tramped in, I should say, on enormous iron feet. I'd done it again. *I had done it again.* And worse than ever; well, no, not worse, the same. . . . (*Not* what you're supposed to do more than once. Or twice, at the outside. Learn by experience, they say. Well, hell to that. I'm not at all sure that's what experience is for.)

No ducking it, though. I had lost every red cent including those dollars that weren't really mine to lose—and I had given three bad cheques. Not one. Three.

And if I had stopped when—(shut up, now, that's the silliest one in the book. Except I *do* know exactly when I should have stopped. Night before last, when I was two hundred *mille* up. A beautiful moment; in love with all the world and only drinking ice-water and telling André that I wanted to live on a *château-ferme* and raise goats. Feeling well, too. . .).

I didn't remember *ever* having felt as ill as this, anyway. Would my hangover be as bad if I'd won? Now there was a thing to think about—for those who could think; I just wanted to lie here and die. But I couldn't do that. At two a.m. the drowning Pollyanna in me had clutched a straw and taken it for a lifebelt: "Livesey's still *here* . . . oh, wonderful—now everything'll be all right."

(And that miserable ten-mille plaque on the bedside table had, as I recalled, made her cheer her stupid drunken little head off. *The lucky things* . . . like the diamond ship in the dream. Oh, this was too mean, really; why couldn't I just lie still and remember the dreams? It is fun when all the old ones come back like that.

Livesey, though . . . the only hope. And now. Which hotel had André said? Dammit, don't say I've forgotten. . . . A queer one—one I know. *Chez François* at Miramar. . . . Clever of me.)

Time? . . . Nine o'clock. No wonder I felt hideous. I could do with another four hours at least. But I wouldn't get them, not without more pills and more Alka-Seltzer. This was the brassy, thumping, agonised wakefulness behind whose screen you stared and stared.

I had no time to stare and stare. (Music to that, wasn't there?) I must get going. But when I stood up, I should probably die. That would save a lot of trouble. Better get Boxer, though. I rang the bell. As a rule in Destine's villa, nobody answers. Now the sort of thing that only happens on this kind of morning happened at once. Destine's maid brought in my breakfast-tray. She carried it triumphantly and the dogs yelled at her and she put the tray down on my knees and there was skin on top of the hot milk.

I lay back, with my eyes shut tightly. I said, "Please take all that away immediately and let the dogs out and send Boxer." I must have frightened her to death. She rushed out, banging the tray against the door as she went; the rattle of china split my marble head.

"I want the green bottle," I said to Boxer. She knows what that means; it's the one I only ask for *in extremis*; an American prescription. I forget the name of the drug in it but the total tastes of pepper, camphor and vitriol. Here it was, in its glass. Boxer's melancholy disapproval came with it, like a fog. There

was fog about, anyway; it smoked off the corners of my eyes
when I moved my head.

'Down with it, now——' I said to myself. I held the glass in
both hands and threw back my chin, the movement setting up
a splendid firework display inside the marble walls.

(Fire down below. A quotation, I believe. Wrestling with a
high explosive in my œsophagus, too.)

"Don't watch me, Boxer. Turn on my bath, please."

"Are you sure you're all right, my lady?"

"Sure I'm *what*?"

"I'm sorry," said Boxer.

"Now go. Put out my clothes and go. Find all my glasses
and most particularly my sun-glasses. And pack yourself the
hell out of here, like a good girl."

The green explosive steadied my heart and held down my
tummy. It did nothing for my head; hurrying did even less.
But I had to hurry. At the dressing-table I dropped everything
once and most things twice. The tips of my fingers sweated.
From the bath to the lipstick appeared to have taken two years.
My reflection in the glass was repulsive. I put on the dark
glasses and then lit a cigarette by mistake. (Like taking coal-
gas and senna-pods through a straw.)

The dogs came to meet me in the garden, sensible creatures
that did not drink nor gamble. Destine's car was parked in
front of André's, so I took Destine's. There would be trouble
about that. It didn't count. No troubles counted, not even
the way I felt. Not beside the awfulness of having lost the
dough.

(All of it, mind you, *all* of it, my thoughts repeated. But why
didn't you *stop*? Could have stopped before you got to the
dollars, at least. . . . *Or* the cheques. . . .)

Just ahead in my mind there was the last ditch. There was
a notice up over the last ditch. It read, the notice, 'You know
what you are? You're a mess.'

No, no, no. I'm not a mess. Couldn't be less a mess. Just a
little careless, that's all. I'm fine, I'm delicious, I'm crazy for
myself, I love me. I want to *tutoyer* myself and lay a cool hand

on my poor forehead and put me back to bed and cosset me.
Poor me; poor, poor me. . . . Gay and brave, that's what I
am. *Damn* brave, come to think of it. Up and around and
driving . . . at least I guess I'm driving; somebody must be;
the car's moving and the dogs don't drive, so that leaves me.
. . . Good show. Very few women over forty would drive
along the Corniche with a hangover like this.

"Dear old Cara—she's such *fun*."

"The time she wrote a cheque on Ryvita."

"The time Muriel Grampian lent her garden for a church-
bazaar and Cara got buzzed and sold Muriel's grandfather-
clock for seven and sixpence."

"The time she stole all Ruth Martineau's jewellery and wore
it to one of Ruth's parties."

"The time she owed her dressmaker thirty guineas for so long
that the dressmaker's lawyer attached her bank account and
found there was twenty-five thousand in it."

"The time she read the whole of *the Young Visiters* aloud
on Max's telephone from Rye to her lover in Geneva."

"Hey—Cara—we were just talking about you. . . ."

Through Cannes now, and past the harbour, on to the long
straight road by the sea. I couldn't look the frog in the face.
If you know this road, you know the frog. A rock-pyramid
(shaped, you'd never guess, like a frog) with the waves beating
around his bottom. On good gambling days he grins from ear
to ear. In the glimpse I got today he was just plain sulky.

Over the two bridges, past the golf-course; past Henry
Clews' castellated villa and now the road climbed. I wished it
wouldn't. The *lacets* and the prevalence of P.L.M. buses com-
bined to make my head swim again. I had put the green bottle
in my bag and I would ask Livesey for some water. If that
were all I had to ask him. 'Hullo, Livesey. Good morning.
I wonder if you can lend me a glass of water? I promise I'll
give it back—any minute now.'

Too common. . . . Vulgar jokes made inside. Awful car of
Destine's . . . just the sort of car she would have; like herself;
expensive and badly co-ordinated. You'd need maps and a

travel-agent to find your way about the dashboard and the
gears are so stiff you might easily break a blood-vessel changing
down.

Thank God—the hotel, with its garden below the level of the
road and the swinging blue sign, *Chez François*. It might have
been pretty before, but today the colours of the garden hurt,
even through my sun-glasses. Why couldn't it rain, for
Heaven's sake? Oh, well, at least I'd got here; my legs now
that they stood on their own feet felt like thin acid string.

("Can't go *on* feeling like this, can I?")

The bar, with its celebrated panel of signed photographs
. . . pity about all those bottles; what a hideous thought a
drink was. Nobody around, not even the sympathetic child
with the principles and the pointed ears. I went along the
terrace in the cruel sun, the dogs pattering after me. At my
elbow an open balcony-window suddenly framed Livesey,
having his breakfast. He looked enormous and well. He wore
a white towel robe and his hair was wet. He had been for a
swim. He would. He was eating *œufs sur la plat*. He would be.

When he saw me his face became surprised and a little sour.

"Hullo," I said—putting all my energy into it. "The top of
the morning to you. Lovely to see you. Adore these rooms
. . . French farm-house type, no? Please don't feed the dogs."

Livesey said, "You don't look very well."

"I know. Something's poisoned me. Disgusting. Everything's disgusting." I sat down.

"What's the matter, Cara?"

"Oh dear, oh dear. Everything is."

He waited. It was no good putting it off. I said, "I'm in the
worst mess I ever was in; you might as well know."

Livesey put an inconsiderate amount of milk in his coffee.
"Oh, I might, might I?"

"Help me, chum," I said weakly.

"Are you ill?"

"Yes. No. I don't know. I don't care anyway."

"Been gambling?"

"Not to put too fine a point upon it, I've lost all my dough and I've given God knows how many bad cheques and I've got to have the money today."

Livesey filled his pipe. About five years passed in silence while he was doing that.

I said, "I'll pay you back."

"What with?" said Livesey.

"Oh, I'll sell my shares——" He made me so nervous that I lit a cigarette and nearly asphyxiated myself. "Shares——" I said. "Just a matter of cabling the New York bank to release them." (They were holding down a loan, so that would mean getting somebody to co-sign for the loan. More cables.)

Livesey's face was, worst sign of all, blankly uninterested. I stubbed out the cigarette.

"Got a hangover too, haven't you?" he asked.

"Yeah—little one . . . I sat up late. . . . Working out figures. Planning—you know. I think the *best* thing would be to go to England now and live in Victoria's little house in Westminster; or do I mean Westminster's little house in Victoria? I can have it for nothing and the servants are on board wages. She's going to Nassau. Odd about Nassau," I said. "Couldn't attract me less. Cheap, I suppose."

"*Cara* . . ."

"Yes, Livesey? Hate people who say your name every time, don't you? They do it in plays. 'John . . .' 'Yes, Margaret . . .' 'I've been thinking, John . . .' 'What's on your mind, Margaret?' . . . Nobody really talks like that."

"*Will* you stop chattering," said Livesey. He looked quite grim. "Mean you've no money left at all?"

"Worse than none. I'd settle for none. It's the cheques. . . ."

"How much?"

"All together, you mean?"

"That's exactly what I mean."

"Eight hundred and fifty."

"Pounds or dollars?"

"Pounds."

"I see. . . . And three days ago you were offering to buy Whiteford."

"I know. It's awful, isn't it?"

"What I do resent," he said, "is your tacit assumption that I'll come across every time."

"You can't say *every* time like that. I haven't done it for ages."

He leaned back, folding his arms. "Remember what I settled on you at the time we split?"

It wasn't a fair question. And I honestly didn't know how much; I knew it was a lot; but there was the cost of living which everybody says has risen by a hundred per cent although, looking back, the cost of my living has always been enormous. And then, I tried to remind Livesey, I had hideous bad luck with the silver mine, "Even *you* said that wasn't my fault."

He shrugged his shoulders, "You don't deny that I've paid your debts at least once every two years—I've handed out God knows what on the side for Gyp—I've made every kind of arrangement to keep you straight and there isn't a damn' thing to show for it and now you're in trouble again."

"I know. . . . I should like," I said, "to lie down on your bed, please."

He looked at me, grunted, then drew up the bedclothes tidily and arranged the pillows.

"Thank you, that's nice. Easier to talk lying down, some-how——" The poodles jumped up beside me. Livesey stood at the foot of the bed, mercifully blocking the sunlight.

"You're forty-five," he said. "Or is it forty-four?"

"I don't know, darling; one or the other. Whichever you like."

"You said to me on Monday that you only wanted to settle down."

"I did, didn't I? . . . Said the same thing to André . . . must be growing on me."

"It had better."

I sat up on one elbow. "Look, Livesey, if you'll bail me out I'll never do it again . . . that's a promise. I'll find a cottage, a really cheap cottage, and I'll just garden and have dogs. And if Gyp doesn't go into an Enclosed Order she can come and be a nun near-by. A Dominican," I said. "So pretty—the white —don't you think?"

He drooped. I saw the lines of his face softening.

Dear Livesey . . . I stopped talking and tried as I've tried so many times before to figure just why I could never live with him. He can be so sweet. But I got him wrong from the start. Crusoe was my friend first, back in the days when the world was young and I felt a bastard for being loved by a boy in a wheel-chair. . . . Because, despite all the laughs I had with Crusoe, I loved the brother who never looked at me.

In those days Livesey—to me—was elusive, get it. . . . An elusive buccaneer, I thought. I fell for the act and it was an act; Livesey loved me and Livesey stood off because he didn't want to hurt Crusoe. Crusoe was a darn' sight more grown-up than either of us. When he saw what went on he gave us his blessing. But he did warn us against marrying each other. And quite right too. His words used to haunt me afterwards when times were tough.

Crusoe said, "He'll drown you. He's so archetypally kind that he's a bore. He's a giver—on an embarrassing scale. But you aren't really a taker. Except in the sense that Robin Hood was a taker. And Livesey likes a quiet life. Whereas the only life that suits you is life on a switchback. Sleep with brother Livesey all you like—but don't marry him, Cara dear."

But one didn't, in those days, sleep. And I wanted to be loved by Livesey and so we married.

Now my head was opening and shutting. He had paced at least three miles before the window. He came to a halt saying, "You're not going to like this. . . . But it's the only thing I'm prepared to do. Will you listen——?"

I listened. It sounded like a miracle. I was to have the money that he'd earmarked for me in his will. Now. It wouldn't affect Gyp's inheritance. It would pay me up, give me a small income. . . . The relief was numbing.

"On one condition. One definite stipulation," Livesey said.

I'd have agreed to wear sackcloth permanently. But he was

saying something about its being the last time; about removing
all temptation. No more bank-account; no more cheque-book;
the income paid monthly in cash from his office.

I said, "Lovely. But won't that be rather difficult and
cumbrous? For bills, I mean. . . ."

No bills, he said. Rent and 'so on' paid by the office . . . a
pocket-money system. "You'll have to come and see my
accountant—plan the expenses out with him, keep in touch all
the time till it's working smoothly."

The words banged like wooden clappers. They meant little.
. . . All I knew was that I was saved.

I said—"Thank you *so* much, so very much . . . you are so
good and sweet and I'm such a mess. Thank you, *dear* Livesey,
thank you. . . ." Now I only wanted to shut my eyes and
sleep. But he came to the bed and loomed.

"Cara. . . . You're so hungover, if you'll excuse my saying
so, that you're not taking it in. . . . You'll hate it, you'll find
it humiliating and exasperating and in two months' time you'll
be cursing me all ends up. Don't you see? I'm making one
almighty effort to protect myself from you. And Lord knows
I ought to have done it long ago."

With an effort I raised myself and peered at him. Something
had changed him in these two days. If my wave-length had
been operating, I might have got a clue.

"What's been happening to you?" I asked drowsily; a voice
outside the window said, "Livesey—have you finished your
breakfast . . . ?" and there stepped over the sill the child
with the pointed ears; Francis Wells's daughter, young and
tanned and healthy. She wore the shortest dark-blue shorts
and a dark-blue handkerchief with a halter, and her brown
feet were bare.

I said "Hullo" to her. She said "Hullo" moodily and stared
with the kind of hostile dignity that is achieved by having a long
neck. She stayed where she was, just inside the window.

I remembered to say, "Sorry about the paper-weight. Were
you cross?"

She shook her head.

I said, "Stealing's rather a servant's crime, isn't it, really—what? What d'you think?"

"I don't think I ever categorised crime socially," said Miss Wells.

Livesey looked from her to me and back again, his brow creasing. He seemed uncomfortable. About the paper-weight? Oh, it was the bed, perhaps. He worried—did he?—about her finding me on his bed.

"You'll excuse me, won't you?" I said to the child—"Livesey and I have just been talking business, and I've gotten rather a headache and so—well, so I'm lying down." It didn't seem to be going well. Which was quite absurd. "After all," I said to Livesey, "we are married. Were, I mean; weren't we? So there's no need to stand there looking like a scruple."

V

Penelope's Voice

'*When you meet a fact head-on, and it hurts you . . . then you'll learn it.*'

The words seemed to be lying about on the bright air in the garden, just below the summer-house; where I had left them in my thoughts, two days ago. Francis' words, highly apposite. The epitaph on a time ended. He was right; I had known all that there was to know, except the facts.

They were the facts of hatred. I knew this, sitting on the steps of the summer-house with my arms around my knees.

She had not gone yet. I could see the new blatant car that wasn't hers, still parked in the drive before the hotel. She was out on the terrace, I thought, with Livesey and perhaps Aunt Anne. Aunt Anne's talk—while Cara went to cure her hangover with a swim—buzzed in my head: Aunt Anne drinking two glasses of vermouth and telling us. Telling us the stories told to her by Crusoe. How witty Cara always was, and how wild . . . and what good fun. How when Cara married Livesey Everybody was Shattered; Everybody Was In Love With Her; she had been engaged to the Aga Khan—or was it perhaps the Prince Regent or Disraeli? . . . And then when she left Livesey and took the daughter Gyp (*Gyp* . . . that was a dog's name, not a daughter's . . .) to live in France, Everybody Was Shattered again. While, when she married Anthony de Bretteville and went to America—well, Cara's Shattering-Capacity, if my aunt were to be believed, would arouse jealousy in a guided missile.

And I could be sure that Aunt Anne had enjoyed dredging out those old stories from the hiding-place in memory where she kept them; enjoyed them especially, told them deliberately, to hurt and humiliate me.

But why (—scuffing up the red sand with the toes of my shoes as I did when I was a child—) should I think that she wanted to hurt me? Was I—God help me—turning into one of the 'Sensitive' people? Like Marius? I who had said proudly that the ego must be hurt once, so that it would never hurt again? Once wounded, having taken the wound, I said, you grew up.

I had not grown up yet. When I aligned the facts of hatred, I knew where my worst wound was. I had to blink in my mind a little before I got to the facts; so obdurate was the untidy, clanging vision of the woman, sprawled on Livesey's bed, haggard and chattering with the poodles by her feet; the peals of hard laughter, the pitiable out-of-date quality that she had. ("Motor-veils," I had said to Francis, but this morning it was more recently rakish; it was like the old works of a certain author who wrote in the nineteen-twenties and whose discovery had made me blush.)

And Livesey standing there like an ox in trouble; but occasionally throwing back his head with the lion's laugh—as though to prove—as though to prove . . .

The facts. I glared at the light-green glitter of the umbrella-pine.

Livesey had been married to the woman who stole the paper-weight. By this fact he was reduced, made ridiculous and accompanied for ever. I could never think of him again without remembering that.

He was still in thrall to her. What he felt for Cara wasn't hatred, not if I knew hatred. (And I did know it now.) When you hated a person you got away from her as soon as you could. You didn't keep her at your elbow all the morning, bringing her glasses of water to mix with some elaborate medicine in a green bottle, arranging her in a long chair in the shade, accepting her presence equably and in due course going down with her to swim. And lunch; he need not have let her stay to lunch.

"Two facts, are there not?" I said to the small bronzy lizard who now watched me, motionless, from a stone at the path's edge. "One, he married her. Two, he loves her. And three . . . oh, three."

It was odd that three should be the worst. It could not be the worst, not in any terms of logic, order or proportion. And yet it was. This was the one that gave the ego a stab. It was Cara who had put me into Livesey's head. That was why he had come here on Tuesday evening. If Cara hadn't come first, with her plan for the dollars, hadn't gone back to Antibes and told Livesey that she saw me (and I was certain she'd made the wittiest story out of my refusal . . .) Livesey would never have remembered my existence on this coast at all.

That hurt. Oh, and how little I wanted to be one of the Hurt. I had not asked for any of this. And it was going to be horribly easy, at any moment, to remember that this was the last day of my holidays, that my train left at five, to plunge into a wallow of self-pity like a schoolchild because nobody was giving me A Nice Last Day.

Thank Heaven at least for the tasks of the morning. Jeanne had come to help me pack and had stayed with me. Competently tactful, she said no word about the chaotic visitor, glancing only once toward the shady corner of the terrace where the two long chairs were placed and then meeting my eyes with a secret, comical *moue*; very comforting.

And now, rising, backing quietly into the summer-house, I saw Cara go. She came out on to the veranda, putting on her glasses. She whistled to the dogs, kissed her hand to Livesey and drove away in a roar and a whirl of dust; as she went out on to the Corniche, making a scream of notes on the fanciful motor-horn, I knew how I should feel if she came into collision with a P.L.M. bus. . . . Was it only the night before last that I had said to him, "I *couldn't* want somebody to die"?

I knew what would happen next. He had seen me; he had glanced up this way from the veranda. I pretended to be busy looking through old papers on the shelves. (Oh, my poor novel, I thought in sudden pity; these two days have killed it with the others. It is now stone dead in its dullness and I don't even care.)

I heard his feet coming up the red rock-path. He stood on the open side, looking at me with a frozen, would-be-jaunty smile.

"Hullo, bush-baby. Packing up?"

"Well . . . yes. Just sorting a few last things."

"I'll be off before you, I'm afraid. Or I'd drive you into St. Raphael."

"Thank you," I said, "but Francis always drives me in."

"You don't mind going back, do you?" There was an echo of the protective solicitude. Then he said, unforgivably, "I remember Gyp always hated going back to boarding-school, but I suppose that's different."

(How they come out into the open now, don't they, Livesey? Gyp—and Cara . . . I suppose if we'd had another day left we'd have talked of nobody else.)

"No," I said icily. "Oxford and boarding-school *are* a little different."

He hesitated. "Better do a bit of packing myself, I suppose. . . . Rather a disrupted morning. . . ." He took his pipe out of his pocket and put it back again, "You—don't want to be sweet and come and talk to me while I chuck the stuff in?"

"No—no, thank you very much, Livesey. I really haven't time."

Had I ever made this person a hero? Perhaps the lesson was that there were no human heroes. But—and here was the devil of it—I didn't want the hero back. I wanted the man who stood before me; the man in the flesh. I wanted the shadowy road again, and the man's mouth and the man's hands. That was the change that I resented. He need not have done that.

It was no seduction in the technical sense. Yet it seemed that my seduction was complete, my solitude invaded. It wouldn't come back, I thought, watching his large shadow fallen on the path; the freedom of walking in this garden and waiting.

> '. . . *Alone with the thought at the back of your head;*
> *till the sunset turns pale and your shadow grows thin*
> *at the edge of the path where the pine trees begin.*
> *. . . But, if anyone asks you, you cannot explain*
> *why you walk to the end of the garden again.*'

And the thought—like a footstep that followed behind? That was now the footfall of the fact, running after me.

I found that I had, for all my intentions, spoken aloud. "You said you hated her."

"Hated her? Cara?" The forehead creased quickly. . . . He looked baffled.

"You love her, don't you?"

"Not any more; not the way you mean. Anyway, haven't *you* ever hated somebody and loved them at the same time?" It was a pleading smile.

"Well, yes. Perhaps. When I was young and used to get mixed up about these things." I admired the swagger of my lie so much that I reeled under it. Livesey's grin grew wider. He said, "She liked you, you know."

That, I thought, with a cold shower of icicles inside, would be all. I held out my hand. "Goodbye, Livesey."

He put both his hands around the one stiff, polite hand; he squeezed it a little. He said, "I won't forget about the type-writer."

"I don't want it, thank you." That was the muffled, sulky answer of a child. And I was ashamed of it at once.

"Don't want it?"

Now, damn everything, I thought, I was sorry for him and for the unwanted typewriter as well. And I was going to cry. I muttered, "Oh, do go, Livesey, please——" and turned to the little shelf above my table and saw the letter from Marius lying there. He would, I remembered, meet my train tomorrow.

Sad, that it should have been Marius. After his side-steps, his moods, his confessed love for me that always seemed to take the form of an accusation. And after my own determinations to escape him.

What sent me to him now? No orderly motive. In my heart there was a tough, jangling salute to chaos. Since all is spoiled, the impulse said, let us spoil still more.

I had known that it was there from the moment that Livesey left the summer-house. It had made discordancy of the last hours, even of my drive to the train with Francis. I felt as though I had nothing to say to him; no life left behind me in the home I loved; no connection with anything that might happen there, now that Livesey was gone from the place. I remember Francis saying, in the car, "Your holy young friend's looking in tomorrow; with Father Lasalle. Shall I give him your love?" There was indifference in my mind; then a sudden flare of mockery for the black robe, the outward sign. "I think he's crazy," I said, "I really do. He doesn't know what he's taking on."

The spoiling impulse. . . .

It lasted all the way to London.

And Marius was in a new role as a refuge, surely. No use expecting him to understand, or be kind. But I was tired of kind people. ('Charlemagne wagging his tail in the *salon*. . . .') And the spoiling impulse did not really need a refuge so much as a solution. Marius, crudely, was the solution to the problem of my virginity that was now no more than a technical fact, an unwanted fact.

Of course I had to talk about it first. Over the table in the Soho restaurant, with a bottle of red wine between us. With the wine it was easy to be brave. I talked with great fluency and Marius gave the impression of applauding. "At least"—commented an onlooker inside me who seemed bent upon cheapening all issues—"he has physical beauty. It is a most visible head, with its black silky hair and Red Indian profile; its radiant eyes. And his hands are better shaped than Livesey's hands—these long fingers. He will be my first lover. How extraordinarily grown-up that sounds," observed the new cheapjack.

I was as frank as I could be within the limits of verbal decency. I was converted, that was all, I explained. Certain adventures in the south had accomplished the conversion. He must not—if he didn't mind—ask me details.

"Naturally not—of course not—what d'you take me for?" said Marius delightedly. Though he clasped my hand below the tablecloth, I could see him hunting around in his mind for an attitude, a phrase that would gibe at me a little. This he would regard as his privilege. 'Search away,' I thought, 'You will not find it. I am immune tonight.' I lifted my glass and looked deliberately at the reflection that I could see in the mirror on the opposite wall. I saw the chin held high on the long neck. There was laughter in the face; not the sort of laughter that I knew or understood, though I admired it. With that laughter, surely, there should be vine-leaves in the hair. ("And then," snapped an unexpected monitor of good taste, "you would look like an advertisement for Empire Burgundy.")

Marius had found his phrase, "What about God's design? . . . You used to talk a lot about God's design. That gone down the can, too?"

If I could stomach those words, and shrug a little, remarking placidly, "It doesn't seem to have much to do with me at the minute," then, I said to myself, I could stomach anything.

"Sure?" he pursued me.

"Quite sure."

"Darling, I see what's happened. Somebody's hurt you at

last. . . . Really hurt you." (Let him have his victory, I said, it is the least of courtesies after all. . . . Nod and smile and spread your hands and signal 'Yes'.)

"Darling . . ." He poured out more wine. "You'll get used to it. After it's happened a few more times. *I've* got used to it."

"Have you, Marius?"

He said with a dark, velvety snarl, "Naturally. That's how one learns to survive. Once one realises that there's no such thing as kindness—true kindness."

I had been in his flat before, the flat in Ebury Street. I knew the room, with its Cocteau drawing and white lamp-shades, its rush carpet; the little row of Mexican pottery figures along the top of the bookcase. When he shut the door behind us I felt my courage going; and now I think that his was going too. He was only a few months older than I.

"Let's have some brandy, shall we?" said Marius—"It's good brandy. I brought it back from Paris, last time."

He set the brandy-glasses on the low coffee-table in front of the sofa. After a moment he rose and with a face of monkish care, chose records for his long-playing gramophone. The solemnity of the preparation made me want to giggle. "Knowing his taste, you will be seduced to a blend of Dvorak, Brahms and Sibelius," said the cheapjack.

It was the determination in me that felt ugly; a striving; intimate, lonely and muscular; a striving that went on through the kisses and the clumsy gestures that we made with our clothes—the proof that I was in a hurry to be rid of the physical fact once and for all. Then the ugly necessity became what I liked. There was no barrier of fastidiousness now. There was the pleasurable clue again; growing stronger, making my bones weak, carrying me away. It came to its climax long before the hurting began.

And now it seemed a measure of weary politeness to endure the hurting. That thing would not happen again and presently felt as though it had never happened. My mind was detached, most horribly, concerned with the weight of his head upon my shoulder, the exasperation of his arm above me, pinioning my hair against the sofa-cushion and pulling it at the roots. The music changed, as prophesied, Dvorak to Sibelius, and a mad giggle shook me.

Nothing, I thought, was ever so slow, so demeaning nor so wrong as this. And when it was over for him, I could think of nothing to say. We dressed like two people who had been bathing from a pebble-beach in an east wind. I could see his eyes looking at me ashamedly, beseeching me, wanting me to love him and to be pleased with him, and then I was shocked. '*By no aspect of human behaviour except cruelty,*' my mind repeated—'and now I have been cruel.'

So I came to limbo in my mind; a grey place that had not even the distraction of chaos; just limbo, flat and smooth and without end, unwinding its sameness through the winter.

I worked hard; there was salvation there, not in any writing of my own; but in the routine work for my Degree; lecture and thesis and essay, deductions from the book of words. I ate of the printed page; it was the only reality. Oxford was a phantom place, peopled by phantoms—one of whom was Marius. We avoided each other.

Such guilt as I felt puzzled me. In speculation, sometimes, I had thought that if ever I did this thing before marriage, I should feel guilty towards Francis and Jeanne, towards the whole cast of my upbringing; towards the memory of Violetta and the thought of my mother. There was none of that; no sense of a secret. There was only a sense of separation from something that I had never clearly apprehended and could not identify now.

Sometimes it looked as though I had betrayed the dreaming freedom of last summer, and the summers before it; the walk in the garden alone, with the thought like a footstep that followed behind. Sometimes it looked—in all foolishness—as though I had sinned against the ignorant worshipper who made a hero of Livesey—my past self. How could I have sinned against that one? The idea was ludicrous; I had as little respect for her as I had for him. But there came, at times, the uneasy knowledge of some assurance that she had possessed; whereas the current automaton possessed no assurance at all. She had merely her isolation, a difference and a numbness.

Certain spectres intruded; spectres that came in reverie, doing grim little dances. Sometimes I pictured Cara and Livesey reunited, with the daughter whom I had never seen, a happy family living at Whiteford. (Certainly Whiteford was not yet sold.) Sometimes I saw their past, the two of them young and happy, in a time that I did not know.

Often the spectre was Cara herself, talking with me, confiding in me, making me her friend. . . . the last thing—I knew when I was out of reverie—that I would wish to be. I used to dream of her. And on my visits to London I caught myself looking for her consciously, expecting to meet her face to face. Somehow I never expected to meet Livesey in London. In reverie his next appearance was a game played constantly. He came to seek me out; I found him waiting in the porter's lodge. I saw his car drive down Parks Road at dusk. I opened a telegram. In one version it was the daughter who came, to plead his cause. I think, in that one, Cara was dead and he wanted to marry me.

October; November; and there were no more leaves on the trees. December—and soon I should go home again. It was on a morning in December that I heard from Aunt Anne. She enclosed, without comment, half a page torn from the local paper.

At first I was angry with her, then I remembered how little she really knew.

Whiteford was sold at last. To a girls' school of repute. There was a picture; there were stories of the family. There was a summary of Livesey's career and a sugar-sweet paragraph about the farewell week-end party that he would give at the Manor itself; this even went so far as to compare him with Cinderella since he would go straight from the junketings to London Airport and fly to the United States.

'Really a mine of unwanted information,' I said to myself as I read it for the second time.

When I went to Whiteford in the spring there would be only a travesty of it; beset with playing-fields and hard tennis courts. There would be a board at the gate, and a straggly crowd of girls in uniform coming and going. Bicycles belonging to the teachers would hurry into the drive. Whiteford as I had known it would not be there any more.

The dismantling, they said, would begin immediately after Christmas. What, I wondered, would become of the furniture, of the things that I had loved? I thought of the white statue in the marble hollow above the staircase. I thought of the little peacock-room where Livesey and I had drunk tepid tea and talked politics. Most of all I thought of the tawny-hued library; the long table that I had made mine by so many cramped hours of work, by so many blotted lines. The library with the white busts of the ancestors and Crusoe's little bronze horse on its stand.

The idea of the pilgrimage began to take shape in my mind.

It was a cold morning. The windows of the third-class carriage were fogged, the floor was dirty and there was an Ancient Mariner in the corner seat. I recognised the doom at once. A pale damp face, a mob of greying chestnut hair, a welcoming smile.

"Goodness, you've got plenty of luggage, haven't you? Going to Cardiff? . . ."

"No," I said, "I'm going to the South of France."

She blinked; she was holding out a packet of Craven A. Passport to conversation. "Like a cig? . . . Aren't you wise! . . . Wish I didn't. . . . Did you say *France*?"

I explained that I was making a temporary detour; leaving my luggage at the junction and then picking it up when I caught the London train in the late afternoon. She accepted the dull details with rapturous nods and twitches. Until she acquired the fact that I lived on the Riviera.

"*Live* there. . . . But do you like it? I mean, I don't know, but I'd simply hate to." And she laughed loudly. Francis and I have sometimes annotated the laughs that happen when there

is nothing funny about, ' 'Fraid we're a bit late—ha-ha!'—
'The elder boy's fourteen now—ha-ha!'—'Don't quite know
where we're going this summer, ha-ha!' and dozens more. I
looked at her balefully. Her comment came into the category
of remarks that I would not dream of making. *'The prideful
gusto with which people announce their dislikes,'* I recalled from
the album of the Duchess; but the memory gave me less
pleasure than usual; Livesey was there; in the summer-house,
turning the pages with me.

I hoped that she would quiet down. I wanted to arrange my
thoughts for the pilgrimage. I had not told Aunt Anne that I
was making this swoop on Whiteford and the omission nagged
at me. There was also the dancing hope, alternatively the
chilling dread, that the local paper had erred in its facts and
that I should find Livesey.

"Penny for them . . .? Don't mind me. I always talk to
people now I'm getting a bit long in the tooth. . . . Used to
be ever so shy."

"I am shy," I said and began to open my newspaper. The
Ancient Mariner said that she wouldn't have thought it, but
that you couldn't tell a book by its cover, as the saying went.
To look at her, she challenged, one would never say that she
was a bundle of nerves, would one? Would one, now? But
ever since her breakdown—well, it wasn't exactly a breakdown,
they said . . . The tale began.

(At least she hadn't asked me to guess her age. For one
hideous moment I had feared this. Being asked to guess anything at all is a horror to me. It was a dread in childhood when
it seemed to be a convention of cosy fun. Now that I am older
it is just as bad, if not worse. According to the Duchess, people
who say 'Guess how much this cost' should be eliminated from
one's visiting-list without reprieve.)

"My legs wouldn't work at all. Honestly. I couldn't even
walk along the passage to the whatsit. . . . Frightening . . . I
thought I was going loopy."

I must not be unkind. Her eyes were still afraid while her
pale mouth went on speaking jocular phrases: "Ah well, one

gets over anything, doesn't one . . . One good thing about
being on the shelf, you can always get down and dust yourself
now and again. . . . And he wasn't really a wrong 'un, you
know . . . just sporty . . . not the marrying kind. First time
I ever set eyes on him, I said to myself—it was at Littlehampton . . . I had a very pretty dress, black and orange, it
was . . ."

The Ancient Mariner. *Why* did it happen? Because, Francis
said, of charitable eyes and an attentive expression.

Be my looks what they may, I thought, charity has taken its
hat and walked out, attention died stillborn. The voice went
on, "I wonder if you'd mind giving me a hand with this
albatross? Ta ever so."

No; she had said suitcase, not albatross. She wanted her
needlework.

"Helps to keep the heebie-jeebies away. . . . You look a bit
down in the mouth yourself. Anything wrong?"

"No—no thank you."

Except that I needed silence. This might have been a physical
thirst and she denying me a glass of water.

"Excuse me a moment, please?"

Her quick grin of understanding accepted my need for the
whatsit. I went out and walked along the corridor until I was
two coaches away. It was even colder in the corridor. I leaned
on the rail that crossed the window, dabbing the wet fog off the
pane until I saw the winter landscape inside.

The Ancient Mariner and I had this in common; *la récherche
du temps perdu*. She in her head, going back to Littlehampton
and the black and orange dress; I in the slow train jogging on
towards the junction ten miles from Whiteford. I had an uncomfortable belief that her method of transport was the more
intelligent of the two.

It is, I said to myself, like a visit to a grave. I knew this
winter face of Whiteford Manor. The trees made black lacy
groves on grass that was brown-shadowed; the lake was steely,
and the façade of the house pale, bleached against the hard

grey sky. There was an east wind, to help the mood along.
My eyes watered with it and my face hurt. I stood at the foot
of the shallow stone steps, looking up.

"I shall be about half an hour," I said to the driver. It was
a wicked cost, the cost of this rattletrap taxi from the junction.
I should have to eat carefully in London tonight and I should
probably run out of money by the time I reached home, as I
have done before.

There was another car parked on the gravel and this gave me
pause. But it was not Livesey's; it was a small grey coupé with
a pale hood; anybody's car. I need make no explanations,
beyond the fact that I was an old friend who wished to see the
house for the last time. Quite reasonable, surely. . . . I met
the chill stare of the stone dogs guarding the front door. The
front door stood open. All the same, I rang the bell.

Nobody came. I thought that I heard a voice raised somewhere inside the house, but it only happened once. I waited.
It was a scruple of good manners, wasn't it, to stand outside
an open door in an east wind? I went in, shutting it behind me.

I stood in the hall, with its marble pillars. At the back the
great staircase went up, dividing below the marble niche where
the white statue stood. The cold was excessive. A chilly
museum today, I thought; an anonymous place; no echoes
here. Feeling suddenly the uselessness of my pilgrimage, I was
tempted to walk straight out again.

There would be echoes in the library, though. That was sure.
I crossed the watery, black-and-white-squared surface of the
marble floor and went up the stairs.

As I reached the branching of the staircase, a voice called,
"In here!"

It made me jump. It came from my left. I turned that way
and saw, when I came to the landing, that the door of the
peacock-room stood ajar. Whoever called was in the peacock-
room.

I went in, remembering: here was the small, circular jewel-
case of a room; and the rainbow-coloured panels; the looped
pelmets; the painted ceiling.

I saw Cara de Bretteville. She was lying on the sofa, with a fur coat pulled up to her chin. There was only a small electric fire, one red bar burning across a steel shell. She had brought this as close to the sofa as the flex would reach.

I stared, realising her but slowly. Yes. There were the poodles, a mound of silvery fur pressed against her side. She lay with one arm doubled behind her head. The face, without the heavy tan, was different. I had seen that brown face in memory so many times. Now it was oddly red and white, the nose and chin waxen, the cheeks heavily flushed; the eyes were bright, glazed a little, as though she were drunk.

"Well, hul*lo*——" She gave me the dazzling, treacherous smile—"It's you. . . . You buzzed my ear—or somebody did. . . . I was expecting——" she frowned—"Who the devil was I expecting?" She held out her hand. "Forgive my not getting up . . . I've only just gotten comfortable—— That is, tolerably comfortable." Her hand was hot and wet to my touch. She said, "So there is a party after all. . . . Glad you've come. . . . That damn-fool maid said it was last week."

"A party?"

"Livesey's party . . . farewell party . . . you know." She turned her head restlessly on the silk cushion; her hair looked darker and quite straggly.

"It was last week," I said.

"Never do get a date right, that's my trouble."

Certainly she was drunk. On the small marqueterie table there was a pigskin-and-silver flask to prove it.

"Hideously inconvenient, isn't it—what?" The smile flashed again—"Does he always leave the place deserted like this?" —She didn't wait for an answer—"Only one old candlestick of a maid; cross, too; she was just going out. I *could* go on to the Davidsons', of course . . . only about five miles from here, but I don't know that they'd be pleased. Anyway, *not* sure I could make it. Although it does seem to have stopped for the minute . . . can't tell, can you?"

She seemed to expect an answer this time. I said, "I'm sorry, but I don't know what you're talking about."

"No . . ." The dove-coloured eyes were blank, "No—course you don't; never mind. He'll be here in a minute. Pull up a chair and help me with this crossword. Where the hell are my glasses?"

I said, "I'm sorry; but I can't stay. I've a taxi waiting. I was just going to the library . . ."

"Library? Were you now? Give it my love. It's a good library. Ever seen it?"

That sent up a flare of anger in my head.

"I know it well," I told her.

"And when you pass the third Raines on the right—that's the one with the Wellington nose," said Cara—"pull it. That's my advice—pull its nose." She shut her eyes. "Have to keep quiet for a minute," she said, "it's coming back . . . not the same, quite, but something."

I hung on one foot, watching her. If she wanted to get drunk and lie around feeling ill in an empty house, I said to myself, it was no business of mine. I took an uncertain step towards the door. Downstairs a bell pealed, loud and long. Cara frowned, still with her eyes shut . . . "What's that?"

"It must be the front-door bell."

"Thought I left it open for him. . . . Must have slammed. . . . Could you go? Sorry——"

Who, I wondered, could be meeting her here? The bell rang a second time as I went down the staircase. On the last step I was suddenly, illogically, certain that it would be Livesey to whom I opened.

Here was a stocky man in an overcoat and muffler, carrying a bag.

"Mrs. Raines . . .? Dr. O'Neill; she sent for me."

(Mrs. Raines? Not the Countess de Bretteville? *La récherche du temps perdu*, for her also? Nonsense. She had come here drunkenly to look for Livesey's party. I wondered how she had the wit to call the doctor and why she should waste his time.)

Crossing the hall, he said, "She's serious about this, is she? . . . I mean—haven't seen her for years, but she was always something of a leg-puller. . . . Sounds a most unlikely story.

. . . Were you with her when she saw the Harley Street chap? Oh . . . oh, I see. Thought you might have driven down with her—sorry. Anybody else in the house? I see." We had come to the landing. He hesitated at the door of the peacock-room, saying, "You want to be off, I suppose?"

"Well, yes, I do. But I could wait a few minutes." I offered. He looked so cold and worried. As he opened the door I heard her say in her most brittle voice, "Sweet of you to come."

I could, I thought, go to the library now, but a twitch of anxiety tethered me. There was the hint of a trapped feeling, the Wedding-Guest feeling. Ridiculous. I wasn't going to let Cara, of all people, turn into an Ancient Mariner; not with my taxi outside and my luggage at the junction, ten miles away.

I began to know, as I waited, that there was no emergency. There couldn't be, not with a person like Cara; just fuss and disorganisation, some silly mystery, nothing serious.

The door opened. O'Neill shot out and collided with me, barking, "Sorry—— Telephone?"

"In the hall. At the back."

He ran down the stairs two at a time, shouting to me—"Try and make her keep still!"

Cara was sitting up on one elbow, smoking a cigarette. The doctor's bag gaped open in the middle of the floor. On the marqueterie table beside the flask there was a thermometer out of its case, a medicine-glass, a round pillbox.

"Looks a little as though I'm cooked," said Cara. She rubbed her hand palm upward across her forehead and drawled, "Oh honestly . . . But what was I to do? Of course it may *not* have burst. . . . Doesn't hurt any more now . . . you'd think that when they burst they'd hurt more, wouldn't you?"

It was the approach of chaos—and panic. But I heard my voice saying steadily, "You must just keep quiet and still and it will be all right."

"My friend in Harley Street didn't think so. Volcano, he said: operate at once; such talk. Told him they've been after my appendix for years. We ought to call him, you know. Took a room for me in the London Clinic—he's waiting, poor little thing." She wiped her face. "Fever must be going down with all this sweat, don't you think?"

"Yes, I'm sure. But why," I asked her gently, "didn't you go to the London Clinic?"

She narrowed her eyes. "The How of Motive, my dear little girl, is less potent on occasion than the Why of Money," she pronounced cooingly and reminding me, to my astonishment, of the Duchess. Then she broke it, "Somebody said . . . True. I mean, how could I pay? Broke; bust. Don't even have a cheque-book any more, *too* humiliating. Livesey said it would be—the rat."

"But there is the Health Service," I pleaded.

"Isn't that just for poor people?" said Cara vaguely. "Anyway it seemed more sense to come straight here and let Livesey fix. Only of course I got the date wrong." She smiled at me lop-sidedly and handed me her cigarette. "Mind putting that out? Rather sick now, for some reason; maybe that's the codeine." She lay back, frowning. "Oh, *honestly*——" she said again.

"I'll get people," I said. "I'll get Boxer. Where's Boxer?"

"No, don't," she snapped. "Wouldn't be fair. Poor old Boxer. Promise not to?" There was still the frown. She shut her eyes.

"Just have a word with this young lady——" O'Neill said at the door. He drew me outside and away, speaking low, "More than one way of committing suicide, eh? Of all the insane behaviour. Where's Livesey? Well, he ought to be told. Can you get on the telephone to his London office? Do that for me, will you? And then I'll let you go. There's a nurse coming with the ambulance."

I felt dazed. I said, "But will she die?"

"Might easily." He looked very angry about it, "I'm damn' sure that appendix has ruptured and I can't get the surgeon till five." I got scattered words, "Peritonitis . . . penicillin. . . . Anyway tell them she's dangerously ill. They can probably put a Transatlantic call through." I started down the stairs. "General Hospital!" he shouted after me. "Laxton General Hospital."

When I returned, Cara was saying to Dr. O'Neill, "Nobody must try to pull them off me, or they'll bite. They'll follow once I'm on the stretcher."

"Listen, my dear, you can't take the dogs in the ambulance."

"Nonsense, I always do."

"I'm sorry."

"Shut up. *Constantly* in ambulances . . . surrounded by dogs. Happened in Barcelona. And Dublin." She looked up at me, "Be an angel. See they put my luggage into the ambulance. . . . Suitcase; white box. Thank you." As I went out I heard her laughing.

The taxi-driver bobbed out of his seat thankfully at my approach. I shook my head at him. I collected her cases from the small car. The white rawhide box was stamped affectedly with a coronet above the initials. There was a pair of gloves on the seat, good gloves with leather palms and white string backs. They were, for some reason, pathetic; I didn't want to feel sorry for her.

"Look here, Miss——" said the taxi-driver.

"I think," I said at last, "you'd better go."

"How'll you get back? You're cutting it a bit fine yourself."

"There must be a later train. And I expect I can get a car from Whiteford Village." It was odd to think that I was within a mile of my second home, within a mile of Aunt Anne. I had begun to feel caught in a vacuum.

"Thirty shillings, please, Miss."

I watched him drive away; and I stood in the cold beside Cara's two cases until I saw the ambulance come up the drive. I had expected a shiny white one, but this was of a shabby greenish colour. It looked rickety too, swaying to a standstill on high wheels. Two men jumped out. They unshipped a stretcher and some red blankets striped with black.

"Where's the patient?"

I said, "Where's the nurse?"

"Sorry—no nurse available just at the minute," they said.

There was a rack where they slid the stretcher in; and a bucket-seat on the opposite side. Now I heard scrabbles and yelpings and Dr. O'Neill swearing, and then the poodles shot in over the little step and the second ambulance-man laughed as he shut the doors.

"Told you so," said Cara in a hoarse thread of a voice.

I sat on the bucket-seat, holding the dogs' leash. On a level just above me her head emerged from the cocoon of black and red blankets. The wet hair had divided and fallen back, leaving her forehead bare. The clefts on the upper lip and chin were sharply shadowed, the face no longer flushed, but pale and sticky-looking.

"Horrid ambulance. . . . Like a very common aeroplane. Sorry. . . . You could have gone in the car with the doctor, couldn't you?" That touched me. I reached up and patted the cocoon, approximately where her shoulder must be. I said, "Don't worry. This won't take long."

"Not nice," Cara said as we moved. "Not far, is it?"

"No . . . under four miles." I kept my hand on her as we lurched along. After a time she wriggled one arm free of the cocoon and I felt her hot fingers clutch mine. I couldn't hear what she said. I stood up, clinging to the edge of the rack, bending close.

"Do something for me? . . . When we get there . . . Find a priest."

It was the latest shock of the day. "I will," I said.

"Can't do it without. . . ." The hoarse voice chuckled gently. "Funny . . . after all these years."

"I'll get a priest."

"And when I say a priest—" the voice strengthened—"I mean a priest—so don't go coming up with a clergyman, see?" She chuckled again. I stayed standing up, because the hot fingers still held on.

I moved about the empty room, unpacking her possessions.

In my mind there were pictures; the faces of the surgeon and O'Neill; kindly, composed faces, talking a language that I did not understand. The man, carrying the tray, who came to type her blood. The nurse bringing the razor and the soap, and afterwards the hypodermic needle. Then the anæsthetist, a visit of introduction. Everybody who was wanted—except the priest.

There was the echo of the voice making drowsy jokes and ceasing. There were the white woollen stockings that they pulled over her legs. There was the stretcher on wheels, rolling away down the corridor. She was gone. And, most clearly now, there was the look of her face, watching the clock, frowning, wondering why the priest didn't come.

She only asked about him once. That was before the needle. After the needle, I thought, she didn't remember. She stared at me, though, when they came to fetch her, opened her eyes and stared, not reproachfully, but seeming a little puzzled, wanting to ask me something.

I emptied the white box. When I had removed the bottles and jars, there was something left; something that felt like a ball, wrapped in wool and tissue. The rabbit paper-weight. I shook it and the red-coated rabbit was masked in snow. 'She does really care for it,' I thought and I sat it on the bedside table.

The nurse put her head round the door, "You aren't going to wait, are you? They'll be quite a time."

I said, "Will she be all right?"

"Now don't start worrying. Mr. Masters is a wonderful surgeon. Why don't you go and have a cup of tea or something? . . . I'll sit here. . . . Not supposed to leave rooms empty." She looked about her. "And she's got nice things," she said—"Not your mother, is she?"

"No; no relation."

"Just a friend? Worrying for you, though. I'd go and have a cup of tea, I really would."

I said, "I promised I'd get the priest for her."

"That's all laid on. Father Briggs. He was out, you know. But he'll come. Shame he couldn't get here before she went up. I know how much it means to them. You R.C. too?"

"No."

"Those dogs . . ." she said suddenly, "I had to laugh."

"I'll have to give them their dinner. I told her I would."

Scraps, I thought, confusedly; would an orderly get me two plates of scraps? It was six-thirty now and the shops would be shut, so I couldn't buy food for them. In the front office, tied to a table-leg, they gave me agonised welcome. Through their noise, the clerk at the desk was trying to tell me something. I untied them and they stopped barking. She said that there was a message from Livesey's London office; they had reached him by telephone in New York and he was flying back.

He would be here tomorrow, then. I thought about it while I patted the dogs. What else was worrying me, besides their dinner? Oh, yes, the priest.

"He'll come. He always comes."

"Is he far away?"

"No, no; just down the street. Past the church on the first corner."

I walked out into the dark, leading the dogs.

'He'll come; he always comes.' He was at her service, just as I was, hurrying to make sure that no time was lost. (And my train? And my luggage at the junction? And my journey south tomorrow? What was I doing, tearing down a dark hill in an icy wind, pulled along by her poodles?)

It was silliness that had provoked this situation; sheer silliness; cock-eyed idiocy.

"Don't even have a cheque-book any more—*too* humiliating."

"Health Service? Isn't that just for poor people?"

Lord, I thought, how could anybody be such a fool?

"*Horrid ambulance. . . . Sorry . . . you could have gone in the car with the doctor.*"

"*She's got nice things.*"

And the rabbit paper-weight.

No. There was nothing touching about it, nothing here to arouse compassion; only the chaotic silliness that could, it seemed, command serious services at will. I saw the doctor racing down the staircase, two steps at a time; the ambulance-men, the anæsthetist, the man who came to take the blood. Even now, while I walked, that silliness focused upon itself the skill and training of a lifetime; back there, under the lamps, the surgeon worked against odds to repair the thoughtless damage. A man in a mask, with the sweat running into his eyes.

I came to the church and the small brick house beside it. A woman opened the door.

"Oh, you've just missed Father. He's gone straight to the hospital." She stooped to fondle the dogs. "Brought your family with you, I see."

I turned and trudged back up the hill.

The priest was talking to the clerk at the desk. He was quite young; small and owlish with his horn-rimmed glasses. "So sorry you had that walk for nothing. I was just coming back to pick you up."

I said, "Is it all right? I mean . . ." my words trailed.

"She's still in the operating-theatre," said Father Briggs. "Awful time you're having. Shall we go in here?" It was the waiting-room; green leatherette chairs and a green leatherette sofa; white walls; a gas fire.

Father Briggs shut the door behind him. "Got to wait a little while," he said and patted the poodles' heads. "Pretty, aren't they? How old?"

"I don't know. They are hers."

"Your friend's, you mean?"

He offered me a cigarette. I took it because it was some-thing to do. He said, "We might as well sit down." He reminded me of the more sober young men at Oxford, solemn and round, with an educated twinkle. It is, I thought, an essentially English pattern.

I was embarrassed, saying, "Look—forgive my asking. You couldn't do it now, go *into* the theatre and do it?"

"Goodness me, no. Wouldn't be allowed. I'd have to be disinfected and decontaminated and Lord knows what all—imagine. We never do." He crossed his short legs and looked

at me sympathetically. "It'll be quite all right; just as soon as
she comes out."

"Can you give her Absolution if she's unconscious?"

"Oh yes; conditional Absolution, and I'll anoint her. Don't
worry about that."

"And if she's dead?"

"Same thing," he said. "There'll be time. . . . It's all very
simple really. It was she who sent for me, wasn't it? Not you
yourself?"

"Oh no. I'm not a Catholic, Father. She thought of it."

"Well then, her dispositions are good," said Father Briggs,
sounding as though he were talking of her heart, lungs or liver.
"So we needn't worry about anything. Just leave it all to
Almighty God. You're staying near here?"

I explained what had happened. He looked sympathetic
again, particularly when I got to the luggage. "Good gracious
. . . what can you do about that?"

"Just wait." I said. "I can get it in the morning."

"But where'll you spend the night?"

He seemed cheered by the fact of Aunt Anne. He offered to
look after the dogs while I telephoned her, but I said I would
rather wait until I knew what was happening. "Awful for you,
really," he said. "Only possible way I can help is with the dog
food. I've got a Welsh Corgi. So if you'd like to bring them
back——" He looked at his watch. "Seven-twenty now. I
don't suppose they'll be much longer."

We lapsed into what seemed an endless silence. I knew
suddenly that I was tired.

"Wish you'd telephone that aunt of yours," said Father
Briggs.

"I'd rather wait, please. Till I know."

He smiled at me, "Is she a very old friend, the patient?
Forgive my saying so—you look too young to have a very old
friend."

"She isn't my friend at all."

"Eh?" said Father Briggs.

I twisted my fingers together. "I know it looks like that, but it isn't like that. I may shock you," I said, "but the truth is I want her to die."

He said mildly, "Oh? Why? Don't you like her?"

"No. I hate her."

"Got rather a funny way of showing it, haven't you?"

There were steps outside, coming to the door. The nurse said, "They're bringing her down now."

The stretcher was rolling towards us down the corridor, with white figures pushing it. One white figure held a bottle aloft and the tube from the bottle ran down to a needle fixed in her arm. The face was white and flat-looking, with an airway distorting the mouth, like a parody of a baby's comforter. So much I saw before they wheeled her into her room. Father Briggs darted in, with his little leather case in his hand. I waited.

Two more white figures strolled up the corridor, the surgeon and O'Neill, swathed, with sweaty faces. I did not take in the words. I heard "No picnic——" and "Might go either way".

"Well there we are," said Father Briggs. "She'll be all right now. What about your aunt? Could I drive you over?" He was leading me down the corridor. I hung back. I had forgotten the number of her room. The corridor was darkened. We came to the lighted window at the end where the night-sister on duty was sitting.

"Father."

"Yes?" I could see his spectacles glimmering as he turned to me.

"I think I'd rather stay here."

"No toothbrush," said Father Briggs constructively.

"Mouthwash. In a hospital. Sure to be."

"What have you got against your aunt? Hate her too?"

"No, it isn't that. It just seems so awful to leave Cara here alone all night."

"She's got her nurse. And God. Or don't you count Him?" He patted my shoulder, "Not fair to tease you, is it? I don't believe they'll let you stay."

"If you ask them, they will."

He didn't argue. He ducked into the night-sister's office. "All right," he said, coming out. "As she's on the danger-list. They'll fix you up with some blankets in the waiting-room. But I insist on your coming back to the Presbytery with me and having some supper."

I hesitated. "It's kind of you, but——"

"Got to feed those dogs, now, haven't you?"

"Supposing she dies while we're having supper?"

"A lot of people," said Father Briggs, "will die while we're having supper."

The sofa was slippery and although there was a blanket between me and the surface I kept sliding off. The cold went with me all the time too, tunnelling up when my feet kicked out of the blanket; playing around my shoulders as soon as I pulled the blanket down over my feet. I did sleep, though; I must have been unusually tired.

I sat up suddenly in a panic. Where were the poodles? I had lost Cara's poodles. . . . What was all this? A nightmare? No. I remembered. I was freezing to death on the sofa in the hospital waiting-room.

I slid to the ground. There were some matches in the fender and I lit the gas-fire, crouching beside it with my coat over my shoulders. My watch pointed twenty minutes to four. As I had expected. According to the Duchess all who suffered from over-indulgence, insomnia or a bad conscience were accustomed to awake at twenty minutes to four precisely. It was, she said, zero hour for the soul.

I was guiltless at least of over-indulgence; I had eaten sausages, mashed potato and stewed apples with Father Briggs. When he said grace he had shut his eyes tightly, like a child praying. In the Presbytery there was a traceable echo from the convent where I went to school: the oilcloth; the plaster Virgin; the Crucifix on the wall. We had talked about books. He had asked me again to telephone Aunt Anne, but when I said that she was the kind who needed explanations, he had excused me.

He insisted on keeping the dogs overnight. I thought that they would be warmer there and more comfortable, but now I wished that they had not whined when I left them.

Father Briggs drove me back, thoughtfully remembering to enquire of the night-porter about the mouthwash. The last thing that he said to me was, "You can pray for your enemies, you know."

But I hadn't prayed.

Really, this was a silliness almost comparable with Cara's, wasn't it? I might easily miss the boat-train from London; thus missing my train on the other side, with its second-class sleeper reserved days ago. I wasn't waiting to see Livesey, was I? Examination of conscience failed to elicit an answer.

I could not return to the inhospitable sofa. I collected my blankets and lay down on the hearth-rug in the circle of warmth. I dozed and dreamed. In one dream the Absolution was coming down out of that bottle held above her head; it went down the tube and into her arm through the needle.

I was half-awake when I heard the door opening and a stiff rustle. "Goodness, there you are. I was looking on the sofa."

I scrambled up quickly. I put on the light.

"Number Sixteen's asking for you. Her Special said you wanted to be called. Know your way, don't you?" she asked.

Had I not known it, I should still have found the room, because of the things outside the door; oxygen-cylinders and some peculiar equipment on a steel trolley.

As I opened the door, I heard the voice, the quiet voice crooning to itself with the note of the doves on the hotel-roof in summer. I stepped past the screen and stood beside the high bed. The nurse sat on the other side, holding her wrist.

I shall not forget the suddenness. It was like walking into a foreign country. The sick-room was a different place on the map. The chemical reek was all the air of this place; there was no other air. The person living here was, for an instant, wholly unrecognisable. I did not know the colour of its face; I did not know the clothes it wore, the stained white cotton gaping at the breast. Nor the things that it needed beside it, the shallow enamel vessels and the towels.

I began to see Cara in the stranger. All that I saw was in rhythmic, fighting movement; her diaphragm with the short breath, the eyelids that fluttered, the forehead that frowned and then smoothed, then frowned again; the lips that twitched, the hand on the coverlet that kept opening and closing as though it badly needed another hand to hold.

The nurse smiled at me. She said, "Is your name Gyp?"

"Gyp——" the voice muttered. The hand opened and shut. I slid my own hand into it and the fingers clung. They were bluish in colour, those fingers.

There came a moment of peace. Then she said impatiently, "Oh, don't put it in without tissue-paper. You drive me crazy."

The nurse gave me a look that I found intolerable; a winking signal that had an amused superiority about it, an acknowledgment that she and I were in possession of our senses. I leaned towards Cara. I said, "I've got all this new tissue-paper, sheets and sheets."

"Oh . . . *that's* nice."

The nurse looked as though she would laugh. She brought me a hard chair and I sat down. "How is it going?" I asked her. She made a face that might mean anything and returned to her own side. I held the fingers closely and they held mine.

For a while she ceased to mutter. Her breast rose and fell more slowly. I bowed forward; it was more comfortable with my free arm resting on my knee. When I looked away from the shaded lamp I saw a greyness beginning in the room. The voice crooned again once, broken unintelligible words. Then she tried to be sick, turning her head to my side; I held the bowl under her chin. "Nothing left on her stomach," said the nurse. The weary mask looked up at me. "She's pretty silly," Cara said in a friendly voice, pushing the bowl away—"Sorry." Her eyes shut again. My left leg began to go to sleep. I straightened it. My arm got cramp but I dared not move my hand. My head nodded. I became aware of the nurse, leaning towards me, muttering.

"Could you hold her arm? Time for her injection."

The fingers didn't want me to go. I kept saying, "I'm still here." I held her arm while the needle went in.

Back in my chair, I could see the drug take effect; feel it also in the hand that still held mine, but less urgently. The nurse took her pulse again, and her temperature with the thermometer under her arm. The eyelids were quiet now. I felt the nurse touch my shoulder, "Cup of tea . . . few minutes . . . you won't be frightened? . . . Nothing's going to happen." She went, creakingly, and I saw that she staggered a little at the door, as I should, I thought, when I stood up again.

Then Cara stirred and smiled. Her voice was low, but entirely audible, "Look . . . the road by the river . . . Coming?" Her hand shook mine gently.

I said, "Yes, of course I'm coming."

"It's pretty, isn't it. . . . See how far it goes? . . . All the way to the house . . . the house with the two ways in."

There was an enchantment here, beginning.

"Sunny today," Cara said. "It's not always sunny. Want to walk on the waterfall?"

I said, "Well, perhaps. What do you think?"

"I wouldn't," she said. "It's all right on the lily-leaves, but after that there's no place to stand." She turned her head a fraction on the pillow. "You can see the fountains through the trees, though, can't you?"

"Yes. I can see the fountains."

It was a moment of communication unknown and, I would have thought, unknowable, the sense of walking across the border into the private territory of a dream. We went on, together.

"Not up there," said Cara. "That's where the giants used to be; not any more, I think, but we don't go up the field. Here——" there was a quick frown and the fingers tightening. "This is wrong."

"Are you sure?" I asked her gently. "It doesn't look wrong."

"But this is the town. How did we get to the town again?"

"Never mind," I said. "We'll go through." There was the sensation of moving with her down an unfamiliar street. My body was still and cramped in the upright chair; my mind prowled on beside hers.

"It's the wall. It's the end of the town. And look—here's Shady Lane—I'd forgotten. Mustn't-Go-Down-Shady-Lane." Though she pronounced it as an edict, she smiled, seeming to make fun of it. The smile stayed on the dry lips as she appeared to hesitate.

"We won't go, then," I whispered.

"But we're there," she said. She sounded afraid. I walked with her down Shady Lane.

"Dark . . . dark . . . It was always dark." She shuddered suddenly, strongly. "Ugh—the spider. Turn back—quick. . . ." Her hand pulled mine. "No good. There's another one—we can't." She shrank back against the pillow, grimacing, the shiver going through her. I could not bear it.

"No, no . . . don't you see?" I pleaded. "They aren't spiders at all—they are just leaves—I promise they are. Look, Cara, I'm touching them; only leaves; nice smooth leaves."

It was a moment of triumph when I saw her relax; she said, "Well, so they are. That's funny. I've never been able to do it before. You're always telling me, aren't you?"

"Yes," I said, not knowing why I wanted to weep—"I'm always telling you."

Where now, I wondered? It was like a spell. If I went on touching her hand, watching her eyes, I could keep up with her.

She grabbed at me suddenly. "Oh, *too* good. . . . The clearing. I did so hope it would be. . . . Isn't it ridiculous? . . . You're there, aren't you?"

"I'm here; and I love it."

"Red toadstools," said Cara, "and fireflies. At least I suppose they're fireflies. It's a kid's place. Wait. If we're very good, the diamond ship will come."

"Come sailing in?" I ventured.

"Like a train. Look, look! . . . Here it is—they're shouting.

All the toys . . . So pretty. It's the luckiest thing. It always was. You know that, don't you?"

I knew it. I could see the lighted ship in the clearing, the childhood place. But the hand was pulling mine impatiently. "We'll get to the palace now . . . you see——" She was moving her feet under the bedclothes, hurrying on. "So very old," she said. "I wouldn't know how old. So old it's blind. Crumbling. . . ." Her voice was tender. "And nobody on the shore . . . just the waves." I saw them, the waves, and the old palace crumbling against the sky. Sometimes I can still see them.

"Oh, but we're wrong—we're wrong . . ." the voice was heart-broken.

I tried to take over. "We're right, Cara—it's the palace—look. . . ."

"No, damn it, *damn* it. . . ." The change in her was sudden and violent. "Look at it—look at them all. The bastards—— Get *away*." She was agonised now, rearing up in the bed, beating with her hands. "Let me through. . . . This is terrible. Help me, for God's sake help me. . . . Let me through. . . . That's the altar, damn them."

As she fought the invisible mob, she fought me too. "I'm here," I said, "I'm helping you." I was terrified of what she was doing to her body and I had to hold her still. Yet so strong was the image in my mind of her enemies that I heard myself saying aloud to these, "In the name of God, depart."

Cara sank down, weeping. "It is all right," I said to her, "it is all right. They've gone, they won't come back." But she moaned and did not hear me.

I do not know for how long I sat on in the hard chair with the hand still holding. I remember the blue tinge creeping up the hand, the mouth fallen open; the yellow-grey shadow across the face, the gap in the breathing that you timed while it endured. And I remember O'Neill coming back. And there was the oxygen-tent that hissed, the white shimmering tent hiding her, so I could not see her face any more. But the hand, beyond the edge of the tent, still held.

As when I walked with her through the dream, my body was in one place, my mind in another place. There was this body, in this place and this chair, aching from neck to ankles, with my bladder hard and painful because I needed to relieve it so badly, my cramped muscles, my eyes hotly sore. And my mind in the other place, making the mad journey with her again. I went along the road by the river, past the waterfall and the fountains, through the town and into Shady Lane. I saw the spiders turn to leaves. I saw the clearing, the child's playground where the diamond ship ran in. But further than that I could not go.

The voice crying "Help me . . ." made too terrible an echo in my ears. That was where I had failed to get through. I had bidden her enemies depart but she had not heard; she had lain still and wept.

Where was hatred now? I could never have hated her. I loved her. I had been close to her; I would be close again. She would come back out of this stupor and tell me that all went well in the fight, that she had heard my voice, that I had not failed her.

Most passionately I wanted her to live. I would make her live. The prayers that had not come all night were groaning out of me. Old prayers, convent prayers long forgotten; Latin words and French and English: Sancta Maria, Sainte Marie, Blesséd Jesus; Our Father; Si quaeris, Passio Christi, Blood of Christ.

For three months my reverie had played variations of its small, favourite game, the next meeting with Livesey. None of them had suggested that he would come like this; flatly, two-dimensionally, a large man in an overcoat, whom I was too tired to see, except as a punctuation-point in time. 'Oh, yes, you're here now,' my thoughts recorded. The arm that encircled my shoulders and hugged me might have been anybody's arm.

And now, I thought (being more awake), I was subject to his rapid organisation; the smooth, expensive gestures that used once to divert me were cushioning my way. The air-ticket for tomorrow, instead of the train. (The Why of Motive and the How of Money co-operating prettily.) No time lost for me, and all consideration shown, even a telegram sent to Francis. Livesey, looking after me.

Of course. It was my right. I had my own part in the drama. We were all in it, but I the most. Mine wasn't the star part because that, for the moment, belonged to an off-stage character, but I had the second lead. After me in importance came Livesey, flying the Atlantic overnight; the daughter with him, the pale child in the nun's habit; and poor Aunt Anne, hurrying to the hospital at early morning. It was I who had watched with Cara.

But I could watch no more. They would not let me. The issue was still in doubt; they could not say for certain whether she would live or die. And if it were still in doubt tomorrow—no concern of mine. I was passing from this picture.

For the moment, within a frame of physical comforts, drama was lulled. I had slept; my body felt well and rested. Here was the circular panelled room in the Dower House; firelight and the curtains drawn; a manservant to carry the silver tea-tray. Before the fire, the poodles cuddled close. Jacqueline—not Gyp any more, but Sister Jacqueline—talked to Aunt Anne. Her face had an unsatisfactory resemblance to Cara, an anæmic likeness between eyes and chin; the brow was Livesey's.

Livesey looked rested, too; shaved, comfortable, a well-mannered host. I was once more the guest at Whiteford. In a few minutes now, I would go home to my evening with Aunt Anne. Livesey and his daughter would go back to the hospital.

The hospital was my place. Mine only. This I knew, sharply and painfully. That was where I belonged, in the room with the chemical reek and the hard chair and the high bed. They had shut me out.

It was, I supposed, a separation no greater than the silence

that walled me off when she cried to me for help and I answered
and she could not hear.

But since I was shut out, I must keep watch still in my mind;
and remember it; the drip of the blood from the bottle; the
white hissing tent; the enamel bowl; the blue fingers. Most of
all, I thought, the feel of the fingers. I would not think of her
dreams or I should come again to the moment when I couldn't
get through. And the prayers? These I kept without meaning
to keep them. It was impossible to stop their clamour at the
back of my head. They clamoured now, mechanically, mean-
inglessly, while I ate a muffin. Like having a tune on the brain:

> '*Si quaeris miracula,*
> *mors, error, calamitas,*
> *daemon, lepra fugiunt,*
> *aegri surgunt fani . . .*'

Really I must try to talk. The others were talking. They
were calm. They had their staff of comfort, each one. Aunt
Anne was no stranger to death, nor was Livesey; they had
been here before. And the child, the novice, was on terms with
it; on Father Briggs' terms.

My only acquaintance with the enemy was the vigil that I
had kept beside Violetta long ago. That memory stayed
enshrined. But not because of death; because of the brief
revelation that came after it.

The Duchess' death, I could say, had put certain things
right for me. Nothing could be right for me if Cara died.
There would be no consolations. I had hated her. I had met
her only to see her tortured. I had loved her too late. She
would leave me nothing but the fact of her death. And death
was another fact, though they said that it was not. Death
ended people. Of this I was sure now, having seen the body
almost lifeless, the mind departed.

And if I had not seen those things, I might still doubt
survival for Cara. Another sort of person might get through
the silence and go on somewhere else. Not Cara. For her to

exist, she must be here. And play with the poodles again, and shake the rabbit paper-weight and pull on the gloves that had leather palms with white string backs.

We were all too cosy, were we not? Livesey rising to offer drinks . . . Cara could come to an end now, while we were doing this—we, the winners . . .

He said, "Could I just have a word with you, Penelope?" And we were alone in the study, where there was another fire burning. We stood on each side of the fire.

He was saying, "You were very great; to stay, to do all that. Would it strike you as cheek" (one of the Smugs' words, I thought, wincing compassionately) "if I said it made me awfully proud of you?"

I took the unwanted accolade. I said, "Thank you, Livesey."

"Mind if I ask you something . . . you needn't answer, but it worries me. . . . Been worrying me ever since the summer. And I'll probably put it clumsily." The deepening lines on the forehead made the look of perplexity complete. "I did hurt you, didn't I? Quite a lot?"

I hesitated, trying to be just; to see if the hurt had been, in truth, as small as it seemed tonight. I must be fair to it, for what it was worth.

At last I said, "That sort of hurt is bound to come. I always knew I'd have to have it some time." I thought of giving him my views about the puncture of the ego; then it seemed too tedious. Why on earth was he talking about me, not about Cara?

"It is quite all right now, I assure you," I said, trying to sound interested and grateful. He looked at me gently, wonderingly. How we all leave him, I thought, Cara first, and his daughter for her vocation and I now, in my heart.

EPILOGUE

Penelope's Voice

I WAS back in the place where I liked to be; in the open summer-house, though it was really no day to be sitting here. Rain washed the garden. It darkened the red earth and sluiced the green umbrella-pine with new lights; it blotted out the distant view. There was just the parapet and then grey mist above; no sky.

I had folded a rug around my knees, reading the letter again while I waited. The envelope was addressed in Livesey's handwriting. The enclosure was one page, pencilled and mis-spelled. I heard an echo of Cara's voice in a comment upon her nurses, "whose ghoolish love appears to be on the wane. They *are* cross once you're better." Then, "You were so good and sweet and I was so repulsive. I still am. And convales-cence is the *worst* bore, no?"

She was, after all, two people. She was a memory that towered. And she was Cara herself, scribbling this. Cara would have no need of me again; nor, I supposed, would I have need of her. Her life would go on, in terms of a slow, expensive recovery, cushioned by Livesey's cheque-book. Then there would be the light-hearted chaos beginning. Perhaps next year she would come to this coast; and it was possible that I would meet her and know the same exasperation as before.

But today the sense of loss was keen. I still loved her. And I would keep the letter. It had more significance for me now than had the ugly little treasures lying cobwebbed on the shelf above my table: a plaster leg, a black wooden ship with pink sails and an ashtray shaped like a mermaid. I had hung the ram's horn on a nail in the wall.

There was a roaring on the road above me and I saw the grey bus come by, the bus with the seminarians from St. Ignace. Despite the weather, they still rushed out, the young men in the black robes. I saw them milling, chattering, pointing, the cheerful penguins. As usually, there was one who stood on the parapet, pretending that he would jump. Today the wind blew the robe right over his head, so that for a moment, as he struggled, he looked like an umbrella gone inside out.

I unfolded the rug from my knees, pulled my mackintosh over my head and went into the dripping garden. I saw him coming, tall and strict, carrying an umbrella and a little suitcase. I met him at the gate. He still had his freckles; it was still the most English of faces; Don Bradley's face surmounting the black *soutane*. But, as I had thought before, he was, in this transformation, a little pitiful. It was because of the uncompromising haircut, the hands that always looked rough and red.

"Good morning, Penelope. Not a very good morning, is it, really?"

I said, "I'm so glad I caught you. I had no idea you were leaving so soon."

"Going to *Rome*——" he said, grinning widely. Drops from his umbrella pattered on to me.

"But not today," I protested, looking at the little fibre suitcase.

"Well, yes, today."

"Then it's very kind of you to come," I said as we paddled down the muddy red path.

"Not a bit. In fact, it's most convenient. When Father Lasalle said you wanted to see me, I thought I'd ride down on the bus with the others. Pick up the next bus—you see—from there." He pointed as we reached the veranda.

"You don't go all the way by *bus*?"

"Only to Genoa; then I get a train. But what's the matter with a bus anyway?" he asked, shutting his umbrella.

We went into the *salon*. There was a fire and we sat down in the two faded pink and gold chairs that flank the fire-screen. "Love this little room," said Don, "I always shall. That's where she lay—isn't it—on the sofa? Always think of her when I come in here. Say a prayer for her."

"The Duchess?" I asked, startled. She is so much my private property; I had almost forgotten that he knew her.

"The Duchess, of course." He grinned, as though I had said something funny. He took out a battered tin case and offered me a cigarette. He said, "Well, now, what can I do for you today?"

I hesitated upon it, looking at the square toes of his boots. "Perhaps," I said, "I just wanted to see you. I mean, I have missed you so often. I missed you at Whiteford, because you were always there when I wasn't; and only hearing about you from Livesey and Aunt Anne. And then, when you've been here with Father Lasalle—well, we've never been very coherent, have we?" Not, I thought, that I was being exactly coherent now.

"No, have we?" said Don.

"I've wanted to ask you about you," I said, "but not in public. I couldn't."

"That's all right. I'm shy too, you know."

"It's always seemed—forgive me—such an unexpected thing for you to do. . . ."

He looked at his feet. "I suppose so. . . ."

"Livesey said your father agreed to it; that surprised me—still surprises me."

"Well, he did and he didn't," said Don. "To begin with, Crusoe's death set him back on his heels, poor old boy. Death does that to people like my father. He couldn't be sorry enough. That was why he didn't make more fuss about the Sorbonne; normally he'd have looked on it as a season-ticket to the Folies Bergère."

I saw Mr. Bradley's face clearly in memory; in this room; a blustering, bewildered face.

"I think my winning the essay prize, and Monsignor Blank, Crusoe's friend, backing me up, dazed him a bit too," said Don. He laughed. "Of course it was a little different when I chucked the Sorbonne after a term and came to the Seminary. . . . All the letters since then have been highly injured."

"They're cross, the—your parents?" I had almost said The Smugs.

"They're *saddened*. My mother's health, among other troubles, is entirely due to my decision. And the deterioration in our bloodstock. *And* Sister Eva's engagement to the wrong man. Spoiling everybody's day again. That's what I'm doing."

I giggled and he smiled at me. "Bless them," he said— "aren't people funny?"

There was a silence between us. I said inadequately, "Don't you miss the horses? You loved them so."

"Well, yes, I do. Enormously. But there's awfully little point in giving up something one *doesn't* miss."

"You couldn't," I said, "tell me how it happened to you? Conversion—in your mind? I need it, very much. Law and order. God's design. If only I could have them. . . . But chaos always seems to win . . . to be the only visible thing."

He looked at me thoughtfully, medically. "You're right there. It is the only visible thing—most of the time. But you can bring yourself to a thundering philosophical halt by asking 'How do we know that it's chaos? Why aren't we all quite happily mistaking it for Law and Order?' We're dissatisfied with the incompleteness of everything in sight, we say. Well, all that means is there must *be* completeness somewhere. Where? Eh? By what light do we recognise chaos?"

"I don't know," I said. "Would you like some coffee? Oh, and Don—I do call you Don, still, don't I? Not Father . . .?"

"I'm not ordained yet. . . . What's troubling you now?"

"Death," I said. "That's too hard to stomach."

"I should have thought very easy."

"*No.*"

When I came back with the coffee, he was standing in front of the fire, looking more authoritative.

"I don't see *how* you can worry about death, I really don't. Everybody has to do it. Even if you don't believe in it as a gateway, but only as a terminus—well, where's the worry?"

"The fact of the body dying," I said, "is the worry."

"Yes, dying will be frightening, probably. I used to think about that."

"I'm not frightened for *me*——" I said indignantly. "But now I've seen it happen—or nearly happen—I can't bear the thought of it for Francis or Jeanne—or anybody I love."

"Well, but you can't die for somebody else, that's sure. No one's going to do *your* dying for you when the time comes."

"Ever seen it?" I asked him.

"I saw Crusoe dead. And when I look at his death—and the Duchess', oddly enough—they give me a clue. I can see a part of the pattern. One doesn't ever see more than a part and that rarely, I'm sure. I'm very grateful."

"You must explain."

"All you mean is," I said presently, "that you can see your own destiny operating. The Duchess and the vow—and the challengers of the vow coming——" (Like my Ancient Mariners, they were. . . .) "And the rest of it. But that's all yours; not theirs. If you see a person's body dying—and Cara really was dying—you know it's the worst thing. For them——"

"How do you know? You couldn't know what went on in her mind. . . ."

(I could, though. I was there. In her mind. Beside her, in her dream. But I would not tell him that; I had told nobody.)

"Anyway," I said, "you can't sell me death, I fear. Death's the enemy."

"No, he isn't. The Devil's the only enemy——"

"Death is, I tell you. . . ."

We were almost at the head-on collision of a children's quarrel, "It isn't." "It *is*."

I said, "At least I prayed her back to life. I know I did."

"Smug, aren't you?" said Don, grinning. It went home. "Of course, I didn't pray for a long time," I admitted, "so she may have been saved already."

"A woman who'd asked our Superior to pray for her intention, and got it, arrived in a keen state of fuss—wanting to know if he'd prayed before the letter with the good news was posted, or after."

I was cross with him for having caught me out in a stupidity. I said, "The concept of Eternity is tolerably difficult when one lives in Time, you'll agree?"

"Very difficult. But if all your prayers are answered as promptly as that, you've little to complain of."

"I am not complaining. All I know is that I'm unworthy and that I'm at odds." I set down my coffee-cup. "Would you say that the sense of sin is a sense of separation?" I fired at him.

"Precisely. Why do you ask, though?"

I was thinking of the limbo, after Marius.

"Well, you see, I think I have had all the revelations I can expect and I still don't know what to do about them."

He put a hand on my shoulder. "You just keep plodding along."

"I don't think I'll ever be really holy," I said in despair. "Not a nun or anything."

Don said, "Well, you're a writer, aren't you? I've seen you in your summer-house lots of times—writing away."

"I don't seem able to finish anything."

"You will, though."

"I know I will. Why does one go on writing, I ask myself?"

"Same reason as one goes on living," said Don—"to the Glory of God."

"Even when I don't feel as though it were that?"

He grinned again. "But don't you—ever, Penelope?"

"Oh, yes, perhaps . . . not in those words, exactly."

"Well just keep on writing," said Don. He glanced at his watch. "I'm sorry, but I'll have to catch that bus. Afraid I've not been much help."

I looked at the haircut, at the black robe, at the fair plain face and the rough hands; seeing, as he had said, a part of the pattern.

"Yes, you have," I said. "Thank you for coming."

We went out into the rain. Don opened his umbrella

and held it over me. We splashed up the path together.

At the gate he said, "You'll be all right. You get there, without realising it. It's walking and seeing a little bit of the view, not knowing that the road's mounting all the time, and that you're really climbing. And then you see a bit more of the view and then more."

He made it sound like Livesey's lessening hill in reverse.

I said, "Until one gets to the top. And then what does one see?"

He looked at me affectionately. "I couldn't tell you, Penelope. I'm not nearly there yet."

We shook hands. I stayed in the summer-house, waiting for his bus to come round the corner. He looked tall and lonely, standing there. Presently it came, the bulky, weather-stained monster, with all the corded luggage on the roof, and bore him away. He waved to me as he climbed up.

The bus went out of sight, leaving the road empty, and I stared at the blanketing mist, wishing that I could see the sky and the line of white mountain far off.

Then I opened the Duchess' rosewood desk and took out a quire of clean foolscap.

I sat still at the table, with the blank paper before me. I went back; I remembered; I thought my way in. It was the sensation of pulling on a diver's helmet and going down deep.

Presently, on the sea-floor, I began to find lost things; to raise the moods that were mine when I was fourteen years old, sitting in this garden, writing my Anthology of Hates.

I would begin there.

VIRAGO MODERN CLASSICS

The first Virago Modern Classic, *Frost in May* by Antonia White, was published in 1978. It launched a list dedicated to the celebration of women writers and to the rediscovery and reprinting of their works. Its aim was, and is, to demonstrate the existence of a female tradition in fiction which is both enriching and enjoyable. The Leavisite notion of the 'Great Tradition', and the narrow, academic definition of a 'classic', has meant the neglect of a large number of interesting secondary works of fiction. In calling the series 'Modern Classics' we do not necessarily mean 'great' — although this is often the case. Published with new critical and biographical introductions, books are chosen for many reasons: sometimes for their importance in literary history; sometimes because they illuminate particular aspects of womens' lives, both personal and public. They may be classics of comedy or storytelling; their interest can be historical, feminist, political or literary.

Initially the Virago Modern Classics concentrated on English novels and short stories published in the early decades of this century. As the series has grown it has broadened to include works of fiction from different centuries, different countries, cultures and literary traditions. In 1984 the Victorian Classics were launched; there are separate lists of Irish, Scottish, European, American, Australian and other English-speaking countries; there are books written by Black women, by Catholic and Jewish women, and a few relevant novels by men. There is, too, a companion series of Non-Fiction Classics constituting biography, autobiography, travel, journalism, essays, poetry, letters and diaries.

By the end of 1988 over 300 titles will have been published in these two series, many of which have been suggested by our readers.

Pamela Frankau

THE WILLOW CABIN

"He came over to her chair, pulled her out of it and stood holding her hands.
'If I were really grown-up now, I should say good-bye to you and walk out of your life. And yet I cannot bear to go'"

Caroline is twenty-two, gamine and vociferous, neither daunted nor impressed by the prospect of a promising stage career. Then she meets Michael Knowles, a successful middle-aged surgeon, and her career slips into second place beside brief meetings, midnight trysts and the welcome anonymity of foreign cities, as they seek to evade the shadow of Mercedes, Michael's estranged wife. London of the 1930s gives way to the Blitz and the pain of separation and the intensity of wartime does nothing to deflect Caroline's obsession with the three-cornered relationship. In America, some years later, she meets Mercedes for the first time. Discovering an unexpected bond with her, Caroline begins to comprehend her own misinterpretation of the past . . .

SHEILA KAYE-SMITH
Joanna Godden
Susan Spray

MARGARET KENNEDY
The Constant Nymph
The Ladies of Lyndon
Troy Chimneys

BEATRIX LEHMANN
Rumour of Heaven

ROSAMOND LEHMANN
The Ballad and the Source
The Gipsy's Baby
Invitation to the Waltz
A Note in Music
A Sea-Grape Tree
The Weather in the Streets

ADA LEVERSON
The Little Ottleys

ROSE MACAULAY
Told by an Idiot
The World My Wilderness

OLIVIA MANNING
The Doves of Venus
The Playroom

F.M. MAYOR
The Rector's Daughter
The Squire's Daughter
The Third Miss Symons

BETTY MILLER
On the Side of the Angels

EDITH OLIVIER
The Love Child

MOLLIE PANTER-
DOWNES
One Fine Day

MARY RENAULT
The Friendly Young
Ladies

E. ARNOT ROBERTSON
Four Frightened People
Ordinary Families

VITA SACKVILLE-WEST
All Passion Spent
The Edwardians
Family History
No Signposts in the Sea

MAY SINCLAIR
The Life and Death of
Harriett Frean
Mary Olivier: A Life
The Three Sisters

STEVIE SMITH
The Holiday
Novel on Yellow Paper
Over the Frontier

G.B. STERN
The Matriarch

LAURA TALBOT
The Gentlewomen

ELIZABETH TAYLOR
The Blush
The Devastating Boys
A Game of Hide and Seek
In a Summer Season
Mrs Palfrey at the
Claremont
Palladian
The Sleeping Beauty
The Soul of Kindness
A View of the Harbour
The Wedding Group